The Perfect Revenge

Also by Lutishia Lovely

The Hallelujah Love Series
Sex in the Sanctuary
Love Like Hallelujah
A Preacher's Passion
Heaven Right Here
Reverend Feelgood
Heaven Forbid
Divine Intervention
The Eleventh Commandment

The Business Series
All Up in My Business
Mind Your Own Business
Taking Care of Business

The Shady Sisters Trilogy
The Perfect Affair
The Perfect Deception
The Perfect Revenge

Published by Kensington Publishing Corp.

The Perfect Revenge

LUTISHIA
LOVELY

Dafina
BOOKS

KENSINGTON PUBLISHING CORP.
www.kensingtonbooks.com

DAFINA BOOKS are published by

Kensington Publishing Corp.
119 West 40th Street
New York, NY 10018

All Kensington Titles, Imprints, and Distributed Lines are available at special quantity discounts for bulk purchases for sales promotions, premiums, fund-raising, and educational or institutional use. Special book excerpts or customized printings can also be created to fit specific needs. For details, write or phone the office of the Kensington special sales manager: Kensington Publishing Corp., 119 West 40th Street, New York, NY 10018, attn: Special Sales Department, Phone: 1-800-221-2647.

Dafina and the Dafina logo Reg. U.S. Pat. & TM Off.

ISBN-13: 978-1-61773-502-8
ISBN-10: 1-61773-502-7
First Kensington Trade Edition: June 2015
First Kensington Mass Market Edition: February 2019

ISBN-13: 978-1-61773-501-1 (ebook)
ISBN-10: 1-61773-501-9 (ebook)

10 9 8 7 6 5 4 3 2 1

Printed in the United States of America

...nowledgments

...fina who make up Team
...azing. From the cover
...group in sales
..., Steven
...the vil-

This book is dedicated to all for whom success, happiness, and a fulfilled life have been your best revenge.

Acknowledgments

Yay! I did it, finished the third book in a trilogy that for me was a very different set of story lines to write. Jacqueline Tate and Jessica Bolton Givens are truly shady sisters, and telling their stories turned all of those hours I spent watching ID—the Investigation Discovery channel—from wasted time to research. And speaking of research, thank God my computer didn't get confiscated while writing these books. My searches would have undoubtedly led the police to believe that I was about to kill somebody, change my identity, flee the country, or maybe all three! Ha! This novel you're about to read will take you on a wild and crazy ride. But anyone who thinks the story line too farfetched has never watched shows like *Snapped*, *Fatal Attraction*, or *Who the (Bleep) Did I Marry?*!

Aside from some of the shows on ID and Oxygen that indirectly inspired this trilogy, I have to thank my mama, Flora Hinton, for the engaging conversations that led to my watching more of these shows. Like her, I find the human dynamic fascinating; how obsession, jealousy, greed, and other low energies can turn an ordinary person into a monster! So for all of you wondering where the crazy characters came from . . . I'm blaming Mama! LOL.

To my angel/editor/friend, Selena James, for your patience and understanding throughout the completion of this series and, especially, this book. Your unwavering support is a godsend, and so are you. As always, the folks at Kensington/Dafina who make up Team Lutishia are nothing short of amazing. From the cover design to the editing team to the super group in sales and marketing, and all the way to the top, Steven Zacharias, I am so blessed to have all of you as the village around my literary children. Hugs and love.

Natasha Kern, my spiritual sister/agent/friend, I'm so excited about all we've discussed and all that is possible. My publishing journey is made sweeter because you are one of the VIPs on it with me.

What can I say about readers that would accurately express my love? Okay, imagine me scaling the Empire State Building, megaphone clutched under my arm, determined scowl on my face, and joy in my heart. I reach the top, spread my arms, and shout at the top of my lungs: I LOVE ALL YOU LOVELY READERS!!!! Sounds crazy, right? But it takes that type of image to in some small way demonstrate how crazy I am about all of you who've embraced this challenge I gave myself to write a different type of story, who've come along for the ride and enjoyed it as much as I did. To my Avenue Angel VIPs (who some would call street team); the members of A Lovely Day Experience, my online love club; the subscribers to the Lovely Day newsletter; every reader who's picked up *The Perfect Affair* and *The Perfect Deception*, thank you so very much. Being who you are helps me get to be who I am. I pray the blessings of Spirit in your life give you the ability to live your dreams and desires, the way I am now blessed to do. If you're sitting on a dream or squelching a desire . . . stop it! Get up, get out, and start doing what it takes to make it happen! Just start, and watch the Universe conspire with you to make that dream/desire a reality. I am living proof that this spiritual law works when you work it, over and over again.

Because they are SO amazing, I've got to give a book club roll call! I LOVE these groups of women and men coming together to discuss my novels as passionately as if they were discussing the news: with opinion, enthusiasm, and attitude. There are many. Here are a few: Characters Book Club (Tanishia Pearson-Jones); Literary Divas; The Reading Divas; Reading Between the Lines; Diamond Divas; Go On Girls; R.A.R.E.; Reading Circle; S.A.G.E.; Friendgirls; Sugar and Spice; Frances & Friends; The Mississippi Magnolias, Gulfport, MS (Antoinette Gates); Divine Sister; Phenomenal Sisters of New Orleans; Readers Circle of Friends; The Reader's Journey Network; Faith's RN Readers; Sistahs On The Reading Edge, Antioch, CA (Lisa Renee Johnson); Readers Paradise, Chicago, IL (Laverne "Missy" Aslam); Literary Ladies; Divine Sister; The Pillars Book Club; Book Talk Book; The Black Orchid Book Club, Houston, TX; 7th Ward Readers, New Orleans; Literary Lunch Bunch; Circle of Color; Divas Divine; OOSA . . . you rock! These days, online book clubs are gaining popularity. A wave and hug to B.R.A.B., Mary Green and Just Read Book Club, and the first online book club with which I interacted, Sistahs' Thoughts From Coast To Coast. Love you!

Thank you for choosing a Lovely novel, specifically one of the Shady Sisters, as your book of the month. If a Shady Sister novel (or any of my others) is one of your book club's selection of the month, selections and you'd like to include me in the discussion via Facetime, Skype, or in person, please send a line to **ALovelyDayExperience@gmail.com.** Your club could be part of the roll call in my next book!

This is the last Lovely novel to be turned in this year, 2014, and I am looking forward to a slower pace during the holidays. This year has been challenging on many levels, but, as always, Spirit and my angels have stayed with me every step of the way and seen me through, as have my friends, associates, and colleagues. I'd like to take the time to thank a few whose words of encouragement and unconditional love kept me focused and grounded, and kept the laughter flowing, sometimes even through tears! Again, my shining example of a mom, Flora Hinton; my always-supportive and lovely aunt, Ernie Jackson; #1 bestie and forever big sis, Dee Turner; Renee Flagler; Orsayor Simmons; Priscilla Johnson; Kim Knight; Reshemah Wright; Tanishia Pearson-Jones; Kenneth Killian; Jennifer Copeland; Ella D. Curry; Lissa Woodson: At one time or another, during the writing of this trilogy, you spoke a word of encouragement, sent a prayer, gave a hug, or talked me off the ceiling. Your love and support are appreciated more than words can say. If you're reading this with a scowl and thinking, "I did that, too," then go ahead and include yourself! I heart you! Getting your e-mail will simply mean I have another book to write, just to publicly thank you, too. J

I also want to mention my eternal love and light for my cousin, Eno Jackson, who this year—quickly and unexpectedly—earned her angel wings. As we talked and laughed during our last Labor Day family reunion, none of us had any idea that it would be our last opportunity to do so. I love you forever my Libra-sister/cousin. I am sure you are enjoying your celestial journey as much or more than you did your earthly one. Soon, I'm going to take more time to "chillax" the way you often suggested.

Hug your loved ones, y'all. Tell them that you love them. Don't let the sun go down on an argument. Leave with peace between you. Yes, they can still hear you on the other side but somehow resolving situations on this side always feels better.

Recently, at the 10th Annual Cavalcade of Authors, I was asked what role spirituality played in my writing career. For me, that's like asking how does breathing play a part in your being alive? I live, move, and have my being in Spirit, am intricately connected to Source and am nothing, have nothing, and can do nothing without this amazing, All-Knowing, All-Powerful Life Force. Spirit is my writing partner, and together we'll pump out #1 *New York Times* best sellers, *USA Today* best sellers, and books that become movies, for a very, very long time. There are those who didn't know Spirit and I have it like that, and underestimated my strength to be in this game, to stay in this business, and to excel in this competitive field. I never pay much attention or respond to the naysayers because you know what? Turning in book number thirty-something makes a pretty loud statement. Success, happiness, and a fulfilling life are the perfect revenge!

PROLOGUE

Raleigh, North Carolina

Two in the morning. With the girth of a bear and the stealth of a panther, the prison guard crept into the private cell at the end of the hall. Everyone—from the warden to those on work release—had an opinion about the prisoner being housed there, one of only a handful who'd spent more time in a single cell than in the dorm, and the only one who stayed there by choice. In just under two years, she'd made quite a name for herself. Along with quite a few enemies. Such could have been the case with the guard now stalking her. But Charlie's attraction for the woman, beautiful even in prison garb with no makeup, hair products, or even a smile, had not been dimmed by the woman's obvious disdain for her. No, it had been heightened. Every taunt had made her obsession more intense. Every foul name uttered that was followed with a sneer had only made Charlie more determined to one day have her. That time was now.

A steady hand reached for the heavy, barred door. A key slid into the lock chamber. Quietly. Surreptitiously. Without a hint of metal scraping against steel. The guard smiled at the ingenious idea of dipping the key in baby oil before placing it into the lock.

Click. Damn. She'd thought about the key but not the bolt. The sound of it settling into the open position ricocheted against the deathly quiet. Quieter than usual, even for this side of the dorm-style prison. New moons were often like that, quiet and steady, as if all of the foolishness brought on by the often chaotic effects of a full moon had sapped the inmates' energy and exhausted their desire to create an imitation of life on the outside while on the inside. She heard a scraping sound. Charlie froze momentarily, breath held, ears alert, listening for unusual movement, senses trained both to inside the cell where her prey lay and the perimeter around them.

Down the hall, a woman coughed. Another snored softly, rhythmically, constantly. The object of her fantasy remained unmoved, a deep sleeper. Charlie smiled. Even if the prisoner reacted negatively and changed her mind, the end result would be the same. Five steps, seven max, and she'd be at the cot. Two seconds and, if necessary, her hand could cover the luscious mouth that might alarm others of her obtrusive presence. Five seconds more and the words guaranteeing the prisoner's compliance could be harshly whispered into her ear. *Felonious assault against a prison guard. Life without parole.* She hoped it wouldn't come to that. But no matter. One minute, and Charlie's dreams of intimacy with the object of her desire—Jacqueline Tate—would become reality.

*   *   *

As Charlie stepped inside, Jacqueline forced her body to remain relaxed and still. She had to, in order for her plan to work. For the past month, she'd begun flushing the psychiatrist-prescribed meds down the toilet. Good move. Every day her mind seemed clearer, her thoughts more focused. She'd even reconnected with her best friend, Kris, who'd encouraged her to end Charlie's flirtations once and for all and had helped her flesh out the details on getting it done. The first part, taunting Charlie into this late-night visit, had been easy. The dyke guard had been sniffing around and drooling over her for almost two years, kept away only when Jacqueline threatened to tell the warden, whose son Jacqueline had slept with while in county jail. The threat was made moot two months ago when the warden had resigned and her son's inappropriate actions no longer threatened her employment. That's when Charlie had reiterated her desires, along with the promise that sooner or later they would be realized. "Tonight," Jacqueline had whispered as the women filed from the dining room and returned to their cells. She'd flashed a shy smile before turning the corner, had glimpsed the brazen lust that filled Charlie's eyes. There'd been no doubt that tonight she'd have a visitor. Now, all she had to do was play the vixen about whom her captor had fantasized, and the hunter would get captured by the prey.

The sight of Jacqueline sprawled against the stark white sheet took Charlie's breath away. In her unconscious, unguarded state Jacqueline's thick dark tresses, flawless golden-brown skin, and perfectly symmetrical features resembled those of a runway model, an A-list actress, or a men's magazine centerfold. Her T-shirt had twisted up above her waist, exposing a smooth, flat stomach. One long leg was bent at the knee, mimicking the angle of the arm above it. The other lay straight and revealed painted pink toenails. For seconds, Charlie simply stood there, drinking in the vision as a parched man would a cool glass of water. Jacqueline changed positions. The shirt rode up a little more. A creamy globe winked at Charlie, who reached out a shaky hand and pushed the material farther up to expose a perfectly shaped breast. Jacqueline turned once more, her eyes fluttered, then opened.

She stared at Charlie.

Charlie stared back.

Time stood still.

"I told you I'd have you one day," Charlie whispered. Jacqueline, wide-eyed, simply nodded. Pants removed, shirt undone, Charlie knelt beside the cot. Her mind took no notice of her knee's complaint about the hard concrete floor. Instead, her mouth watered as thoughts of the pleasure that would soon be hers flooded her mind. She looked at the barely hidden hairy lips between the enchantress's thighs. That's what Charlie determined Jacqueline must be, to so fully consume her thoughts every single day for the past two years. So much so that her fourteen-year partnership had disintegrated and Charlie had chosen nipple suckers, Venus butterflies, and Jacqueline-fueled fantasies to replace her lover in their previously shared home.

Charlie reached out a tentative hand and touched her. Softly, reverently, she ran first one finger and then two down the length of Jacqueline's arm. Up and down again. Jacqueline watched, but Charlie could no longer meet her eyes. Suddenly, she felt like the dorky schoolgirl who got the jock. Jacqueline hadn't rebuffed her, hadn't been teasing, hadn't changed her mind. Unbelievable.

With no sound other than the harsh rush of breath through Charlie's nostrils, she gingerly sat on Jacqueline's cot and gazed at the length of what lay before her, once again gently placing her fingers on Jacqueline's flesh. Her thighs were silkier than gelato, softer than a newborn's bottom. She touched with her fingers, then tasted with her tongue, buried her nose into the crotch of Jacqueline's panties and inhaled harder than a crack addict on a two-dollar pipe. She lifted her head, placed a finger just inside each side of Jacqueline's panties and began to pull. She couldn't believe her luck when Jacqueline not only failed to stop her but rolled to the side and made it easier to remove them. For months, she'd thought that it might take rape to get what she'd promised herself she'd have if it was the last act she performed on earth. Yet here she was, staring at the triangular treasure being offered before her. She smiled, gently parted the gates to the golden pearl, and bent her head.

That's when Jacqueline stabbed her.

Unfortunately the concrete-sharpened letter opener swiped from an unguarded station penetrated enough to end the unwanted assault but not enough to kill the woman Jacqueline had hated from day one since being transferred from county lockup. Hated for her lustful gazes and cocky threats. Hated for having the keys to Jacqueline's freedom, and her lockdown.

Charlie's scream and Jacqueline's attempts to beat out the life that hadn't been stabbed away quickly awoke everyone on the floor. Other guards rushed in, too quickly for Charlie to put on her pants or to make up a lie that would clear her completely.

The official story was that Charlie had willingly gone into the cell and then been viciously attacked. As far as Jacqueline knew, Charlie's only disciplinary action was that she was transferred to a different prison. Charges of felonious assault were never filed. Jacqueline believed this due to one of the injuries she'd managed to inflict, and the possible difficulties of Charlie explaining how a prisoner's teeth imprints ended up on her buttocks unless they'd been exposed. Jacqueline earned three months in solitary confinement and an additional twelve months tacked on to a lifetime sentence with the possibility of parole after serving fifteen years. They'd thought putting her in the hole was punishment. But for her, solitary confinement became both boot camp and university. Push-ups. Planks. Crunches. Yoga. Prolonged leg lifts. Meditation. Twenty-three hours to plan out what she was going to do to all of those who'd wronged her; and once she was reintegrated into the central population, three hardened criminals—murderer, armed burglar, drug trafficker—to teach her all they knew.

And then, the break of a lifetime. Freed on a technicality. A new, more sympathetic judge had ruled that the evidence used against her had been illegally seized and was therefore inadmissible. The Atwaters had gotten her arrested and put into prison, had petitioned to have her stay there, and had thought the key forever thrown away. Her sister had tossed her aside like yesterday's trash. But Jacqueline Tate's attorney had earned the enormous fees he charged her. She was now a free woman. And there was only one thing on her mind. Revenge.

CHAPTER 1

"Where to, pretty lady?"

Jacqueline knew exactly where she wanted to go. She also knew she wouldn't travel there in a straight line; one of the reasons for walking two miles from the prison she'd just been released from to a gas station and getting the attendant to call her a cab.

"That's a good question."

The taxi driver viewed his passenger from the rearview mirror and was rewarded with a genuine smile. Two years, eight months, four days, and seven hours ago, Jacqueline would have ignored this stranger, maybe even cursed him out for attempting to flirt. But after so long with so little contact with people in general and men in particular, she allowed herself a moment to relax, and feel grateful to breathe free air.

It wouldn't last long.

"You new in town?"

"Just passing through. You?"

"Raleigh, born and raised."

"So you probably know where I should go to get a good meal."

The driver's smile increased. "I know all the places you can go."

Jacqueline laughed.

"Do you like soul food?"

"Love it." Actually, she could take it or leave it. But for her plans it was the location, not the food, that mattered most.

"What do you want? Ribs, fried chicken, pork chops, greens, mashed potatoes and gravy, macaroni and cheese . . ."

"Please stop! You're making my mouth water."

"There's this place tourists like to visit. It's in the heart of downtown. The food's good there."

The last place Jacqueline wanted to be was in a heavily populated area filled with cameras to chart her moves.

"Is that where you go when you want a good meal?"

"Naw, baby. I go to my mama's house."

"Well, I wouldn't dare think of bothering your mom. Where's the next best place?"

"It's a little hole in the wall in the hood but I don't think you want to—"

"That's exactly where I want to go."

The driver nodded, reached the corner, and turned left.

Jacqueline noticed how the driver kept glancing at her through the mirror. He was obviously smitten. *Good.* "I like your hat."

"Ah, yeah?" He pulled the ball cap off his head and looked at the logo. "Got so many of these things I forgot who I put on this morning."

"The Carolina Panthers are my favorite team."

They'd been so for a whole minute or two, since seeing a billboard a few miles back.

"You like football?"

Not at all. "Don't know much about it but, yes, I'm a fan. I'm only going to be here until the morning. Maybe I can find a Panthers cap somewhere besides the airport. Everything's so expensive there."

"I'd give you this one if it weren't so dirty."

"Really? That's so sweet of you. I'd love to have it!"

"Oh no, darling. A woman as pretty as you don't deserve to wear a cap holding this much of a working man's sweat."

"I'll wash it before I wear it." She reached for her bag and eyed him through the mirror. "How much?"

At the next light the driver removed the cap, brushed it against his pant leg in a failed attempt to remove grime, and handed it to her. "You've just paid for it with that pretty smile."

"You sure?"

"Positive."

Jacqueline made a big deal of admiring the cap. "Thank you."

After a cab ride made shorter by the driver's running commentary on the place he'd only left a handful of times since birth, they arrived at the aptly described eatery located on a corner marred by trash and weeds. Jacqueline paid the driver and went inside. It was early. The place was almost empty. Though her stomach growled at the smells that assaulted her, she ordered a glass of tea, waited ten minutes, and called another cab. After walking out of the eatery, she casually donned the dirty ball cap. Once in the cab she just as casually braided her hair and stuffed the twists beneath it. That the driver had spent the entire ride on his cell phone, engaged in what seemed to be a heated conversation (not knowing the language he spoke, she couldn't be sure), worked to her advantage. If asked, she doubted he could give anything other than the most basic description of the passenger he'd dropped off at the post office five miles away.

While behind bars, Jacqueline had eventually cut ties with all but three people. Phillip was a longtime fellow Canadian friend with whom she'd stayed during a three-month US-based assignment. She'd reconnected with him several months ago, right before he'd moved to Europe and just before the illegal cell phone she'd used was discovered and confiscated. The first call was mere chitchat. Thereafter, the reasons for their communication became crystal clear. She'd laid them out with the precision of a general planning a sneak attack on a terrorist group. By the time she'd finished giving Phillip her side of why she'd been sent to prison, the only side of the story that mattered, he'd been more than willing to help her. As she retrieved the items from the post office box, the calculated decision to trust her old friend with a secret or two proved to be a wise one. Now she had what she needed for the games to begin.

Four hours later, a casually dressed woman possessing an understated elegance and pulling a small carry-on bag approached the counter of a five-star hotel, one of only a handful in Raleigh.

One of the employees, a tall, good-looking Black man around twenty-five, straightened his posture and flashed a dimpled smile as the guest approached. A pronounced Southern accent added to his charm.

"Good evening, ma'am, and welcome to our hotel.

How may we provide you with quality service this evening?"

"You're off to a good start." The woman gifted the smitten young man with a pearly dazzle of her own while reaching into an oversized designer bag and retrieving a driver's license and credit card. "I have a reservation." Her clipped British accent was flawless.

The young man took the cards and entered the information into the computer. "Ms. Smith . . . Alice?" He looked up.

She nodded.

"It shows here that you've prepaid for the room, so your credit card will only be charged for incidentals." He quickly finished the reservation and handed Jacqueline two card keys. "We're fairly light this evening, so I've provided you with a complimentary upgrade to one of our suites."

"I appreciate that, but it wasn't necessary."

"It's just our way of thanking you for your business and hopefully leaving you with a favorable impression that you will share with others when you return to England."

"I certainly shall."

Jacqueline scanned the lobby, but her steps did not slow until she reached the elevator. Moments later, she placed a key card into the double-door entrance. Once inside, she shed "Alice," a persona created with a short blond wig and black reading glasses that resembled the picture on the best fake driver's license money could buy. Tossing them on a table, she removed the clothes she'd donned in a mall public restroom, and after ordering room service, took a long, hot shower. Not long enough to wash away the memories of prison, but enough to make her feel more like herself.

While she was blow-drying her hair, room service arrived. Wrapping her luscious black locks in a towel and donning the black glasses, she welcomed in the sumptuous feast she'd ordered. With a satiny nightie caressing her skin, Jacqueline enjoyed her first meal of the day: radicchio salad with pears, pomegranate and ham; seared foie gras, and a Kobe beef rib eye, perfectly medium rare. As the news hour approached, Jacqueline turned the television to a local channel. There was a breaking news story.

"Police have no leads and are asking for the public's help in determining the cause of death for Charlotte Stockton, known as Charlie to her friends, a guard who held various positions within the North Carolina Corrections system for the past ten years. Stockton was discovered by a concerned neighbor after the guard's beloved dog exhibited highly unusual behavior, and seemed to be locked outside of the home, something that according to the neighbor Stockton would never do.

"'That dog was her child,' the neighbor said, still clearly shaken. 'He kept barking and running between their yard and mine. I knew something was wrong.'

"While Stockton's sudden death seems suspicious, police have no theories as to what might have happened, and no suspects or persons of interest. Anyone with information is asked to call the number that appears on the screen."

Jacqueline picked up the bottle of champagne she'd ordered along with her meal, popped the cork, and filled a crystal flute. "One down, seven to go." She lifted her glass.

"Cheers."

She drained the flute and reached for one of three burner phones she'd purchased at the mall. It was time to contact the other two people with whom she'd kept in touch, and begin the next phase in the big payback.

CHAPTER 2

Carroll, New Hampshire

Laughter mixed with flurries of snow as four water-proof-nylon-clad skiers removed their skis, stomped the snow from their feet, and entered their private Snow Ridge home, where a blazing fire was the perfect welcome.

"That was fun!" The twelve-year-old boy rubbed his hands together, still basking in the aftermath of his successful run down a pretty tough hill.

His fourteen-year-old sister gave him a playful shove that sent the unsuspecting lad tumbling to the floor. "Ha! You conquered a snow-covered mountain but can't handle a hardwood floor!"

The boy jumped up, ready to defend his honor and give his sister a taste of her own medicine.

Their parents intervened at once.

"Albany, stop it."

"All right, Aaron, cut it out."

The Atwaters—Randall, Sherri, Albany, and Aaron—

were enjoying an impromptu yet much-needed vacation at the Bretton Woods Ski Resort, a trip born out of a dinner discussion about whether more fun could be had in snow or sun. The men said snow offered more opportunity, while Sherri and Albany said it was sun, hands down. This trip had been planned immediately so that Randall and Aaron could prove their point. Later in the year, when the family went to their home in the Bahamas, the women would get their turn.

Aaron removed his shoes and began peeling out of his snow suit. "I'm hungry, Mom."

Randall laughed. "You're always hungry."

"I think that ski slope worked up an appetite for everybody. Y'all go on up and shower and change. By the time you come back downstairs, I'll be well on my way to a killer pot of chili."

Aaron punched the air with his fist. "Yes! That sounds good."

"That does sound good, baby," Randall agreed, pulling off his snow pants before padding over in his sock feet to give Sherri a kiss.

Albany walked to the wall mirror by the door, checking to make sure the woolen cap she'd worn to protect her shoulder-length locks hadn't smooshed her fluffy hairstyle to the point of no return. "Will it be made with ground turkey?"

"No, sweetie, ground round."

"Then could I have baked chicken, please? I've given up red meat and pork."

"Since when?" Aaron's face was a mask of disbelief.

"I guess since she finished that bacon she gobbled up this morning," Randall replied.

Albany gasped. "Stop teasing, Daddy. That was

turkey bacon. Right, Mom?" Her eyes begged Sherri to agree.

"Sorry, sweetheart. That was good old thick-sliced oink."

Aaron snorted rhythmically as he strutted toward her.

"Eewww, I'm going to be sick!" She rushed out of the room and up the stairs, with Aaron the Irksome Pig hot on her trail.

Randall watched Sherri retrieve peppers, onion, and garlic from the refrigerator and walk over to the cutting board on the counter. He let her get in a few good slices before easing over to embrace her from behind and nibble her neck.

"Ooh, that feels good. But if you want to have chili in an hour, you should probably follow your children upstairs and take a nice hot shower."

He ground himself into her and mumbled, "Right now, I need a cold one."

"There's beer in the fridge."

"Ha!" With one last kiss on her neck, Randall leaned against the counter and continued to watch Sherri slice and dice.

"Are you going to stand there until everything is in the pot?"

"I like watching you. I like this . . . you in the kitchen fixing our dinner, the kids bonding upstairs. Quality family time, with just the four of us. Life has been so busy the past couple years. We need to do this more often."

"I agree." Sherri poured a generous amount of olive oil into a pot before adding the peppers, onions, and garlic. She walked over to the refrigerator and retrieved the ground beef. "And as much as I believe Mama loves living with us, and we love having her there, I think she's enjoying her time in Raleigh, visiting her former church members and catching up with Miss Ridley."

"I think you're right. You want a glass of wine?"

"That sounds good."

Randall walked over to the cabinet, retrieved two wine glasses, and grabbed the corkscrew from a nearby drawer. "It's good to see Aaron playing around and being silly again," he said as he pulled the cork from the wine bottle and poured two full glasses. "The therapy sessions have definitely helped."

"I'm just thankful his teacher was astute enough to recognize what we didn't, or as she and the therapist said, what he'd kept mostly hidden. That incident traumatized him more than any of us realized, and continued even after the handful of family therapy appointments we set up. Trying to hurt us is one thing, but what Jacqueline did to my kids makes her the lowest type of human being that I can imagine."

Randall looked up in surprise, looked toward the stairs and back at his wife. "We're speaking her name now? Since when did this become okay? I remember a conversation as recent as a couple months ago when I forgot your rule and got punched in the chest."

"That may have been an overreaction."

"You think?"

Sherri reached over and gave him a quick peck on the lips. She stirred the meat mixture that was gently sizzling in the pot before opening a cabinet door and pulling out a chili seasoning packet and a jar of tomato sauce. "Mom and I were talking the other day. What she said made me realize that my demanding that her name not be uttered reflected the fear and hatred I still harbored against her. She pointed out that as long as these feelings remained, Jacqueline was still controlling a part of my life. She suggested I forgive her, not for anything I owed Jacqueline but for what I owe myself. So while I pray there will be little reason to mention her name in the future, the rule against doing so is gone. Jacqueline is in prison, where she belongs, and where she will be for a very long time. I have no need to fear her, or that name. And by the way, I didn't hit you that hard."

"You did, but it's okay. Later tonight, I'm going to punch a part of your anatomy with something hard. So we'll be even."

"I look forward to it." Sherri added the rest of the ingredients to the pot, then lowered the fire so the chili could simmer. She picked up her glass of wine and reached for Randall's hand. "I'm going to let that simmer about thirty minutes and in the meantime, go take a shower. You want to join me and start delivering a few of those punches you promised?"

A sexy smile crept onto Randall's face. "Oh yes, I most definitely want to do that. Or, as the kids would say, mos def."

"Kids don't say that anymore, Randall. Men trying to hang on to youth long gone say it."

"Oh."

"Ha! I love you mos def, Randall."

He placed his arm around her shoulders as they mounted the stairs. "I love you, too."

CHAPTER 3

Atlanta, Georgia

"Hey, baby. You about ready to get out of here?"

Jessica Givens looked up into hazel-brown eyes set in a pretty-boy face. On a day like today, when hormones gone wild had kept her mind locked in the past and brought on a pity party, that the owner of this gorgeous face was her husband felt surreal.

"I've been ready to leave since I arrived this morning." She switched the company phone lines to the night answering service, placed the file she'd been working on in a drawer, and reached for her purse. "All right, let's go."

The elevator arrived. Vincent held the door, allowing his wife to enter first. As the door closed, he used his body to maneuver Jessica against the back wall, and sent his mouth in search of hers.

"Stop, Vincent."

He frowned. "What's wrong, baby?"

"I don't feel like being mauled in the office elevator where the door can open at any time and we can get busted."

"We're married, Jessie. A little PDA every now and then I think is allowed, even in the workplace." He leaned in again but when she turned her head, he gave up and moved to the other side of the elevator. The car stopped at the next floor. Several people got on, effectively ending the conversation.

But Vincent started it right back up as soon as they'd reached the parking lot and gotten into the car. "You've been in a bad mood all week, babe. What is going on?"

Jessica pulled out her cell phone and began checking e-mails.

"Oh, you're ignoring me now? So this is one of those times where you're mad at me and I'm supposed to figure out why?"

"Nothing's wrong, Vincent. I just didn't feel like being attacked in the elevator, all right?"

"I try to steal a kiss from my wife and you call that attacking you? All right, then. I'll be sure and keep that in mind. Wouldn't want my shows of affection to be misconstrued as some type of domestic violence."

Jessica heaved a sigh, wishing she could exhale her mixed up feelings as easily as she had the air. She slipped her cell phone back in her purse, propped her arm against the door, and stared out the window. She observed the passing Atlanta scenery through eyes blurred with tears.

"I'm sorry," she said, her voice low and forced. You don't deserve how I'm treating you. You're the best thing that ever happened to me. The only true friend I have in the world."

He glanced at her. "Are you crying?"

Swiping her eyes, she answered, "No."

"Look at me."

"No."

She saw movement from the corner of her eye, felt his arm come around her shoulder and his fingers begin to knead the tight knot in her neck.

"Baby, if you don't tell me the problem I can't help you."

"If I tell it, you still can't." His hand slid from her neck to her shoulder and down to her thigh, where he offered an encouraging squeeze. Seconds passed, punctuated only by the faint sound of music coming from the car speakers and the windshield wipers moving the rain that all day had fallen over northern Georgia.

Eventually, Jessica was able to staunch the flow of tears that rolled down her face. Still looking out the window, she reached for and found Vincent's hand, took it, and squeezed. "I don't know why I let her get to me like this."

"Who, baby?" Vincent felt he knew that the answer to this question was her locked-up sister, Jacqueline Tate, but asked it anyway; hoping, praying, that he was wrong.

"Sissy."

He was right. Damn.

Anguish coated every letter of a word made raspy by the strength it took to be pushed through Jessica's taut throat. "I dreamt of her last night. In the dream we were talking, hugging, happy. Even though it shouldn't, even though I haven't seen her face-to-face in over fifteen years, it made me miss her so much. She did everything wrong to me that one can do to another human being—lied, betrayed, used me—and then when I failed to accomplish the unthinkable favor she'd asked, walked out of my life faster than she'd come back into it. She cut me off without a backward glance." Shaking her head to try and rid it of those painful memories, she felt tears threaten again. "I still can't believe the person I looked up to for most of my life could hurt me so deeply, so much so that just the thought of her and what she did can take me there, put me in a depressed, funky, horrible mood and make me take it out on you." She turned to face him. "I don't deserve you."

Vincent lifted her hand to his lips and kissed it. "You deserve everything that makes you happy." He released her hand, flicked the signal and exited the freeway. They'd almost reached the day care center to pick up their son.

"Don't beat yourself up, Jessica. We can't always control our emotions or help how we feel. Our heads might say one thing but our heart might say something totally different.

"No matter how it ended, at one time you considered her your sister, the only family you knew. She made you feel loved and needed, as though you were the only thing that mattered and everything she was asking was so the two of you could be a family again. After spending your life in foster care, those words had to sound wonderful, amazing . . . they were probably the ones you always wanted to hear. You built yourself up to have a wonderful future with the only person of whom there are fond childhood memories. We all want to feel connected to family, we all want to belong. When that dream got snatched away the cut was deep, to the bone, to the soul. Only time will tell how long it will take for that type of wound to heal."

He pulled into the day care center's parking lot and

cut off the engine. Reaching up, he tenderly wiped the lone remaining tear from Jessica's face.

"In time, I hope that memories with the family you have now—me, Dax, and one day maybe even more children—will help to heal that scar. Not that you'll ever forget what your sister did, but so many new, happy memories will fill your mind that there will be little room left to remember the unhappy ones."

Jessica leaned toward Vincent. He met her halfway. The kiss was poignant, heartfelt, filled with promise of more love to come.

"Hey, get a room!" The gruff command was accompanied by a knock on the driver side window. They slowly pulled apart to see a smiling face partially hidden by a large, black umbrella.

Vincent lowered the window. "Hey, Carl. What's up, man?"

"Given what I just walked up on, you're probably better equipped to answer that question."

"Ha!" He turned to Jessica for one last peck on the lips. "Be right back."

Carl stepped back as Vincent opened the door. The two men walked into the day care center like brothers, sharing Carl's umbrella against the drizzling rain.

Jessica watched their easy rapport as they walked inside. Vincent had met Carl some months ago when daddy duty had him picking up their sick toddler midday. Turns out Carl, a real estate agent, was on the same assignment. They'd first bonded over a shared belief in naturopathic medicine and later over beers and a love for the Braves. Vincent was like that though, a man with charisma, confidence, and charm, who never met a stranger. She remembered thinking that from the moment she laid eyes on him, how during those first days at the law firm he'd been a big flirt, and then a nuisance, but finally a friend, lover, and more. After spending ten years married to a monster who made her believe that no one else would want her, Jessica had given up hope that good men existed. But they did. And one of them loved her, which to her was quite amazing.

"You're a good man," she whispered as the men held open the door for a mother who was leaving, before ducking inside the center. "Way too good for me."

Jessica felt this way because of how patient Vincent had been since the news of Jacqueline's betrayal had caused her life to all but unravel. But that wasn't the only reason. It was also because the child, Dax, who Vincent was so crazy about, was beginning to look more and more like his true biological father, the man with whom Jessica was still in love and had also been dreaming about, the invisible yet constant intruder in her mind and her marriage.

CHAPTER 4

Raleigh, North Carolina

"I still can't believe this—you, here, lying next to me. I've dreamt of it so many times, it's hard to believe the dreams have become reality."

Jacqueline sighed. "I can't believe it either."

And really, she couldn't. But not for the reasons she assumed her boy toy imagined. Not long ago, no one could have told her that now she wouldn't be the constant companion of a handsome, award-winning scientist.

Thirty-year-old Jacqueline looked at the twenty-five-year-old hunk beside her, propped up on an elbow, chin in hand, looking at her as though she were the goddess of all goodness or Mrs. Clause. She could assure him that she was neither, but decided not to burst his bubble. Instead, she threw back the covers and got out of bed, dramatically tossing her raven locks before strolling across the living room to the kitchen of their Extended Stay suite in all her naked glory.

"Get up. We're checking out."

"What?" Eric Martin, now known as Todd, rolled out of bed equally unashamed of his naked bod. At six foot three and a toned two-fifteen, the ex-marine, former guard at the county jail, and son of an ex-North Carolina prison warden definitely held his own. "Why?"

"What did I tell you about that, Todd? Stop asking questions. The less you know, the better." Jacqueline washed her hands and then reached for a container of ground coffee. She poured a liberal amount into the filter her boy toy had just placed into the coffeemaker.

Eric mumbled something under his breath as he left the kitchen for the bathroom.

Jacqueline was right behind him. "What did you say?"

"I said I hate that name." In that moment he looked more little boy than man, frowning as he relieved himself with perfect arch and aim. "I understand you wanting to change your identity and get a brand-new start. But I don't understand why I have to do it."

Jacqueline posed against the doorframe, eyeing him speculatively. "You don't have to do anything you don't want to do: change your name, leave this state, or be my man." Another dramatic toss of the raven mane punctuated her statement as she walked back toward the kitchen.

"Jacqueline, wait!"

She whirled around. "What did you just call me?"

She was in his face in an instant, finger pointed toward his chin, eyes blazing fire. At a slender five foot eight, Jacqueline was no match for the well-built ex-soldier, but he wilted like a daisy in the desert sun.

"Sorry!"

"What's my name?" she growled through gritted

teeth in a manner that suggested there was no room for error.

"Right now? It's Alice."

"For the sake of simplicity, it's always Alice. No matter what I look like. Got it?"

"Okay, Al." Jacqueline raised a brow but otherwise ignored this slight disobedience. "Alice what?"

"Alice Smith."

She crossed her arms. "Go on."

"You're from a small town outside of London, England. We met at a bar about a year ago, where I fell hopelessly in love."

That part of the spiel was true.

Jacqueline smiled, lightly rubbed her breasts across his chest, and watched the stars burst in his eyes.

"And from this moment on you are Todd Dern, former member of special forces until you denounced violence, moved to India, adopted some obscure religion and basically disappeared . . . until now."

He placed his arms around her. "Now I, as Todd Dern, am back to live in the country I protected for almost ten years and also to take care of the woman who turns me on like none other."

Everything about Todd Dern was true. Thing was, the real Todd still lived in a hermit-like community in India, where he'd moved after leaving the military. Todd and Eric had served together in Afghanistan. When a convoy had been blown up, killing the man who drove the Jeep in which Todd and Eric were riding, something in Todd had mentally snapped. After his tour and to everyone's surprise, he didn't re-up. Instead he told Eric he was moving to India to be with a girl he'd met while on leave. For a while, they kept in touch by email but lately he'd gotten no response. He wondered if anything had happened to him but knew there was no one else that he knew who'd have that answer. Todd had been raised by a grandmother who died when he was sixteen. He'd joined the marines a year later. His comrades had become his family, Eric was his best friend and, until he'd met her, the military had been his life.

The day Eric had shared this story was the day he earned a spot in Jacqueline's life, a role in her drama, and eventually a new name—Todd.

She questioned Eric about a second persona she'd also secured through fake ID and other documentation, the persona she'd used when Alice needed to be on the low. He answered every question correctly.

"You're a smart guy. That turns me on. I'm glad I turn you on," she whispered, rubbing her full lips across his thinner ones as she felt his nature rise against her thigh. "Because when that happens . . . I know exactly what to do."

Two hours later, the satiated and rehydrated (sex, shower, two pots of joe) couple tossed their minimal luggage into the white compact car Jacqueline had rented online as Alice Smith. "Alice" was driving, hitting the highway ramp at fifty miles an hour while blasting Katy Perry's "Roar." For the umpteenth time she thanked her lucky stars for an attorney as hungry for success as she was for freedom. Because her case had been thrown out on appeal, she was a totally free woman. No probation. No parole. No constraints to her traveling where she needed to go and getting business handled.

"If you're wanting us to stay under the radar, honey, this isn't how to do it."

"Oh, thanks." Jacqueline eased her foot off the gas. "I've got so much on my mind."

"I wish you trusted me more to share what's going on in that pretty head of yours."

"You know more than most."

Eric nodded, and pulled out the burner phone Jacqueline had purchased for him. The radio switched from roaring to rapping. He bobbed his head as he scrolled the Internet. "Where are we"—Jacqueline's head whipped around, her eyes off the road for a full two seconds while she glared at him.

"All right, girl, damn. Watch the road!" He shook his head, slouched down in the seat, and engrossed himself in whatever was on his cell phone screen.

"You're going to D.C."

"Me, not us? Oh, another question. My bad."

"Between the two of us, patience is a commodity that's in short supply. Grab my bag from the back."

He did, set it precariously on the console without a word.

"Look in there and get the notepad. It's the one from the hotel."

He retrieved the notepad, scanned the words scribbled across three pages, then looked at Jacqueline with a raised brow.

She laughed. "Very good, soldier. It looks like oral gratification isn't the only area where you're able to catch on quickly."

"Please." Said with a confidence undermined by the subtle shade of red creeping from his neck to his chin and still moving.

"You'll be flying out in a couple of hours. That top number is your confirmation code. Memorize it, as well as everything else I've written there. I'll need that paper back."

"Look, I know you don't want to be found out. I know how to tear up shit when I need to."

"I'm sure you do, but that won't be necessary since I'll be burning it as soon as you exit the car and I get to a rest stop. It's the way we're rolling, so get used to it. No paper trail, no electronic stamp. Ever. Got it?"

Eric looked at the paper. "So this is where I'm staying?" Jacqueline nodded. "What about a car?"

"Take a taxi to the hotel, then use their computers and find a rental company nearby."

"Why not just rent one from the airport?"

"Never perform nefarious activities in a straight line. Makes it harder to connect the dots. Even better if you don't leave dots to be connected."

Eric nodded. "What's Capitol Intelligence Security?"

"The firm where you're going to apply and get hired."

"I thought I was working for you."

"Ah, the truth comes out. I'm just your employer, eh? And all this time I thought it was my witty kitty that kept you close by. Now I know it's the appeal of the dollar bill."

"Babe, your pussy hypnotized me from the moment you first put it in my face."

"So I don't need to give you the envelope inside the bag before you leave, the one filled with money?"

"I'd be lying to say I don't need money. That's what makes the world go round, you know that." He took the hand that had been resting on the bottom of the wheel. "I'll always be grateful to you for rescuing me from that boring, dead-end job. My mom's dream of my following in her footsteps and carving out a career in the penal system wasn't the future I saw at all. It would have been as bad as being behind bars. Meeting you, though? Made those two years that I worked at county well worth it."

"I must admit your dick saved my sanity. But that's enough talk about past life. Alice Smith knows nothing about life behind bars. Never talk to her about it again."

Eric laughed, thinking she was kidding. A look instantly told him she was not. "So what's this job, as a security guard or something?"

"Yes. Among other properties, they guard a medium-sized office building on the outskirts of D.C., on the way to Alexandria, Virginia."

Thanks to Jacqueline's photographic memory, she'd stored away this tidbit of information, the security firm for Randall's office building, during a visit to his office. That there had been job openings posted while she was doing her research last night had been a stroke of luck.

"And what makes you so sure that I'm going to get hired?"

"One, I did my homework. Two, there's a five-thousand-dollar bonus once you seal the deal and become a CIS employee."

"Five g's? You might as well go ahead and deposit that in my bank account."

"Get hired and I'll deposit two point five. Get assigned to that specific office building and you'll get the rest."

"How am I supposed to do that?"

"That's for you to figure out." She tapped her finger against the wheel as he kept reading. "If you have time, I want you to . . . never mind."

"What?"

"I was going to put another piece of the plan in motion, but I don't want to get ahead of myself."

She paused as the GPS informed her that the ramp leading to the airport was two exits away. "That manila envelope in that bag's side pocket?" She cocked her head. "That's yours."

Eric pulled it out, flipped through the stack of green inside.

"That's enough for food, transportation, a little entertainment. There's also a debit card to secure the car and hotel. Don't worry. There's enough in the account to handle the large deposits they require when using a debit card, and anything that comes up. I don't want to constrain your movements too much, but I do need you to keep a very low profile. No using those killer green eyes to catch a female, or that thick, wavy shock of brunette hair—"

"That I'm still getting used to—"

"That makes you look amazing."

He pulled down the visor and looked in the mirror.

"You know you look good. Blond is overrated."

"I look all right."

"You look amazing."

He smiled.

They reached the airport's departure area. Jacqueline maneuvered the car until they were next to the curb.

"Give me the paper." He passed the notepad to her, his eyes lowering from her eyes to her lips. "Get out of here. I'll join you in a day or two. Don't worry about where I'm going," she added, correctly reading his thoughts. "Just place an application ASAP and get that job. I'll explain more when I get back."

"Damn." He leaned over and brushed her lips. "You're harder than a drill sergeant."

She swept her eyes over his body, stopping at his crotch. "So are you."

She watched him walk into the airport, then pulled back into the late-afternoon traffic heading south on I-85.

Though never having traveled to Atlanta, Georgia, Jacqueline had heard great things about one of the Southern state's most cosmopolitan zip codes. Chances were on this quick trip she'd miss much of what made the city so special. Sightseeing and club-hopping were not the focus of this visit. She was driving from North Carolina to Atlanta for a family reunion that was long overdue.

CHAPTER 5

Alexandria, Virginia

Sherri looked up from the papers she was grading. She sat in the front office of the palatial, fifty-five-hundred-square-foot home they'd purchased a year ago, endured three months of renovations to make it their dream home, and where they'd finally returned to a sense of normalcy and security following years of upheaval. In the end, all of the stress involved with relocation and renovation had been worth it. The Atwater family's home, which now included her mother, Elaine, was indeed their castle. And she thought she'd heard the king, her Ph.D., award-winning husband.

"Randall?" She listened for a second, placed down her papers, and rose from the desk. "Baby, is that you?"

She walked down a wide hallway that boasted the same dark mahogany wood prevalent throughout the lower floor, passing through a sitting room with French doors leading to a well-landscaped side yard, and met

Randall as he came through the garage entrance into the keeping room, where a low-burning fire gently halted the frigid November air.

"It is you! To what do I owe this pleasant surprise? You home before the kids on a weeknight? Wait, did I miss an appointment we had, or a meeting or . . . babe?"

Randall had taken off his coat and hung it in the closet and now sat to remove his shoes. He hadn't spoken.

Sherri walked over to the bench. "Babe, what's wrong?"

"The kids home?"

"No. What's the matter?"

"Just because I'm home early something's got to be wrong?" Said while placing his shoes on the rack. He got up to leave the room.

Sherri was right on his sock-covered heels. "Not because you're home early, but because of that itty-bitty crease in the middle of your brow, and the slight strain that shows around your eyes when something heavy is on your mind."

"Ah, she knows me so well." He turned down a hall and entered his office, which was located across the hall from hers, and perused a stack of mail. "Got a call from the attorney today."

Sherri frowned. "Which one?"

"The one who's been keeping us abreast of . . . you know who."

She crossed her arms. "Do I want to hear it?"

"Probably not." Randall walked around to the chair behind his desk and sat down. "But I'll tell you anyway."

He picked up a piece of mail and slid the opener between the envelope folds, slowly cutting through the paper.

Sherri sat and watched him, exhibiting the patience of Job while awaiting the news.

"She's out."

Everything about Sherri stopped: breath, heart, all motion, for a good five seconds.

"What do you mean . . . out?"

"Out as in released from prison."

The pitch and volume of her voice increased along with her blood pressure. "How? When?"

"A few days ago. He's got a call in to the judge to find out what happened, and a call in to the prosecutor to find out why he wasn't notified."

"She was convicted of murder, with a sentence of fifteen to life. How in the heck does something like her get released?"

"You mean someone?"

"That wasn't misspoken. I meant some*thing*."

Randall shook his head. "I wish I knew." He stood and walked behind the chair where Sherri sat. Her shoulder muscles were as tight as he'd imagined. "But I don't want you stressing about this. Chances are she's had enough of the States and is already back in Canada."

"How can we know for sure?"

"I've already contacted Nathan and asked him to get in touch with his friend the detective, to ascertain her whereabouts."

"Which means as much as you're telling me not to stress, calling my brother is proof that you're obviously concerned."

"More cautious than worried. Not putting enough importance on seemingly innocent details is what got us in trouble the last time. I just want to make sure we're not caught off guard again."

"We shouldn't have to make sure of that! That witch should not have been released from prison, especially without our attorney's knowledge. Knowing where she is isn't good enough for me. I want her back behind bars. What can we do to get this decision reversed?"

"I don't know, but we need to do something. At the very least, our attorney should be able to file some type of appeal, based on the fact that he wasn't informed. Trust me, I want her back behind bars as badly as you do."

Sherri placed her hands on top of Randall's. "Thanks, Ran. I needed that." She turned to face him. "Should we tell the kids?"

"I don't think so." Randall crossed over to the window and looked out on the snow-covered front lawn, the bare, shivering trees, and darkening sky. "No need to alarm them unless there's a reason, especially with Aaron finally returning to his old self and Albany doing so well."

"I agree, and feel the same way about Mom. With your phone call to Nathan, he obviously knows. We've moved since we had contact with her, and with the way this community is secured, getting beyond the gate isn't easy."

"More like impossible without a key or a code."

"Exactly. So I guess we're good for now."

She said this, but an hour after her conversation with Randall, Sherri was still uneasy. The papers she'd come into her office to grade still lay unread. The kids had come home, but aside from quick conversations, with their heads stuck just inside the room, there'd been no real conversation. She didn't want to alarm them, but it was hard to fool them when something was wrong. She decided to call the one person besides Randall and her mother who could talk her down when needed. Now was one of those times.

After closing her office door, she hit the speaker button and the most used number on her speed dial.

"Good afternoon, Renee Stanford speaking."

"You can drop the professional persona, Nay. I don't need information on the city of Las Vegas. I need some sistah-girl advice."

"One moment, please."

In the silence, Sherri turned down the volume on her phone. Her best friend had one of those voices where even whispers carried.

"Okay, girl. I shut my door. What's up?"

"That 'B' is out of jail."

"Whoa, what 'B'? Girl, start at the beginning."

"Really, Renee? How many women do we both know of who're incarcerated?"

"Okay, Sherri. I get that you're upset. But you're talking fast and I just came from a two-hour lunch with a grateful client, which involved lots of good food and a bottle of champagne. That after kicking it with my mister until three this morning. So I'm six kinds of sleepy and halfway drunk. Don't judge me."

Sherri could hear Renee take a breath in an attempt to get it together. She took one too.

"They let the woman we thought behind bars forever, the one whose name I swore would never again pass my lips, out of prison."

"What?!"

"Exactly." Sherri told Renee what she'd learned from Randall. "Somehow all of this happened without our attorney getting wind of it. Knowing what that witch is capable of has my stomach in knots."

"That's understandable, Sherri. The news has almost made me nauseous, and I've never met her. No one knows where she is?"

"Not yet. We're waiting to hear back from Nathan, who's getting in touch with his detective friend, the one who helped him out with Jessica."

"Lord have mercy, the crazy-ass sister."

"Yep, two straight-up loony tunes. We want to hire someone we can trust to do the job and to keep it confidential. We're also in touch with our lawyer to try and get her probation or parole, or whatever she's out on, revoked."

"Good for you. Where is Jessica? Has Nate seen her since everything went down?"

"Since getting married and having her baby, I think he's only seen her a couple times. And both from a distance, thank God."

"From the moment I met her at your house on Thanksgiving, I knew there was something about that girl that warranted very close observation."

"I felt it, too."

"Remember how when I tried to make small talk she cut me off and left the room? And how she barely left Nathan's side all that day? I'm still trying to figure out what it was about her that had him so twisted."

"I don't know but my brother loved him some Jessica Bolton, or whatever her last name is now. Make no mistake about that."

"Oh, there was no mistaking it. He loved her so much she almost became your in-law!"

"Whew! Our family dodged a bullet for real."

The women were silent a moment, remembering one of the times in their lives when the truth had been stranger than fiction.

"Do you think there's a chance that she'll go to Atlanta—Jacqueline that is—maybe get Jessica's help to get back on her feet?"

Sherri turned to look out the window. "Honestly, I don't know what to think, except that two crazy heifahs like that on the loose are two crazy heifahs too many!"

"I agree, but there's no need getting your blood pressure up imagining the worst when you don't even know where that chick is. Maybe Randall's right. For all you know, she could have purchased a one-way ticket back to Canada, and be as determined as you are to put what happened a couple years ago behind her."

"I sure hope so, especially if our attorney finds out that we have no recourse, if the judge tells him the early release decision is final. The last six months have been amazingly normal. Everyone's doing so well."

"Then let's think positive and believe that normal will continue."

Sherri took a deep breath. "Thanks, Renee. I'm going to try and do just that."

She ended the call and entered the hallway to the sound of laughter between her husband and son. It put a smile on her face to hear Aaron happy, when for months after the incident with Jacqueline he'd been quiet and withdrawn. Renee was right. There was no need imagining trouble where so far there was none.

She had a beautiful home, a rewarding job teaching elementary school kids with the possibility of an even more exciting position, an awesome family, and no time at all to waste on the whereabouts of Jacqueline Tate.

CHAPTER 6

"Wow!"

Nathan Carver took one look at his friend's wide eyes and slack mouth and shook his head. There was no doubt what had gotten his good friend Steve's attention. Atlanta, Georgia, was full of beautiful females.

"Love at first sight again?"

"Dog, you don't even understand. This girl who just walked in is so bad, I feel like going over to propose."

"You might want to get her name first, and find out if she's married."

"It don't matter. She looks so good I'll be the other man."

"Wow, she must be special." Nathan gave a casual look over his shoulder and got a glimpse of an ivory-clad angel: cropped sweater, tight jeans, thigh-high boots, short blond haircut. He turned back around and drained his beer.

"What I tell you?"

"You were right."

"She's never been here, that's for sure. There's no forgetting somebody like that." Steve frowned.

"What?"

"Vultures circling already."

Nathan turned again and saw the winter wonderland holding court with three goofballs. "Ha! I'm not surprised. Calvin hits on anything female and breathing."

"He needs to go home and hit on his wife."

"I don't know how a woman stays with a man like that. He hides his affairs in plain sight."

"Rumor is she gives as good as she gets, just does so with more discretion."

"Then why even get married?"

"Ooh!" Steve placed a fist to his mouth, his eyes bright and gleeful. "Brothers just got served!"

"Man, why don't you go on over there and introduce yourself? It's clear she's who you'd rather spend time with."

"Can you blame me?"

"Not really. Just remember what happened the last time I picked up a woman in here."

"Naw, Nate, I'd rather forget about that."

Nathan laughed. "Me too, Brothah, me too." He pulled out his wallet and tossed a twenty on the table.

"You out of here?"

"Yeah, man. It's been a long week." He stood, and after exchanging a soul brother's handshake walked toward the door. He passed the object of his friend's desire on the way.

Their eyes met. The moment was brief, mere seconds. But Nathan got the distinct impression that she liked what she saw. He damn sure did. But memories of a woman named Jessica, the woman behind the warning he gave his friend, caused him to keep it moving.

Besides, Nathan had been in a long-distance relationship for over a year and was not on the prowl for a thing on the side. But he'd be lying if he said the woman didn't move his manhood.

Hours later, he was still thinking about her.

Jacqueline eased out of her chair, aware that the man who'd been talking with Nathan was coming her way. She had no idea who he was. Nor did she care. But the pictures she'd seen on the Internet of her sister's ex hadn't done him justice. Nathan Carver was not only handsome, he had that type of swagger that couldn't be taught. It had to come with a brother when he was born.

"Excuse me, miss."

Jacqueline feigned not hearing the man behind her, put her phone against her ear on her way out the door, and engaged with dead air in an intense conversation about an emergency. "No, I'm not that far. I'll be there as quickly as I can."

She ended the "call," while making sure not to look in the direction Nathan had walked. That way no one would suspect her of knowing that he got into a navy blue BMW, or that her photographic memory had captured the license plate number.

She hadn't met him, as she'd intended, but they'd made a connection. That raw look of hunger in his eyes made her sure of that. So all in all she was glad she'd gone to plan B when she'd not been able to reach her sister, and had gone by the sports bar where she knew Jessica and Nathan had initially met. Plans for the demise of all the others had already been formulated. For the most part. Nathan's was the only one still being thought out.

Jacqueline retrieved her newly purchased tablet computer from beneath the front seat, typed the name *Nathan Carver* into a search engine and pulled up his picture. "You are most definitely a sweet temptation," she murmured, smiling and running her manicured nail across his lips. "I just might have to make ours a more intimate acquaintance and find out what's so special about what's between your legs"—the smile slid into a sneer—"that it came between me and my sister."

She x-ed out his image so hard with her fingernail that it scratched the face of her computer. That same nail tapped the contact feature and tapped again on a one-word entry—Maple—Jacqueline's code name for the woman she'd seen leaving the workplace along with her husband. Wanting their first meeting to be private, or at the very least without her man around, she'd remained in the confines of her car. Tomorrow would be soon enough for this sibling reunion. Tomorrow, bright and early, Jessica Givens would get a blast from her past.

When Jacqueline returned to her hotel room, she got one, too.

"Oh my gosh . . . Kris!" She ran across the room and enveloped her best friend in a big bear hug. "I didn't know if you'd meet me."

"I almost didn't."

"Please don't be mad at me for not keeping in touch. I wanted to but . . ."

"But what?"

"I couldn't! Between the guards, the other inmates, and those crazy meds that kept me feeling like a zombie, it was all I could do to just function. I didn't begin thinking straight again until I decided to stop downing their stupid pills, something I should have done a long time ago. Will you forgive me?"

Kris took in Jacqueline's vulnerable expression. "I'll think about it." She brushed the hair from Jacqueline's face. "I've really, *really* missed you."

Jacqueline smiled, relieved. "I missed you too, you crazy Canadian. And I'm so glad you're here. Come on. Let's sit down. We've got a *lot* to talk about."

The next morning, Jacqueline, feeling as confident as ever following the powwow with Kris that lasted till dawn, sat in a downtown Atlanta parking structure and watched as Jessica and the man she now knew was named Vincent exited his sporty black ride and walked to the elevator.

"Yesterday, a tall, dark, and handsome businessman, and today . . . this." Jacqueline sat motionless and sans disquise, her breathing deep and even as she watched the handsome couple cross the underground parking lot. Today's vantage point gave her a much clearer picture of the duo she'd eyed yesterday from across the street. Then, she'd been more focused on making sure the woman she scoped out through a set of high-powered binoculars was indeed her sister. There'd been no mistaking Jessica Bolton-Givens—five-foot-five, curvy frame, curly black hair, attractive round face—just like the pictures they'd exchanged via a contraband cell phone when Jacqueline was in prison. Today she took in the full measure of the man who walked beside her sister, noting his lean frame, boyishly handsome face, and confident strides. Where Nathan was handsome enough in a corporate cool sort of way, the medium-built glass of water her eyes now drank in was a pretty boy/playboy if she'd ever seen one.

You've got great taste in men, Sis, I'll give you that. And you're a pretty girl. "But pretty girls are a dime a dozen," she murmured under her breath. "Especially in this town. So how does your simple-minded self manage to wrap such prizes around your finger?" Her eyes narrowed. She watched Vincent hold open the elevator door, lightly place his hand at the small of Jessica's back, and guide her inside. Unconsciously, she shifted her head to the left, trying to continue monitoring their actions as the doors closed. She strummed her fingers against the steering wheel, mind whirling. With each passing day that she'd spent in prison, hatred for her sister had increased. Not only had Jessica foiled the job that Jacqueline had asked her to do, the one that could have potentially gained her an earlier release, but she'd then moved on without a backward glance, happy to leave her sister to rot in jail. It was time for baby sis to learn that bad things happened when people crossed Jacqueline Tate. The question was, how should she go about teaching this lesson? Should she go through with her first plan of taking her sister out with an arsenic-laced liter of cola as she had the prison guard? A sniper surprise, perhaps? Or would that be too quick a death, painful but soon over? Or should she opt for the riskier yet eminently more rewarding option of leaving Jessica alive but killing all of what seemed to matter in her life, starting with her idyllic marriage to that hunk of a man, and followed up with the death of their child, another valuable tidbit she and Kris had gleaned in the two days they'd searched online. While pondering this thought, Jessica pulled out the tablet computer, plugged in Vincent's license plate number, and soon had more than enough information to aid in her continued strategic planning: date of birth, home address, current employment, college education, professional memberships, and more. What she learned helped seal the decision to not end her dear sister's life. At least not right away, and perhaps not literally. But before Jessica's head hit the pillow tonight, Jacqueline planned to shake up the younger woman's perfect world.

The opportunity presented itself four hours later.

Jacqueline watched her sister walk across the lobby after exiting the elevator. Head down, she had no idea someone got up to follow her as she passed through the revolving doors. Thankfully, she was alone. Quickly replacing the magazine she'd pretended to read for the past forty-five minutes, Jacqueline adjusted her oversized sunglasses and tightened the belt on her coat as she followed Jessica outside. She stayed back, wanting to make sure that Jessica wasn't meeting someone. Jessica walked to the door of a popular restaurant, casually looking behind her as she opened it and went inside.

Jacqueline quickly averted her gaze. She reached into her coat pocket for her cell phone and after sending a quick text to Eric, called a twenty-four-hour weather information recording and pretended to engage in conversation as she entered the busy eatery. Recently she'd ascertained that talking on a cell phone was an easy, surefire way to blend into a crowd. A quick glance around yielded no sign of her target. Bypassing the hostess stand, Jacqueline moved into the main dining area, carefully scanning the faces of those enjoying a midday meal. Finally she spotted Jessica sitting in a booth, alone, busily texting on her phone.

Without a moment's hesitation, Jacqueline walked over to the booth, positioning herself in a way to make the encounter as private as one could have while in a public place.

"Excuse me. May I join you?" Jacqueline used a Southern accent to throw Jessica off guard.

Jessica looked up and around. Every table seemed to be taken. "I really need some alone time but"—she shrugged and smiled—"as long as you're not looking to strike up a conversation, I guess it's okay."

"Thank you." Jacqueline quickly removed her coat and sat down. She watched Jessica for a moment, took a calming breath, and said, "I know you're not up for conversation but—"

"No, I'm not."

"And I don't want to be rude." Jacqueline took off her glasses and spoke normally. "But you're more beautiful than I remember. And your pictures don't do you justice."

She watched as Jessica's expression went from agitated to perplexed, and finally to recognition.

"Sissy?"

Jacqueline braced herself, imagining any number of reactions: being cursed out, water in the face, an all-out brawl, all of the above.

What she didn't expect was for Jessica's eyes to water, or for her to get up and come to Jacqueline's side of the booth, scooch her over, and envelope her in one of the sincerest, warmest hugs she'd ever felt in her entire life.

Nor had Jacqueline expected a squiggle of a feeling she vaguely remembered as love stir within her own heart. She hadn't expected that . . . at all.

CHAPTER 7

Jessica pulled back and looked into the face of the person she'd either loved or hated her entire life, the face she'd imagined seeing again, in person, for more than fifteen years. But never like this. And never after all the owner of that face had put her through. Quickly recovering from her unexpected reaction, she returned to her side of the booth and picked up the cloth napkin to wipe away tears. For a torturously long moment she just sat there, staring, swallowing the sob that threatened to call all the diners' attention to the drama unfolding in booth number ten.

Finally she regained control of her emotions and found her voice. "How did you get out of prison? I thought you were in there for life."

"So did I. Thankfully, the truth finally came out and I was cleared, just as I told you I'd be."

"You told me a lot of things, most of them lies. I can't believe the nerve you have in coming here and surprising me like this."

The waiter arrived at their table. Jessica ordered quickly. "Vodka, double shot."

Jessica wasn't much of a drinker, had never, ever drank in the middle of a work day with four hours left. But she quickly absolved herself of guilt. She'd never sat across from the devil, either.

Jacqueline answered before the question was asked. "Nothing for me, thanks."

Jessica watched the waiter walk away, precariously close to totally losing it until she saw one of the office busybodies get seated across the room. Any thoughts of causing a scene fled at that moment, much like she wanted to do.

"So you say they cleared you of all charges? You mean they were dropped?"

"Not exactly."

"Then I don't get it. How are you out?"

"Legal loophole, inadmissible evidence, the stars aligning in my favor . . ."

"Your. Favor?" Jessica felt her voice rise along with her anger. She ground her teeth and clasped her hands together in an effort to stop her body from shaking and to resist the urge to jump across the table and choke the smile off this woman's face. She lowered her voice and spoke through gritted teeth with a vitriol that surprised her. "No one who kills and tries to get others killed should ever be allowed to walk free."

Jacqueline's poise was unruffled. "I deserve every ounce of hate you have for me. But not because of what you just said. One of the reasons I'm sitting across from you is because that of which I've been accused is based on circumstantial evidence and hearsay. There's no telltale fingerprint, no strand of hair found at the crime scene, no smoking gun to prove without a reasonable doubt that I'm guilty of murder. It's my word against all of you.

"What I am guilty of, and take full responsibility for, is hurting the one person who's ever truly cared for me and believed in me for all of the right reasons. That's why I'm here."

"Look, I don't need this. Not your confession, not your apology, not your presence. I've gone on with my life. I'm happy, something that after you reentered my life two years ago I never thought I'd be able to say again."

The waiter returned with a tray bearing two ice waters and one double shot of vodka. Jessica stood, reached into her purse, pulled out a bill, and tossed it on the tray. "I won't be staying. Keep the change."

She walked out of the restaurant with her head held high, kept it together until she reached the parking garage and slid into the backseat of Vincent's car. There, she rolled herself into a fetal position, cried like a baby, and placed an incredible amount of stress on a child she didn't even know she was carrying.

Jacqueline grabbed the tall shot glass of vodka and tossed it back like water. A toast of sorts. The reunion nearly two decades in the making hadn't gone as dreamily as she'd hoped, but it could have definitely gone worse. She waved away the waiter and reached for her vibrating phone.

"What's up?" She slid on her sunglasses and headed out of the restaurant. "Oh, really? This is interesting news." She reentered the office building where Jessica worked. "Tell me more."

As she listened to the caller, the tension between her brows was replaced by a sunny smile on her face.

"Excellent work, dear. And well worth the extra two point five."

Jacqueline entered the elevator and pressed the button for the floor to her sister's office. The news she received reminded her that she was one bad biscuit who not only controlled her destiny but the ones of those who dared mess with her. She, not Jessica, would decide when their meeting was over.

Once the elevator doors opened, she walked to the reception desk with a spring in her steps, growing only slightly concerned when she didn't see her sister.

"Hello, I'm looking for Jessica Givens."

"She's still out to lunch." The woman behind the desk couldn't have looked less interested. She'd barely looked up at all.

"Darn. I was hoping to surprise her. I'm an old friend of hers, in town for the day. Oh well." Jacqueline turned to leave. "By the way, love that haircut. It really makes your eyes pop." She turned toward the elevators.

One sincerely delivered compliment and the middle-aged worker two weeks past pretty and a day beyond don't-give-a-damn perked right up. "You like it?"

Jacqueline turned around. "I do. It's cute!"

"I wasn't quite ready to let go of the yak, but my hairdresser is trying to get me to go natural."

"I think you should." She flashed a smile and once again turned to leave.

"Uh, do you know Vincent?"

Jacqueline waited until she reached the elevator doors. Wouldn't want to appear too anxious. "Her husband? Of course. Well, not technically, since it's been so long since I saw Jessica. But I know she got married and they have a child."

The woman rolled her eyes. "Anyway, he's in his office if you want to talk to him."

"You know . . . that's a very good idea. You're pretty and smart, too."

The woman obviously hadn't been complimented much. She hurriedly reached for the phone. "What's your name?"

"Oh, um, can you just announce me as a client?" She winked. "That way I can surprise him, too."

The woman pressed a couple keys on the switchboard. "Vincent, there's a client here to see you." She listened. "One moment." Placing the call on hold, she whispered, eyes twinkling, "He's asking for your name."

Whispering as though they were conspiring schoolgirls, Jacqueline answered, "Um, Ms. Blank."

"It's Ms. Blank, Vincent. Okay, thanks."

"You can have a seat, Ms. *Blank*." The receptionist winked. "He'll be right out."

"Thank you."

Instead of sitting, Jacqueline walked over to where a large painting of the Atlanta skyline hung, where her back was to the receptionist and her eyes were on the elevator doors. Her hope was to ride this wave of unexpected luck and get to Vincent before Jessica returned from lunch. She popped the top button on her blouse and eased her hand behind her head to release her hair from the band that held it. While shaking out her hair, she heard him.

"Ms. Blank?"

Jacqueline turned and walked to him, her voice so low that not only could the receptionist not hear the words spoken, but Vincent had to strain as well. Though having him lean forward and catch a glimpse of her cleavage and a whiff of her perfume was as good as she wanted it.

"Mr. Givens. Forgive me for not making an appointment. If I can have five minutes to explain why, I believe you'll understand."

"Sure, come on back." And to the receptionist, "Where's Jessica?"

"Lunch." Said to Vincent while eyes beneath a raised brow took in Jacqueline's sudden change in appearance.

"Okay, thanks. Please hold my calls."

They reached his office. He closed the door, motioning for her to have a seat in front of his desk while he walked behind it and sat down.

Jacqueline remained where she was by the door, ready to make a quick escape if things got ugly. Lowering her eyelids in an expression that reflected vulnerability and a hint of fear, she made the announcement straight out.

"I'm Jessica's sister."

Years of training as an attorney kept Vincent's expression bland. But a measure of surprise managed to flash in his eyes before they too came under disciplined control.

"Jessica doesn't have a sister, and the woman who pretended to be her sister is in prison."

For Jacqueline, these were fighting words that chased away feigned fear. "When it comes to me and Jessica, there is no pretending."

She strode to the chairs in front of his desk, sat, and leaned forward. Her hands were clasped in a prayerlike plea.

"She hates me, and she has every right. But there's so much she doesn't know, starting with the fact that I've never killed anyone. The evidence against me was circumstantial, which is why I'm no longer behind bars. Since getting out, finding my sister and making things right has been the only thing on my mind.

"After . . . everything that happened . . . I almost went crazy with worry and regret. Not a day went by that I didn't hate myself for what I'd gotten her into."

These words came out in a rush, and since he'd not interrupted or called security, she hurried on.

"I've not always been a very nice person. I've done horrible things and had things that were even more repugnant done to me. But I've got to let her know that through all of it she has been my one and only source of light. If I could take it all back, I would. I love her. That's all I wanted to tell her just now, when I saw her at—"

"What? When you saw her?"

"Yes, I saw her leave for lunch and followed her to a restaurant down the street."

Vincent reached for his phone and tapped the screen. The call went to voice mail. "Babe, where are you? Call me as soon as you get this."

His countenance was no longer expressionless. It now showed anger and concern. "What exactly did you say to her?"

"I didn't get a chance to say much of anything. As soon as I told her who I was, she left."

Vincent looked at his watch. He stood. "I've got to go find her, and you'd better hope and pray that she's okay."

"I didn't do anything to her!"

"You showed up!" He reached the door and placed his hand on the knob. "Get out of my office," he demanded, his voice low. "And do not come near me or my wife again." He opened the door.

Jacqueline reached into her purse and placed a newly made, generic card containing a phone number on the desk. "In case she ever wants to call me . . . and get the whole truth."

She stood and walked to the door. In heels, she matched Vincent's five feet ten with no problem. Stopping directly in front of him, she looked deeply into his eyes. A classically trained actor could not have shown more raw emotion, or more easily caused their eyes to shimmer with tears.

Nervously licking parted lips, she allowed her gaze to slip from his eyes to his lips for the merest of seconds before she placed a hand on his chest.

Hot breath touched his face with her whispered parting. "I'm glad she has you."

She walked out, aware that he was behind her, confident that the rapid heartbeat she'd felt when she touched him wasn't solely because he wanted to find Jessica but because he wanted her.

Jacqueline reached the lobby. Still no sign of Jessica. Totally ignoring the smiling receptionist, she walked to the elevator and pushed the button. All the while, in her mind plans were shifting, changing, adjusting to a new reality.

She was sure Vincent was turned on by her. She was attracted to him, too. She'd already planned to get a sample of Nathan's lovemaking skills but now knew she wanted a taste of Vincent's prowess as well. After the way he and Jessica had treated her, seducing him and scorning her would be Jacqueline's pleasure.

Reaching her car, she pulled out her cell phone. "Todd, call me back when you get this message. Looks like I'll be in Atlanta a bit longer than planned."

CHAPTER 8

Randall reared back in his seat, removing his glasses and pressing fingers against weary eyes. He had at least two more hours of work before he could even think about going home. But he and his research partner, Dan, being on the verge of another breakthrough discovery, one that would not only complement his plant-based stem cell success but possibly change the face of how contagious diseases were treated, gave him the energy and enthusiasm to count his sixty- to eighty-hour workweeks as blessings. Seeing that it was nearing the dinner hour, he pushed the speaker button on his phone.

"Hello, sweetheart. How's your day so far?"

Sherri huffed in response. "I'm getting ready to ground your daughter and take away her electronics."

"Why? What has she done now?"

"She's not home yet."

Randall looked at his watch. "It's only seven o'clock. Did she have some type of practice or was there a game at the school?"

"Nothing was on the calendar, which, after the last time we went through this, we decided would have to be the case for us to approve her attendance at any event."

"Did you call her?"

"Of course. She didn't answer the phone but instead texted me back and said she was on her way. I called again. No response. Albany is really feeling herself these days, but she just doesn't know. I am not the mom to mess with. If she keeps being this defiant, she'll find herself in an all-girl boarding school somewhere in Montana."

"Dang, baby. Why Montana?"

"Because it's closer than Idaho. I'll send her anywhere they don't have a slew of tall, dark, testosterone-driven sports stars strolling around to sidetrack our daughter's attention."

"How are her grades?"

"Slipping. Not by much, but last year she was 4.0. Now she's hanging on to 3.8 by a thread."

"That's unacceptable."

"Exactly."

"If she didn't have the intellectual ability, it would be different."

"But she does have it. She's very smart. Unfortunately she has little common sense, as proven by the fact that she thinks she can outsmart a mother who's forgotten more about gaming a parent than she'll ever know to remember."

"Whatever discipline you decide, I'm with you."

"I appreciate that."

"We've got to be a united front, babe."

"Speaking of united, have you heard back from Nathan? I've tried to honor your request that you handle everything concerning that witch, but quite frankly I'm running out of patience. I want to know, no, I *need* to know where she is."

"I'm sorry, Sherri. After that unexpected conference call on Sunday and the news from my partner about the bacteria working, I just . . ."

"Forgot to call him?"

A long pause. "Yes."

"So the detective still hasn't been contacted? No one has looked into her whereabouts?"

"I'll give Nate a call on my way home, promise."

"No need. I'm calling him right now. Bye."

Randall tapped the End button and blew out an exasperated breath. He then struck a key to bring his computer back to life. But the conversation with Sherri had thrown him off track. He couldn't focus.

Maybe a bottle of water and a quick walk around the lab will help. He popped up from his chair, headed out of his office, and stopped short.

One look at the uniform the stranger was wearing and Randall relaxed. "Whoa, security. Y'all aren't usually up here at this hour."

"Sorry if I alarmed you. This is my first week and I'm trying to get acclimated." The handsome young man extended his hand. "Todd Dern. I'm the new manager of this detail."

"Randall Atwater."

"Nice to meet you." Todd looked around. "What is this, a research firm or something?" He turned to fall in step with Randall, who continued toward the break room.

"We do a little bit of everything here. What happened to Patrick?"

"He got promoted to manager after the previous

one relocated. Luckily this happened just before I put in an application. Because of my military background and previous security work, I got the job right away and was hired to cover the buildings that Patrick covered.

"I look forward to gaining your trust and proving to you that your company is as secure with me as it was with my predecessor."

"As an ex-military man, I'm sure you'll do fine. What branch?"

The two men entered the break room. Randall walked to the refrigerator while Eric stopped just inside the door.

"Marines, sir."

Randall nodded and offered Eric a bottle of water. "What's your name again?"

"Todd, sir. Todd Dern." Eric tried to look pleasant while using the alias he hated.

"Todd, around here we're at ease. You can knock off the 'yes, sir' 'no, sir' routine."

"Yes . . . sir. Sorry, that's a hard habit to break."

Randall's smile was tight but genuine. *I wonder if I should tell him about . . . no . . . I refuse to let Sherri's paranoia get me going as well.* "Good to meet you, Todd. Hey, listen. It's rare to see security up here. You guys usually make the rounds once we've all left. Is there something going on that I need to know about?"

"Not at all, sir. I'm just taking a week or so to become familiar with all the employees' faces. That way it's much easier to spot someone who doesn't belong."

"That's a very smart move." Randall slapped him on the back. "I think you're going to work out fine."

When they reached a T-shaped hallway, Eric walked

toward the lobby and the elevators. Randall continued down the hall to his lab. Had he lingered, he would have seen a sly smile spread across the new security manager's face as he pulled out a cell phone and tapped out a three-word message.

I'VE GOT NEWS.

When Sherri saw her daughter pushed up against a tall, handsome boy wearing a skull cap, oversized down coat, jeans, and Jordan sneakers, she tapped the car's Bluetooth and ended the voice mail she was leaving for Nathan, veered to the curb, and stomped on the brakes. The frustration of not being able to reach her brother had been replaced by something much more irritating.

"Albany!" She was livid. But she wasn't gripping the steering wheel out of anger. It was to prevent herself from getting out of the car and slapping the smile-turned-sulk off her daughter's face. "Get in this car . . . now." The demand came out in a tone that was a third growl, a third threat, and a third Terminator-style directive. I'll be back. Get in the car. Same vibe. Matter of fact, even her eyes blazed much as had the machine Arnold Schwarzenegger portrayed. When she saw Albany laugh, then turn and wave a flirty good-bye to the tall boy she'd been glued to, Sherri looked into the rearview mirror to be sure no steam poured out of her ears. They felt just that hot.

Albany got in the car without speaking and immediately pulled out her phone.

"Give me the phone, Albany."

"Why, Mom, I—"

"Give me that phone!" Sherri reached over and

snatched the phone from her daughter's hand, then put a finger in her face. "And don't you dare ask for it back. Since you can't answer when I call you, and think a text message will suffice? You obviously don't need it."

"But, Mom, I was in the middle of something."

"Uh-huh. I saw what you were in the middle of."

"No! I was—"

"Shut up, Albany. I don't want to hear the lie that's getting ready to come out of your mouth. It doesn't matter what you were doing. I'm your mother. You are to answer that phone *every* time I call you, no matter what you're doing. That phone could be on the moon and your ass on the sun, but if that boy who was all up on you when I pulled up was calling, you'd find a way to answer it. You're fourteen with a bullet and don't think fat meat's greasy, but you're about to find out. Having a phone isn't a requirement of being a teenager, it's a privilege. One that you've just lost."

Albany opened her mouth in protest, but took one look at her mother's blazing eyes and instead stared out the window.

After a couple minutes, a calmer Sherri spoke. "You have no idea how angry I am right now, Albany, nor how disappointed. You have a life that some children can only dream of, with every comfort one could ask for and almost everything you've ever told us you wanted. The only thing your father and I have asked for in return is for you to do your best scholastically and maintain a moral compass in your social life. What I've never asked for, because in my mind it goes without saying, is respect. I won't ask for it now. I'm demanding it. You will respect me. And in case you don't know, I'm going to tell you what that means.

"If I ever decide to give you back this phone, you will answer my calls and never, ever again ignore my calls and respond with a text. By doing so, you're saying there's someone or something else more important happening. At your age, that should never be the case. No one should occupy a higher position than your parents. If someone does, you need to make an adjustment. Now. Not only because it's the right thing to do and something I'm demanding, but so that if, heaven forbid, something happened to you, I'd know it. By your ignoring my call, it sets up a precedent where if something happened to you, hours could go by before anyone knew it because hey, she ignores her mom and doesn't answer her phone all the time anyway. So how would anyone know something was wrong? Do you get what I'm saying to you?"

"Yes."

"Is there anything you'd like to add to that?"

"I'm sorry."

Sherri relaxed against the car seat. "Who was that guy?"

"Nobody."

Sherri's hand once again gripped the wheel.

"His name is Corvales. He goes to my school."

"How long have you had a thing for him? And please don't say you're not interested. How much you're enamored of him is written all over your face. Which means he's read the book and knows he can get you for a wink and a smile." Silence. Sherri once more tried to relax, knowing that as angry as she was with her daughter, the information being requested was important to know. She lightened her tone. "What position does he play?"

Albany looked at her. "How did you know he plays basketball?"

"Because he has the same kind of cocky aura as my first heartthrob, who was the star of my high school team. All athletes have it. So is he a guard or forward?"

"Guard."

"Where does he live?"

Albany shrugged. "I don't know, but it's somewhere in the city. He was recruited to play on our team."

"Which means he's probably from a lower-income family and attending on scholarship. My guess would put him in a single-family home with little supervision and lots of time to learn how to game little girls, and make no mistake, I know you think you're grown and know it all. I did too at your age. But you have a great deal to learn, Albany. The first lesson being that if you keep fooling around with Mr. Slick back there, you won't remain a virgin for much longer.

"Here's how it will play out. He'll string you along for another month or so, get you good and ready to do whatever he asks. Then he'll ask to have sex with you and promise you the moon, stars, and sun in return. He'll swear that no one makes him feel the way you do. You'll give it up because he's your first love and you believe every word he says is gospel. The euphoria will last a few months, until having sex with you becomes routine. Then he'll seek out a new thing for excitement.

"By the time he gets to college—that is, if he goes—he'll forget all of you high school honeys because he'll have a whole campus of new flowers to pluck. That's probably where he'll meet his first child's mother. If he's lucky, she'll be the only one, though statistics show that if he looks pro-worthy, there might be two or more.

"If he's lucky enough to get into the pros, his children's mothers will join the likes of you and the other girls stupid enough to believe this man was thinking about anyone other than himself. You'll be scarred from this hard lesson, but in time, hopefully you'll heal. Or even better, you'll believe what I'm telling you right now and not have to learn this lesson the hard way."

They reached the house where, with the help of her computer whiz son, Sherri proceeded to restrict Albany's access to anything that wasn't school related on her laptop. The television cord was removed from her room and the iPad was also taken away. Dinner was a quiet affair. Aaron was all too aware of the tension between Albany and Sherri and made quick work of his plate of spaghetti. Albany pushed around more food than she ate before asking to be excused from the table. Sherri had opted for a large salad and no spaghetti because the ten or so pounds she'd lost last summer were trying to reclaim their spot on her hips, but after her bout with Albany had no appetite. Finally, she remembered the interrupted call to Nathan, excused herself from the table, and retrieved her phone.

Once again, the call went straight to voice mail. She left another message. "Nate, we need a favor. Give me a call as soon as you get this message."

Randall came home shortly thereafter. Once he finished dinner, he and Sherri retired to the master suite for an Albany-inspired powwow. Randall expressed a desire to pull out a can of kick-butt on the young man who'd groped his daughter. While the feeling was mutual, Sherri talked him into a more rational response, exhibiting the united front they'd talked about by agreeing that he would have a chat with his firstborn. Their action-packed day had left both of them too exhausted to do anything but take a quick shower, get into a comfortable cuddle, and go to sleep.

Throughout all of this, Nathan never called.

CHAPTER 9

Nathan told himself he was going to the sports bar to unwind before going home. He reminded himself that the establishment was on his way home, so it wasn't like he was going out of his way. Even though he rarely, if ever, went there on Tuesday nights, he told himself that sometimes it was good to change up the routine. He told himself all of these things even though he knew the real reason his car was now pulling into a half-full parking lot at just past seven. In hopes of seeing her.

Forcing himself into a casual stroll, he entered the establishment and headed straight to the bar. What he'd wanted to do was stand at the front door and scope out the joint, turning around and leaving if he didn't see her there. But how would that look to anyone watching? How would it look to her if she were watching? Like it was: a man with something on his mind looking for the woman who'd occupied it ever since their eyes had met. He'd have been okay had they not locked eyes for those mere seconds before he'd walked out the door. Her eyes were beautiful, light.

They shone like cat eyes. Something in her brief yet penetrating gaze had sent shivers down his spine and a message to his sex: If you can get that, hit that.

"Hey, Nate! What's up, dog?" The bartender gave Nathan a fist pound, then continued wiping down the bar. "What brings you in here on a Tuesday night?"

"Long day at the office, man. I just stopped through for some wings and a cold one before I head home and put in some more work."

"Must be nice Mr. Business Consultant, living the executive life, making the big bucks."

"Yeah, well, you know . . ." Nathan made a show of straightening his collar and pumping his shoulders. The two men laughed.

"Anything else with those wings?"

"I guess I should get a salad."

"House or Caesar?"

"Neither. I said I *should* get a salad. But I'm going to have a large order of those homemade fries."

"Can't go wrong with the home fries." He punched in the order. "One cold one from the tap coming right up."

Nathan checked his e-mails until his beer arrived. Mug in hand, he leaned back and viewed one of three television screens behind the bar. Somewhere in the world Serena Williams was beating up on an Amazon of a woman who looked to have a pretty good tennis game herself. To his left was a recap of last night's football game. The screen to his right showed a boxing match, something that would normally have held his attention. But not today. With a slight shake of his head, he took a long swig of beer. He wasn't a snot-nosed teenager enjoying his first crush. He was a grown man who needed to remember that there was a very lovely woman in the Bahamas with whom he was enjoying a relationship, one that had begun casually but lately was becoming more serious. The M-word had even come up.

Matter of fact . . . He reached for his phone, saw that Sherri had called, and made a mental note to call her later. Seconds later a wonderfully lyrical voice was filling his ears and replacing the stranger's image that had dogged his mind for the past twenty-four hours.

"Hey, gorgeous." Ten minutes later, when his food arrived, he was still chatting with Develia, his Bahamian friend. "Listen, baby. I've got a plate piled with spicy wings in front of me and the bartender just set down another cold beer. Can I call you back when I get home?" He laughed at her saucy response. "I'll hold you to that, okay? Good-bye."

He'd just finished his sixth wing and was right in the middle of a finger lick when she walked in looking like the Georgia Lottery. A faux fur, oversized jacket covered what he imagined to be a skintight, black jumpsuit, imagined because since he couldn't seem to look away from her mesmerizing eyes, he couldn't be sure. Somehow she managed to look supersexy and ultraclassy at the same time. Next to her was a clearly enamored young man. An assistant perhaps? Nathan sat there like the snot-nosed teen he'd earlier sworn he wasn't, hand in midair, sauce threatening to drip onto the shirt-covering napkin, until at the last minute he remembered why his hand was heading to his mouth and he carefully licked the sauce off his fingers.

Her smile widened as she watched him. Her strides never slowed. He tried to smile back but his face was frozen. His friend was right. This girl was something else. She approached him. He thought she'd passed him by. But just as she passed his left shoulder, she stopped, leaned in, and whispered, "What I wouldn't give to be licked like that."

Nathan was in trouble, knew it the moment he heard that clipped British accent. Dev's lyrical inflections had wrapped themselves around his heart the first time he heard her speak. But there was something about such naughty words being spoken in a clipped, matter-of-fact tone that was a total turn-on beyond anything he'd ever witnessed, including the baddest stripper working the stage of Atlanta's finest gentlemen's club. That girl was trouble. This, he knew for sure. He couldn't wait to get into whatever havoc she was planning to wreak in his life.

Ten minutes later he used a napkin to wipe the last vestiges of sauce from his hands and mouth. He finished the remainder of his beer and walked toward the bathroom to take a leak before hitting the road, hopefully with her phone number in his cell. She was sitting at a table by the window, laughing at something her companion said. Their eyes locked, her head turning brazenly to follow his movements, his head turning in likewise manner in acknowledgment. When he finished handling his business she was in the bathroom hallway, waiting, business card in hand.

"Would you prefer to play cat and mouse, or cut to the chase and go for pole in the hole?"

Her forwardness surprised him; pleased him, too. It had been a long time since he'd had a one-night stand. "I'd prefer the latter."

"Good. My hotel and room number are on the card. I'll be there in fifteen minutes."

"What about the guy you're with?"

She laughed. "Hardly worth your interest or my

time. He saw me in the parking lot and demanded to buy my drink. Had I not saw you here, at least I would have eaten and drank for free."

"So you came here looking for me?"

"Yes, I did. Are you glad I found you?"

"Indeed."

Nathan made it to the hotel in ten minutes. He grabbed a *Wall Street Journal* and took a seat in the hotel lobby with a bird's-eye view of the front entrance.

She walked in a half hour later. Even though she didn't look in his direction, he felt she knew that he was there. He waited ten more minutes, just because, then walked to the elevator, trying to slow his heartbeat as each passing floor brought this rendezvous closer. The elevator stopped. He checked the numbers and began walking down the hall on the left. For a brief second, sanity snuck through his lust-filled determination.

Man, what are you doing?

You don't even know this woman's name.

Right. He stopped and pulled out her card. *Alice Smith. Now I know it.* He reached her door and knocked.

She opened it wearing the faux fur he'd seen earlier, the high-heeled boots, and nothing else. "Good evening, my name is Alice. Please come in."

She didn't have to ask twice. With his coat already off and his manpower getting harder by the second, there was no point in delaying what was about to go down. Caught up in the excitement of the moment, he dismissed the lessons learned from past events with Jessica and totally forgot about returning Sherri's call.

CHAPTER 10

The next morning during the company exec breakfast meeting, it was sheer determination and a little luck that kept Nathan's forehead from greeting his bowl of oatmeal. He couldn't remember a time when he'd been so tired, worn out, wrung out, from an endless night of sex. Everyone was familiar with a headache, but a dickache? There was a first time for everything because the wildcat he'd had in the bed last night had screwed him so hard it hurt.

But it had hurt so good.

"Nathan? Any comment?"

"Oh, excuse me, boss. What was the question?"

His boss, Broderick, glanced at one of the other VPs and then back at Nathan. "I just added my two cents on the topic on the table. Do you have anything to add?"

Since the only thing on the table Nathan knew about was his remaining orange juice and the oatmeal bowl, he shook his head. "No. I'm good."

"All right then, guys." Broderick reached for the

check that had been placed near the center of the table of six. "I guess that's it. I'll see everyone back at the office."

Nathan wasn't surprised when fifteen minutes later, Broderick knocked on his open office door. "You got a minute?"

"Sure. Come on in."

Nathan watched his friend and business associate for the past seven years, and boss for the past five, shut the door. It was going to be one of those conversations. He didn't wait for Broderick to take a seat before starting it up.

"What's going on, boss?"

Broderick cocked a brow as he took a seat. "That's what I came here to ask you. I don't know where your mind was this morning, but it sure wasn't at the breakfast business meeting. Is everything okay?"

"Man, I'm sorry about being MIA this morning. I stayed up late working on that report . . ."

"Which is excellent, by the way."

"Thank you."

"But hard work has never had you so distracted. What else is going on?"

"See, this is one of the disadvantages of being close to those you work with."

"If it's something too personal, Bro, I understand. I don't mean to pry. I'm just concerned."

"No, it's not that. There are a couple of family situations going on around me, but personally, I'm good."

"How's your Bahama mama?"

Nathan laughed. "Good, man. She's good. I'll be seeing her in two weeks, matter of fact. The whole family's going down there for Thanksgiving."

"Must be nice to own an island."

"Or be the brother of someone who owns it."

Nathan's cell phone rang. Broderick stood. "Oh, it's all right, man. This can go to voice mail."

Broderick waved off the comment as he walked to the door. "Someone's got to get to work around here."

"Ha!" Nathan tapped the answer button as he got up to close the door that Broderick had left open. "Sis!"

"Don't sis me, sounding all happy-go-lucky. I called you last night and asked you to call me back."

"Got sidetracked, Sherri." This said around a yawn. "But I'm here now. What's up?"

"As tired as you're sounding in the middle of a workweek, with your lady miles away, that sounds like something I should be asking you."

"Why is everybody trying to get all up in my kool-aid?"

"Maybe 'cause I want to know the fla-vah!"

They cracked up at the sparring language dating back to their teens. Nathan looked at the clock. "Girl, what do you want? You're married to a balling biologist, but I've got to work for a living."

"No, you didn't go there. You're not the only one with things to do, so I'll be brief. My balling biologist husband was supposed to do this over the weekend, but he's been swamped with a new project that has him living at the office. So I'm following up on our conversation about having your detective friend find out where the witch's broom landed."

"I put a call in to Ralph, but his office said he was out of town. He's supposed to be back today, so don't worry, I'll stay on it."

"Thank you."

"Do you really feel it's necessary to get ourselves

involved in this again? Maybe it would just be better to let sleeping dogs lie."

"Calling her a dog disparages the canine community. A woman like her is way lower than an animal. Hopefully I am overreacting. But I won't rest until we find her."

"No problem, Sis. I'll call Ralph when we end this call and get back with you by tonight."

"If I don't hear from you tonight, I'll be at your front door tomorrow."

"And you'll do it, too."

"Think I won't when I will?"

"Stop acting like my older sister. I'll hollah at you later."

"You'd better."

"I promise."

Jacqueline had experienced many intimate encounters. Last night's romp was definitely top ten. It was the only reason this disciplined, always-in-control woman had hit the snooze button several times before turning off the alarm altogether. Her ringing cell phone woke her with a start. She was shocked to see it was ten o'clock. Normally, she would have four hours of work behind her by now.

"Todd." She cleared her throat but the frog remained. "Good morning."

"Is it? You're usually the one waking me up. What did you do last night?"

She rolled out of bed. "When are you going to learn to not ask questions?" She stumbled toward the breakfast nook in search of coffee. "What's the news you have for me?"

"I met Randall Atwater."

This announcement stopped Jacqueline in her tracks. *Why would he think Randall mattered to me?* She'd purposely not mentioned Randall's company, Progressive Scientific Innovations, nor the Atwater name to him yet. Had she underestimated Eric's interest in why she'd been arrested and been too confident that he hadn't read her court transcripts? Her brows knit in concentration. Jacqueline didn't like surprises. She didn't tolerate slipups. Even from herself.

"Who's that?" The question sounded lame in her own ears. She didn't like that either. "I mean, I know who he is. But why are you telling me?" Eric laughed, actually laughed at her, which for Jacqueline was akin to slapping her face. "Oh, I'm a joke to you now?"

"Whatever, Jacqueline—oops, I mean *Alice.* You're obviously forgetting that a woman I know quite well, a mother figure you might say, used to be the warden where a good friend of yours, Jacqueline Tate, was—"

Okay, so he did know. Jacqueline hung up the phone, livid. Eric had broken five rules in five seconds. One, laughing at her. Two, using her given name. Three, calling her out. Four, mentioning Randall Atwater. Five, being too dumb to realize that she was not one to be messed with, that what had been done to others could happen to him.

The phone rang again. Eric. She started not to answer but decided the more information she had, the better her position would be. "You have one more time to defy me. Just one."

"These phones are not traceable. You need to lighten up."

"Just share what you've learned using as few words

as possible. Can you do that, or have you been struck with a case of diarrhea of the mouth?"

The silence lasted so long that Jacqueline looked at her phone to make sure they were still connected.

"A private investigator is being hired to find out where the witch landed."

This time, he hung up.

Had it not been for the value of the information he'd given her, she would have been angrier. Right now, that emotion was not productive. She needed to move, fast, and get back to D.C.

Kris walked into the room. "I don't like him."

"Who?"

"Todd."

Jacqueline smiled. Kris, her best friend since the age of five, hadn't liked any of Jacqueline's boyfriends. She'd always felt they were using her, and didn't show the kind of loyalty that she did. Kris was right. They didn't. But not everyone could be like her single, financially-secure, carefree friend, able to drop everything on a dime and meet up. Kris had done that, and in just a couple days had made plans to meet her the moment she'd called.

"How can you say that when you two haven't even met?"

"I don't know. Just something about you two being so cozy."

"Don't worry about him. He's a temporary fixture who soon enough will be out of my life. You're a permanent spiritual sister who I can't imagine not having in my life."

Jacqueline put on the pot of coffee and took a quick shower. Ten minutes after drying off, she was packed and ready to make her move. A quick stop by the business center to use the public computers was all that remained for her to do here.

Nathan was a tasty lollipop she'd have to lick again later. Aside from the e-mail, regaining Jessica's trust while seducing her husband would have to be put on hold. Getting a grip on Eric and his cocky attitude was something that required immediate attention, as did the fact that those being hunted were trying to find the hunter. That they were looking wasn't what concerned her. That would work in her favor.

But when they found her, she wanted to make sure it was when and where she wanted it to happen. For her, the time was later this week. The place was Washington, D.C.

CHAPTER 11

"Vincent, are you asleep?"

It was six a.m. on Wednesday. Jessica had gotten very little sleep. She had no appetite, yet her stomach growled. Probably because a few spoonfuls of soup were all she'd been able to push past the knots that had been in her stomach ever since she'd seen Jacqueline.

"Baby, you up?"

Vincent grunted and rolled over, rubbing his eyes. "I am now."

"I want to call her."

"Jessie, I thought we got this straight last night. Nothing good can come from allowing your sis—that woman, back into your life."

"I'm not saying I want her back in my life. I'm saying I want to call her and have a conversation. She's the only blood family I have. Sissy and I weren't super close as children, but she was still my big sis. I haven't seen her since I was eight and she was thirteen. But both times we've reconnected, first right before my divorce and then again after she was arrested, we made progress in establishing a real relationship. I felt love there!

"It may be senseless, but I want answers. I want to know why she lied about so many things. Why she went through so much trouble to find me. It couldn't have been just about the crime she wanted me to commit. The right amount of money could have made that happen with no problem, using someone who could have done a much better job than I, considering that I failed. Miserably. I want to ask her about what our old neighbor Mrs. Hurley said, and about all that stuff Mrs. Hurley sent me. And I want to know why she went through so much to supposedly get us back together only to turn her back, instantly and completely, when things didn't go the way she wanted. I want to try and understand how any human being can do that."

Vincent sat up next to Jessica, now perched against the headboard. "Jessie, baby, she has all the traits of a sociopath. People like her have only one reason for doing anything, to satisfy themselves. The answer to all of your questions is, it's all about her."

He placed an arm around her. "I remember your sharing how happy you were when she reentered your world, how you couldn't wait for the two of you to begin the life in the beautiful picture she'd painted. Miami, wasn't it, where y'all were going to buy a house and be best buds? She told you everything you wanted to hear so that you would carry out her plan. She had no concern for your well-being. She didn't care that what she asked you to do could have landed you behind bars for the rest of your life. She was self-centered then, and she's self-centered now. I guarantee you that whatever reason she has for trying to once again worm her way into your life has nothing to do with you. Trust me on this. It's about her."

"You're probably right."

"I'm definitely right." His tone softened. "You never followed up on what Mrs. Hurley suggested. She was your family's neighbor for a long time and from what you told me, has lived in that town her whole life. She could very well provide additional insight on issues that continue to bother you. Maybe it's time to take that trip to Canada and talk with her in person, time to explore the possibility of having family there that you don't know about."

"I don't want to put any hopes into that being true. More than likely, I'd just end up being disappointed again."

Vincent leaned over and kissed her ear. His hand reached beneath the covers as his lips moved to her cheek.

Jessica threw back the covers and hopped out of bed. "I'll take Dax to day care this morning."

"You?"

"Yes. I'm driving my car today and going in early. I want to make up for taking off yesterday afternoon."

"Are you sure?"

"Yes. Now try and go back to sleep. I shouldn't have woken you up."

Vincent lay back down but Jessica's conversation had chased sleep away. He'd never loved a woman like he loved his wife and he would do anything to protect her. But that wasn't the only reason he'd discouraged her from reconnecting with Jacqueline. The way his body had reacted when she'd turned around in the lobby, let alone when she ran her finger across his chest and blew her breath in his face, was enough for him to know she was one dangerous female. Vincent was protecting himself.

Jessica was at work by seven thirty, an hour before her usual start time. Unlike some of the secretaries trying to climb the executive assistant ladder, arriving early and staying late, she was content to be where she was and do what she did. Right after she gave birth to their son, Dax, Vincent had begged Jessica to quit work and let him take care of the family. But after enduring a bad first marriage where her ex used money to control her, she'd vowed to never be totally at a man's financial mercy ever again.

So here she sat.

After transferring the switchboard from the nighttime answering service to manual control, she fired up her computer and decided to check her personal e-mails before starting work. One of the reasons was to see if she'd received the link a woman at the gym where she took Zumba classes had promised to send her. This exercise partner had joined the gym around the same time as Jessica, both doing so because they'd just had kids and wanted their bodies back. Jessica had pretty much lost her baby weight but hadn't been able to get her stomach as toned as it once was. She hoped to find something that would help her with that. Instead what she saw in her in-box was an e-mail address that caused her stomach to tighten more than a crunch ever could: somebodyssissy@gmail.com.

Sissy.

Jessica looked around, glad the lobby was deserted.

She hurriedly clicked on the e-mail boasting the subject "I'm Sorry," and began to read.

Jessie, I'm very sorry for upsetting you yesterday. It was the only way I could think to try and connect. After everything that happened, you have every right to want nothing more to do with me. I get that. I spent much of the past year in solitary confinement, with nothing but time to think long and hard about everything I've done, not only to you but to others. So I totally understand why you hate me. On all but the rarest of days, I hate myself.

Last year, when I stopped writing, was a very dark time. I thought I would never again see freedom, experience life outside prison. Of course I blamed you and everyone else. Everyone but myself. In the space of solitude, however, I had to finally face my biggest enemy: me.

My first sexual abuse memory is from three years old. My last is right before the fire. There's more I want to share on that. But not here, in a cold, impersonal collection of letters and spaces. Our tough childhood taught me to look out for number one. For the past two decades, that is exactly what I've been doing. I will not apologize for that. It's how I've stayed alive.

I will, however, apologize for hurting you, for betraying you, for pulling you into my mad, mad world. I am sorry for what I asked you to do. Forgive me.

It is good to see life worked out all right. I met Vincent. He seems to care for you very, very much. And he's hot!

I'll understand if you don't, but here's my number should you ever want to contact me. Even with all that's happened, we have so very much to talk about.

All my love, Sissy

Just as she read the last word, she heard the elevator ding, announcing an arrival. She quickly closed the screen and raced to the bathroom to avoid eye contact with whoever had made their way to work. With the way Jacqueline's words had made her bawl, Jessica was sure she looked a mess.

Five minutes later she was back at her seat, looking fairly normal except for slightly red eyes. Otherwise the cold water splashed on her face had done the trick. Or so she thought. She finished her coffee, along with a Danish from one of four boxes of treats that had been left in the break room. Seconds after her last bite, her stomach heaved, and she was back in the bathroom— throwing up.

CHAPTER 12

Juggling three personalities in eight hours wasn't easy, but Jacqueline had pulled it off. Shortly after Jacqueline had checked out of her hotel room on her way to Atlanta, she'd pulled into a busy road stop. Walking into the handicapped stall as blond, short-haired Alice Smith, sans cat eyes, she'd walked out as Kate Freeman, the cutie with curly auburn hair who'd initially rented the car in North Carolina. After arriving at the Raleigh-Durham International Airport by way of the rental-car shuttle, curly-haired Kate had walked into a stall. An hour later the sexy, head-turning, confident Jacqueline Tate walked out of the restroom and made her first true public appearance. Every wigless moment until now—from the shady shenanigans of her first hours of freedom conducted under the cover of darkness and a dirty baseball cap to purchasing the cheap clothes, wigs, and other transforming paraphernalia—had been on the down low.

Not anymore. When she gave her real ID to the admiring security personnel, pushed out her breasts as she posed to be scanned, had a gentleman promptly purchase her drink when she sat at the bar, and took her seat next to her chatty fellow passenger in first class, there was one thing about which there could be no mistake.

Jacqueline Tate was back on the scene.

The airplane wheels had barely bounced on the runway in Washington, D.C., before Jacqueline pulled out her phone and sent Eric a text: Meet me at the Liaison in two hours.

There was a bit of a line at the taxi stand, but she didn't mind waiting. In fact, it put a smile on her face, reminding her of another time, and another taxi line. On that rainy California day, she'd waited patiently at the airport for Dr. Randall Atwater's flight to arrive, and had followed him downstairs to baggage claim. She'd positioned herself in a way to chart his movements once he'd grabbed his bag and proceeded outside to the lane for passenger pickup. And after another five minutes, during which she saw him look around impatiently before speaking to the man in front of him and checking his watch, she'd strolled across the wet pavement to join him, the innocent damsel who wouldn't dare infringe upon his privacy by accepting a ride. Ha! He'd been so gullible, like putty in her hands. Her plan had worked to delicious perfection, all the way up until the moment his dowdy wife dared to go up against Jacqueline and play for keeps.

Once settled into the back of the taxicab, she took a deep breath and allowed herself a moment of quiet reflection. Hard to believe that this time last week she was dressed in a prison uniform, stuck behind a chain link fence. In less than a week she'd managed to set up several credible personas, fulfill the first of several eliminations, reconnect with her sister, however messily, and get her sister's ex-lover—who was also her nemesis's brother-in-law—into the sack. All while hardly breaking a sweat. And the best part of all of it? Kris was back! Getting off those meds was the best thing Jacqueline had done since the jailhouse doc had put her on them following an outburst last year. A clear head allowed her to remember why it was so important to keep trustworthy friends in her life. *Kris! That's my girl!* The merest trace of a smile ran across her face. Everything was running smoothly, as planned. That was one thing all of her bosses had loved about her. She was a highly efficient organizer and an expert at multitasking.

As she did right now, when one of three phones she had in her purse began ringing. Not wanting to pull out her British accent, she waited until the call went to voice mail, listened to Nathan's message questioning her whereabouts, and responded via text.

ONLY IN ATLANTA TWO DAYS, ALL BUSINESS. WELL, ALMOST ALL. MEETING YOU ADDED AN IMMENSE AMOUNT OF PLEASURE TO THE ITINERARY. WILL DEFINITELY CALL YOU WHEN OR IF I RETURN TO YOUR TOWN.

Seconds after her response, another question. Where are you?

Jacqueline tossed the phone back into her purse. She ran a frustrated hand through her luxuriously thick tresses, and worked to rein in her temper. Men and their exasperating need to know everything! Why couldn't they just work and fuck and keep their mouths shut?! So much for a relaxing ride and gentle reflec-

tion. Jacqueline all but growled when she reached her
destination and the cab driver flirted as he took out her
bag. She snatched it away, flung several bills into the
trunk of his cab, and marched into the lobby of the
quaint boutique hotel without a backward glance.

She entered one of four king suites the hotel offered and immediately found it to her liking. Unlike
many hotels that opted for bright, some would say
cheerful, colors with feminine fluff, the Liaison's classic brown, black, and tan combination, with a pop of
red here and a touch of ivory there, was the type of understated elegance she could appreciate. Reaching into
her oversized bag, she retrieved the tablet computer
that had quickly become the central workstation for
her multipronged operation and practically attached to
her body. She opened one of the bottled waters provided in the suite, checked her watch, and then fired up
the computer and Internet using the hot spot provided
by the hotel. She updated a couple charts and refined
her to-do list. Now that she was back in the area she
planned to use as her base for these upcoming operations, she could set up a post office box in nearby
Union Station for the array of spyware and surveillance items she'd be ordering soon. Her growling
stomach informed her there was something else she
should be ordering. But dinner could wait until Eric arrived.

A soft tap at the door came as if on cue. She briefly
closed her eyes, made a mental adjustment, and then
walked to the door. She peeked through the peephole.
He'd covered it up, an action that reminded Jacqueline
of the kid Eric, aka Todd, really was. True, he'd spent
four years in the military, but at the end of the day he
was a cocky middle-class kid whose tall, lean frame

and more-than-adequate erotic equipment gave him an air of maturity that had in actuality not been realized.

She opened the door.

He walked in and tossed his leather jacket onto a nearby chair. Taking in the room with a three-quarter turn, he ended facing her. "It's about time you called me. Damn, Jacqueline. I don't like being in the dark about what's going on."

She stood there, eyeing him. No words. No movement. Two seconds passed. Three. Five. He crossed his arms, his look defiant yet hungry. She took a step, slow and measured, and then another, until she stood directly in front of him.

Then slapped him so hard it broke a blood vessel in her hand.

He barely flinched, just brought his face back around from where the velocity of her hit had sent it. The only other reaction: a subtle clenching of the jaw that now bore a red palm print.

Before he could blink, it happened again. The left hand this time, connecting with the right side of his face.

His chest heaved, eyes narrowed. But still, not a word.

He was ready for the next move, caught her wrist as a fist zoomed toward his chest. She lifted a leg. He deflected her kick by turning his body and hers in the process, basically tying her up by her own arms and walking them to the king-size bed.

"Let me go," she growled, trying to bite the hand he kept just out of reach.

"Calm down," he demanded. "What the hell is wrong with you?"

They fell on the bed as one. He continued to subdue her with sheer weight and strength. She capitulated, became limp. He raised up to look at her, but her eyes were closed. Another few seconds. He felt her heartbeat begin to slow. He rolled off her.

Wrong move.

She pounced on him like a cat on a mouse, pushing words through gritted teeth as fists flew. "You. . . . irritating . . . impertinent . . . thickheaded . . . owww!"

With another tight grip against the windmill of fists, Eric flipped them once again. Jacqueline twisted and turned against him. Her thin, lithe frame was stronger than it looked. Those long legs that felt so good when wrapped around his waist now kicked and shook until she planted her feet and did an acrobatic backbend that sent them tumbling to the floor. Jacqueline's skirt had morphed into a leather belt around her waist as she fought on. Eric's T-shirt was ripped, and so was the skin beneath the tears. He returned the favor of her fingernails by pinching and then slapping her now bare ass. Once, and again.

She grunted against the pain, tried to claw out his eyes.

He flipped them over, pinning her arms out to her sides.

She twisted, turned, hoping for one good shot at the family jewels.

Eric got the memo and protected the legacy.

"I hate you!" she hissed, clearly defeated.

"Screw you," he snarled.

"Good idea," she panted, still squirming. "Too bad there's no one here to do the job."

His eyes narrowed. He put her arms together and

grabbed both wrists with one hand. With the other, he reached for his buckle.

Her chest heaved, placing her cleavage on prominent display.

His body reacted, bringing his appendage to the forefront as well.

Pulling the belt from the loops in his jeans, he secured one end around her wrists and the other around the leg of a nearby desk. His eyes scanned her face to gauge her reaction. Her eyes darkened. She licked her lips. "Motherfucker."

He smiled. "Bitch."

He pulled down his jeans zipper and released the anaconda.

"Give it to me," Jacqueline said, tied up yet still in control.

He tore off her flimsy thong and obeyed her command. This was an order the soldier gladly followed.

The sex was hard, fast, and dirty.

Sometime later the two lay on their backs, naked, catching their breath while still pressed against the hotel's carpeted floor. Clothes thrown haphazardly before, during, and after copulation decorated the chair, desk, bed, even a lamp. The smell of sex permeated the air. Jacqueline's empty stomach growled again.

"I'm hungry."

Eric spoke up. "Me too."

"Let's order room service."

"Sounds good to me." Their breathing had returned to normal. Eric glanced over and cleared his throat. "Don't get mad at me, okay? But I have to ask a question."

"What?" Framed with annoyance, punctuated with impatience.

"Why in the hell did you attack me like that?"

Two seconds passed. Three. Five. "To you my name is Alice, or Al, or whatever I tell you to call me, but never Jacqueline." She jumped up, walked over to the desk, and picked up the room service menu. "Every time you forget, I'm kicking your ass."

CHAPTER 13

Sherri walked into a rare sight for her kitchen: Albany and Aaron cooking. But there they were, complete with aprons and chef hats, up to their elbows in flour and seeming to love every minute of it. Her mother, Mom Elaine, was instructing this crew of two on the art of making homemade cinnamon rolls. Sherri's heart warmed as she took in the happily messy sight that, given her fashionista daughter and computer-geek genius of a son, she might not ever see again.

"Be right back."

She left the kitchen, walked around the corner, and pulled out the cell phone from the bag on her shoulder. She turned on the camera and was able to get off a couple great shots before her paparazzi moves were discovered. By Albany, of course.

"Mom!"

"Oh, come on, honey. These are memory-making moments for the family album. I won't put them on Facebook . . . promise!"

But it was no use, she'd been found out. Albany removed the hat and hid her face. In typical geek fashion, Aaron pulled out his phone and began filming his mom taking pics of him.

"Y'all, this is Mom, looking all fancy because she's going out on a date with this dude she likes."

"Aaron!"

He aimed at her feet. "I think her heels are too high, and her dress is kinda on the short side."

"Boy, if you don't stop!"

"Just taking a little film for the family collection, Mom!"

"Man, are you bothering my wife?" Hearing what was happening from the hallway, Randall had entered the kitchen from the other side and ambushed his son. "I will take you down." They tussled for a moment.

"If y'all fool around and knock over this bowl of dough, I'm going to take both of you down." Randall and Aaron stopped play fighting. Mom Elaine ushered Randall and Sherri out of the kitchen. "You two lovebirds get on out of here and go on y'all's date."

"Thanks, Mom." Sherri gave her a hug. "You going to be all right?"

"Child, we'll be fine."

"Okay. Albany, come here a minute."

She joined her parents as they walked down the hall to the garage. "Blair's off tonight, but she's around if you need her."

Blair, the Atwater's nanny-turned-personal-assistant, now going to college close to their home, lived in the guest house. While the weekends found most teens partying, Blair could usually be found wrapped around an anatomy, chemistry, or nursing science book on a Friday night, studying hard toward a nursing degree. With Sherri's concern for her basically healthy but aging mother, it was an arrangement that worked out well for both of them.

"Aaron and I can watch Grand. We'll be fine."

"All right."

"Mom, can I ask you something?"

"What?"

Randall walked ahead to the car. Sherri followed a minute later.

"What did she want?"

"To know if she could get her phone back."

Randall shook his head as he drove out of the garage. "Can't blame her for trying to cash in on your good mood."

"Can't believe someone so academically smart could have such poor street cred."

"Street cred? Listen to you! Trying to sound hard, as though you have some. And don't give me that South Side of Chicago mess. Mom Elaine had you on lock and all of us knew it."

"Don't say that too loud when the kids are around. I've got them pretty convinced I know how to roll."

"Not talking like that, you don't. Kids don't *roll*, and they most definitely left *street cred* back there somewhere with the Jheri curl."

Sherri burst out laughing. "Yes, right next to your 'mos def'."

Randall turned up the music. New jack swing and nineties R & B singers provided the soundtrack of the Atwaters' dating lives and to this day was their music of choice. Blackstreet's "No Diggity" got both of their heads bobbing—the well-respected, award-winning biologist and his educator wife. Nights like tonight took them back to before they were married, before their names changed to Mom and Dad.

"Man, I needed this break. Thanks for guilt-tripping me into taking you out."

Sherri smiled at him sweetly. "You're welcome."

He glanced over. "That was too easy." He merged onto the interstate, giving her a couple more quick glances on the way. "Come to think of it, you've had a gleam in your eye ever since I got home. What are you keeping from me?"

"Nothing."

"That was the fakest *nothing* I ever heard."

She laughed. "We'll talk over dinner."

They entered Washington, D.C., and drove to an area not far from where Randall worked. "Why'd you choose this hotel anyway?"

"Well, when we thought James and Debbie were going to be able to join us, I thought this would be a nice middle ground. Union Station isn't far away, Capitol Hill is just down the street, and it houses the restaurant of a man who used to be one of Oprah's private chefs."

"Uh-huh. That's the real reason."

"I must say it gave this place an edge. Who knows? I might meet Art Smith and have only one degree of separation from a woman I admire and have always wanted to meet." She looked out the window at the crisp, cool night. "I sure hope James's father pulls through surgery. Drunk drivers have no idea how many lives they threaten when they decide to get behind the wheel."

"No doubt. James's father is a trooper, though, so if anybody can pull through, he can."

"You and the good doctor have been best friends for a long time."

"Twenty years or more. He and Nate are getting close now, too. He contacts him whenever he's in Atlanta, which lately is quite a bit. A hospital there is waving big bucks in his face to join their staff. He and Debbie are toying with the idea of relocating. For them to think of leaving their beloved New York, the price must be right."

"That he and Nate would become friends doesn't surprise me. When a man plays a hand in saving your life . . ."

"I still can't believe that Jacqueline's hatred of you and me would extend to enlisting her sister to go after my brother, to try and harm him just because we're related. One has to be a special kind of evil to think like that."

Conversation stilled as the two remembered how close Nathan had come to dying last year at Jessica's deceitful, poisonous hand. Had it not been for the additional tests James ran following a routine physical, things could have ended much differently.

"What do you think about inviting them to spend Thanksgiving with us?"

Randall looked at her and smiled as he stopped in front of the hotel's valet. "I think that is an excellent idea."

Not long after checking into their room, which boasted a picturesque view of the Capitol building, Randall and Sherri sat in front of appetizers that paid homage to the restaurant owner's Southern heritage.

"How are your crab and crawfish cakes?"

Randall wiped his mouth. "Delicious. What about you?"

"The way Renee went on about shrimp and grits, I

was expecting something different. It tastes good, don't get me wrong. But I wouldn't drive out of my way to have them again."

Randall picked up his glass of wine, sat back, and gazed at his wife as he took a slow sip.

"What?"

"Nothing."

She picked up her glass and sat back, too. "That was the fakest *nothing* I ever heard."

"Can't I just sit back and adore my wife for a minute if I want to?"

"Absolutely."

"There are days I thought we wouldn't get here again."

"Where, back to a place called normal?" He nodded. She put down her drink and placed her chin in her hand in a thoughtful pose. "Me too. We have so much for which to be thankful, starting with the fact that Mom finally agreed to come live with us. Not having to worry about where she is, who she's with, and whether or not she's okay is a huge burden off my mind. And that you could move your mom into the condo she wanted? She never saw that Christmas gift coming!"

"It made last Christmas worth everything."

"Which is why I will not rest until we take care of the Jacqueline situation. Did you talk to the lawyer?"

"Yes, and he's going to file a motion to bring an appeal before the judge based on the fact that we weren't properly informed."

"Good. How long will that take?"

"He didn't say, but he knows that for us this is a priority. I don't want to have to worry about something happening to my family, especially when Dan and I are so close to another scientific breakthrough."

"I know you love what you do, Randall. But please try not to keep working so hard. When you agreed to a lighter travel schedule I didn't know you were just going to replace that time with more office hours."

"I didn't either. This new development that happened by a mere fluke really is something I didn't plan and can't ignore." He looked around, lowered his voice. "It could literally change the way we approach vaccines, the way we handle contagious diseases; it could be a huge breakthrough in treating common, reoccurring illnesses."

"From your actions, I'd say this was highly confidential."

"Absolutely. This is the type of information you definitely don't want in the hands of the competition. Which reminds me about the gleam in your eye and the reason behind it."

"In short, I'm being considered for what to me would be a dream job."

They continued talking. Sherri shared more about the newly created executive director position at an alternative education organization and Randall expressed his happiness that she was once again using the intelligence that had so attracted him to her in the first place.

"You mean it wasn't my big booty?"

They laughed. Their entrées arrived and conversation shifted again.

The woman sitting directly behind Randall reached for her fork and took a bite of the pork belly confit that at the sound of the voice behind her had grown cold on the plate. The odds of this chance encounter had to be something like a million to one. But it had happened. Jacqueline Tate was sitting directly behind the couple she believed was responsible for her going to prison, thanking the gods that her hair was down and around her shoulders and that they couldn't see her face. She had caught just enough snatches of the conversation to know four things. One, she had to get into Randall's office and find out more about the confidential project being cooked up in his lab. Two, she needed to turn that witch Sherri's chance at a dream job into a nightmare. Three, with the possibility of her being dragged back into court, she had to move fast to ruin their lives the way they'd ruined hers.

Four, once done, she'd need to leave the country, ASAP.

CHAPTER 14

It was almost midnight when Randall and Sherri arrived back at the hotel. They were as exhilarated as they were exhausted. Both of them plopped on the bed. Randall lay back still wrapped in the euphoria of the amazing music they'd just heard. Sherri reached down to take off her "sit down" pumps. Those shoes that are great for sitting, but for walking? Not so much.

"Man, I'm going to have to thank James for turning me on to that dude. Gregory Porter is the truth!"

Sherri stood, began removing her clothes. "I can't believe I'd never heard of him. It just goes to show you how many amazing singers and musicians are out here doing their thing that the world doesn't know about."

Randall rolled over and got off the bed. "I think I'll take a quick shower. Care to join me?"

"No, you go ahead."

Randall gave a brow raise and shrug and walked out of the room. Sherri smiled. She knew that was his way of being romantic and she had no intention of disappointing him. A few seconds after hearing the shower

being turned on, she went to her toiletry bag and pulled
out the edible lotion she'd recently ordered, shimmied
out of her underwear, and spread the gooey chocolate
all over her body. She was wracked with a touch of self-
consciousness when she touched her freshly waxed sex,
the first time those lips had been so exposed since hair
began to grow there. "It turns my man into an animal."
That's what Renee had said earlier in the week when
Sherri had mentioned her upcoming date night and that
she'd ordered the lotion Renee had told her about. "A
wife in the living room, a hooker in the bedroom.
That's how you keep your man."

That conversation is what had sent Sherri to a spa
two days ago. She'd walked out with skin as soft as a
baby's, and as bare. Why was it so important that she
please her hardworking husband? Because a few years
ago someone had come along and tried to not only take
said husband but destroy their marriage. The incident
was traumatic for the whole family, but it ironically
proved a bit of a blessing as well. Both Sherri and Randall had acknowledged that after two kids and fifteen
years they'd become complacent in several marital
areas. Jacqueline Tate had reignited the spark between
Randall and Sherri, which in turn had made their union
better than ever.

But if Jacqueline was holding her breath waiting
for a thank-you from Sherri, she'd be waiting for a
very long time.

Sherri took one last glimpse of her chocolate-covered
skin before turning to join Randall in the shower. She'd
just taken two steps when the room phone rang. She
looked at the phone and frowned. *Who could that be?*
No one but Blair and Mom know where we are and

she wouldn't call unless . . . Sherri raced to the phone. "Hello?"

Dead air.

"Hello?"

Click.

Sherri's frown deepened. *Who would call the room just to hang up?* A shot of air swirled around her body, reminding her that she was standing butt naked, covered in rapidly drying edible goo.

She shook away the troubling feelings brought on by the weird non-call, picked up a bar of strawberry-flavored soap, and walked into the bathroom. She opened the door and struck a pose. "Care for a little chocolate?"

Randall's hand stopped in mid-scrub. He slowly turned around, giving Sherri the once-over. "Mrs. Atwater, you look good enough to eat."

Sherri allowed the merest spray of water to touch her body before wrapping her arms around Randall's neck and rubbing her body against his in a seductive sway. "Now," she whispered, licking some of the lotion now smeared across his chest, "so do you."

She rubbed her body across his again. This time when she licked the lotion off his chest, she pulled his nipple into her mouth. He hissed, a sure sign she was turning him on. He shifted, and in one smooth move had her body up and against the subway tile. She wrapped her legs around his waist as he nibbled, sucked, squeezed, and licked.

Later, she'd have to thank her friend. Tonight was going to be good.

He left her breasts and found her mouth. The kiss was hot and sloppy, the taste of chocolate sliding off their tongues. Randall eased a hand beneath them and found her heat. He slid a finger between her folds, brought it out, and licked it.

"Um. You taste good."

"Ooh, I love it when you talk nasty."

"Baby, I'm getting ready to do more than talk."

He eased her down just enough for her wet pussy to meet the thrust of his thick dick. They'd gone all week without much loving. The first release came quickly. They washed off the chocolate lotion with the edible strawberry soap. But their sexual hunger was far from satisfied. They moved to the bedroom.

"My turn," she said as they neared the king-size lair. "Lie down."

He did.

Sherri climbed on top of him, teasing him, taunting him, rubbing his throbbing hot dog between her toasty buns. She leaned forward and was immediately rewarded as Randall eased a nipple between his teeth, alternatingly sucking her areola and squeezing her cheeks. He tried to enter her, but she had another thought in mind. Randall was about to protest, until she slid off of him and kissed her way to his strength. He wisely decided to lie back and enjoy her power. When he was about to go over the edge he eased her up into their favorite position, got behind her, and sheathed his sword. They went from fast to slow, shifted side to side. Randall thrust as though in search of a buried treasure. Sherri hoped he'd never find it, that he'd search forever. Chocolate lotion was replaced by sweat. He kept searching. The beautiful spread slid off the bed. She encouraged him to go farther, dig deeper. Sherri gripped his buttocks as an orgasm tore through her.

Randall barely broke stride. He kept going—pump, swerve, grind, stroke—until he too went over the edge.

And after a while, they did their thing all over again.

The shrill of the ringing telephone awoke him with a start. Randall's head shot off the pillow. It took him a few seconds to remember where he was and to realize what was ringing. With one eye open, barely, he groped for the phone. He heard Sherri groan and felt her roll over as he found the source of the intrusive blaring and ended the annoyance.

"Hello?"

Sherri scooted closer to him, trying to hear who was on the phone.

"Who?"

"Who is it?" she whispered.

"Look, I don't know what you're talking about. You've got the wrong room." He slammed down the phone and fell back on the bed.

"Who was that?"

"Some stupid chick talking about this is her room but she can't find it. Her words were slurred and all mixed up." He yawned. "She sounded drunk out of her mind." He reached for Sherri, pulled her body against his, and covered them both with a sheet. She messed with a pillow and adjusted her body until she'd nestled into a comfortable position next to him.

"Ran."

"Hmm?"

"I just remembered something."

"What?"

"Someone called last night too, right before I came into the bathroom."

"What'd they say?"

"Nothing. Just hung up."

Randall grunted but said nothing.

"Don't you think that's strange?"

Her answer was the soft, even sound of Randall's breathing, punctuated with the slightest of snores.

She'd always envied how quickly he could fall asleep, and how easily. Now was no exception.

They'd stayed in dozens of hotels across the United States and in other countries. Yet she could count on one hand the times that the room phone rang with a wrong number. So what was up with their getting not one weird call but two in less than twelve hours?

By the time Sherri finally fell back asleep almost an hour later, she'd not figured out an answer to that question.

"Sleepyhead, wake up." Sherri tried to shake off Randall's hand but he was persistent. "Come on, now, baby. It's time to go."

"Go?" She rolled over, blinking her eyes against the sun streaming in through the open blinds. "What time is it?"

"Almost noon."

"Noon!" She sat straight up, a move that matched parts of her hair.

He laughed, sitting down beside her and running his hand through the hair she'd finally allowed to grow past her shoulders, a style he preferred. "I tore that stuff up, didn't I? I wore my baby out." She purred. "It's all your fault. You and all that chocolate and strawberry goodness."

"You were amazing, baby. I mean you always are,

but last night? Whew!" She shifted until she could place her head in his lap. "I wish we'd kept the initial reservation to stay one more day."

"Do you want to?"

"I do." She sat up, yawned, stretched. "But we should probably get back. Albany was none too happy when we left yesterday and Mom is in no shape to be the teen police."

"Call Blair. Tell her to keep an eye out."

"Sounds like I'm not the only one who could use an extra day in our love nest."

Randall turned and gave her a hug. The casual embrace lengthened. Randall did, too. "I love you, baby."

Sherri gave him a peck on the lips. "I love you more."

She kissed him again. He kissed her back, taking them down to the soft mattress. She spread her legs in eager anticipation. He rose up and entered her with one long thrust. She moaned. He hissed.

His cell phone rang. Both ignored it. The ringing stopped. Randall swirled his hips and set up a rhythm. Sherri matched him stroke for stroke. Her cell phone rang.

"Don't worry about it, baby." Randall picked up the pace. "Let's get this."

To the rhythm of ringtones, they rode a hastily built road to ecstasy. Randall's rod still twitched and Sherri hadn't stopped shuddering when his phone rang again.

"Randall, you need to get that."

"Yeah, I know." He hopped out of bed, grabbed the phone, and didn't even check the ID. "Hello?" He looked at Sherri. "Good afternoon, Ralph." Pause. "Sorry about that." He placed the call on speaker. "We were both . . .

handling another matter. I assume you're calling with information?"

"We've located her."

Sherri's jaw tightened as she got out of bed and came to stand next to Randall.

"Where is she?" Randall asked.

"Not far from you, I'm afraid. She's in Washington, D.C."

Sherri's eyes widened as she and Randall exchanged glances. "Ralph, this is Sherri, Randall's wife. Where exactly in D.C.?"

"At first she was at the Liaison." Sherri's jaw dropped. "But for some reason she moved from there to The Hay-Adams hotel."

"Ralph, we may have a problem."

"Why?"

"Sherri and I are at the Liaison. We checked in last night."

"Hmm, interesting. She checked in yesterday and checked out several hours later. Still . . . that's almost too crazy to be a coincidence."

Sherri chimed in. "I don't know how she knew we'd be staying here but I believe somehow she did. We got a couple weird phone calls last night."

"What time?" Ralph asked. Randall told him. "According to the hotel records she checked out around eight, more than an hour before you got the first call."

"I don't care," Sherri said. "It was her. I'm sure of it."

"But if she'd planned for something to happen to you two, why change hotels?"

"Because she's devious and shady. She may have set something up and then left so that she couldn't be blamed. Don't put anything past her, Ralph. Don't think anything's too far-fetched for her to try."

"Listen, I'll have one of my guys come over and do a sweep of your hotel room. Make sure there are no video or audio spying devices in your room. We'll go over your car as well for GPS equipment that may have been recently installed. I don't want you guys to get too worked up over this. If anything has been planted anywhere near where the two of you were this weekend . . . we'll find it."

Randall looked at his watch. "You say she checked into another hotel."

"Yes, the Hay-Adams."

"Is she there now?"

"She was until five minutes ago when she got into a taxi. My guy is following to see where she goes."

Randall nodded. "Stay on her."

Sherri swung into gear. She walked quickly to the closet, pulled out their luggage, and began tossing their clothing inside.

Randall watched her frantic movements. "Listen, man, thanks for the info. Keep an eye on her and keep us posted, all right?"

"Will do."

Randall ended the call, walked over to Sherri, and enveloped her in his arms. "Baby, I know it's hard, but try not to get too upset. Just because she's out, and just because she's here, it doesn't necessarily have any-thing to do with us."

"Seriously, Randall? You're that naïve? It was that witch who called last night, and again this morning. I'd bet my life on it. But even if it wasn't, no one is going to tell me that her being here, less than ten miles from where we live, is coincidence. Oh, no. I'm not about to sleep on that crazy chick."

Sherri headed to the shower, reached the bathroom door, and turned around. "But I tell you what. If she brings crazy, she's going to get crazy, South Chicago style, gangster style, you understand me? It won't look pretty. It will not be nice. But I'll be damned if she messes with this family again and thinks she'll get away with it. Before that happens, I will take her out."

Randall tried to be the voice of reason. "And then it will be you going to jail."

"So be it."

No room for reason when a mama's rage ruled.

CHAPTER 15

"You screwed up." Kris lounged on the bed watching Jacqueline pace. "That's not like you."

Jacqueline whirled around. "Do you think I need you to tell me what I already know?"

"Hey, don't get mad at me. I'm just saying."

"Well, quit just saying, all right? Be the quiet mouse you were during all of those years I was locked up."

"And whose fault was that?"

Her pivotal question deflated Jacqueline's anger. "Look, no matter how angry I was with you, I'm glad you're back in my life."

"What are you going to do?"

"Be more careful, for one thing." Jacqueline walked over to a window that provided an unobstructed, stunning view of the Washington Monument. "Your idea to check out of that hotel and into this one before making the calls was the best call all night. Since I made them from the courtesy phone, there's no way they can positively trace them to me."

"What about surveillance?"

Jacqueline gave her a look. "You saw how I was dressed last night. If they caught anyone on camera it was a Black man with a short 'fro, ball cap, slacker jeans, and Timberlands—a description that in this town fits ten thousand men."

"What about Eric, or Todd, or whatever you call him? What are you going to do about him?"

"What do you mean?"

"I've told you, I don't like him. You've never before enlisted help in your . . . activities."

"Yeah, well, I had to this time."

"You're taking a risk."

"To get the desired outcome, it's a risk worth taking." She returned to the bed where Kris lounged. "I can handle Todd."

"You sure about that?"

"As sure as one can be about anything. But if he ever becomes less an asset and more a liability . . . he'll be eliminated."

Jacqueline worked from afternoon to evening and well into the night implementing new strategies, adjusting plans, and relocating the base of her operations to Baltimore. After overhearing Randall and Sherri's plan to try and get her dismissal reversed, there was no time to lose. To further muddle her identity, she set up two more: a big girl named Jasmine Baker, and a guy named WaKeem. She'd rather liked the gangster persona and felt in the future it might serve her well. Right now the aliases she currently possessed were enough but a criminal could never have too many masks to hide behind. She'd also set up another one for Eric. He was on his way to Baltimore with credentials identifying him as Bruce Clarke. She'd so wanted to name him Kent, but felt the irony of the moniker might arouse suspicion. Bruce Clarke was a real human being living in Idaho, whom Eric greatly resembled. It had taken an extra two thousand dollars to get the forged documents within such a short time frame, but once again, her guy had not disappointed. The driver's license looked genuine. Watermarks, holograms, were all in place. Jacqueline had drilled Eric on the forged documents' information, and he'd memorized it in minutes. His military training provided the discipline needed to handle, with accuracy and precision, every curve ball that had been thrown at him. Jacqueline truly hoped she wouldn't have to kill him. It would be a waste of such a multitalented young man. Tomorrow, he'd rent her an apartment in his name. The day after, she'd have all of the new paraphernalia for Jasmine and WaKeem that she'd ordered online and had shipped to that address.

Her raw, primal reaction to seeing Randall and Sherri had surprised her, and their plans to get her rearrested scared her, leading to actions that had momentarily thrown her off her game. It was rare that Jacqueline lost control, but it had happened. She shouldn't have called the room even once, and definitely not twice. Kris was right. It was a mistake in a game with no room for error. She lay down for a couple hours of sleep, knowing one thing for sure.

It wouldn't happen again.

The next morning Jacqueline awoke with a response to her late-night text to Nate. As expected, he couldn't wait to see her. She placed a few items in an oversized bag, left the hotel, and went to a mall. Two hours later, after losing the man who was obviously following her, she ducked into a bathroom stall and reemerged as Alice, caught a taxi to the airport, and was on time for her flight's two p.m. departure to Atlanta. As much as Todd pleased her, she looked forward to spending time with Nate. For partly personal reasons but mostly business. This was an important visit, where several things needed to be put into place. The most critical item that she could not control was whether or not she'd get inside his house. That she'd have the opportunity to bug his phone and GPS his car was not a question. But having a bird's-eye view of his most private surroundings and an ear to intimate conversations was the goal. Having such would potentially eliminate surprises.

Not that all unexpected happenings were negative. When they landed and she took her phone out of airplane mode, the unexpected message that greeted her was as positive as it was timely. It was her sister, Jessica, and she wanted to talk.

Jessica heard Vincent pacing just outside their bathroom door. As fate would have it, he'd stepped out of the elevator just as she was returning to the receptionist desk for the second time in ten minutes. One look at her face and he knew something was wrong. He went to his office and canceled a few appointments, rescheduled others, came back out to where Jessica sat, and demanded she let him take her home. Her car now sat in underground parking because the dear, concerned, overprotective husband, currently wearing a hole in the carpet, cared so much.

"Jessica, what is it? What's taking so long?"

"Just a minute. I'm coming out." She flushed the toilet, washed her hands, and picked up the pregnancy tester.

She opened the door and handed him the stick. There were two lines.

He looked from the stick to her face. "There's two lines. Does that mean you're pregnant?"

"Yes," she said, her voice soft and unsure. "We're pregnant."

"Woohoo!" Vincent scooped her up and spun her around, then remembered her earlier nausea and placed her down quickly. "I'm sorry, baby. Are you okay?"

His joy was contagious, chasing away the worry lines from Jessica's face. "Yes, Vincent. I'm feeling better. Don't look so worried, babe. I'm pregnant, not dying of cancer."

He hugged her tightly, then stepped back to gaze at her.

"So you're happy?"

"Happy? Baby, I'm overjoyed, and overwhelmed. Being a father is one of the best experiences I've ever had. Dax is the reason I get up in the morning. Most men would be okay with having a son, but I've always wanted a daughter, too." He placed an arm around her shoulder and a hand on her flat stomach. "This time . . . I hope there's a girl in here."

I hope whatever's in here doesn't look too different from your son.

"Will you join me in the living room?" Vincent asked. "There are some things I want to discuss."

"In the middle of a workday?"

"For me, yes, but not for you."

"I already missed work yesterday. You know people are watching."

"Let them watch. In a few weeks, it won't matter. Come on, let's sit down."

He reached for her hand and started down the hall. She resisted. "What do you mean, it won't matter?"

"Baby, I don't want to fight. Can we just sit and talk peaceably?"

She followed, a bit grudgingly, chaotic thoughts vying for attention. They walked into the sunny living room of the cottage-style home Vincent had lovingly had restored to its former glory but with all the bells and whistles that come with modern upgrades. They sat on a love seat facing the window. She observed what looked like the beginning of snow flurries dance across the panes. He took her hand in his, tried to disarm her with a killer smile.

Her stiff posture gave the impression that she remained armed.

"I want to talk to you about quitting work at the firm."

"Vincent, we've already—"

"Talked about it. I know. I want you to please hear me out, with an open mind, and then sleep on what I've said for twenty-four, no, forty-eight hours before you say no. Will you do that?"

She offered a vague nod.

"No, Jessie." He gently placed his hand under her chin and lifted her face to look at him. "Right now, you've got your mind made up. Is it possible for you to put aside feelings and opinions based on past experiences, and consider what I'm about to say based on what's happening in your life right now?"

He'd asked so nicely. How could she say no? She nodded her head. "I'll try."

"This past year has been very stressful on you, mentally and emotionally. Just a few days ago you admitted how much your sister's actions affect you still.

Then, as if you conjured her up, she shows up at our office, putting you right back into an emotional whirlwind. Even though our child is an embryo, no bigger than what, a quarter or something, her DNA is coming from your DNA, baby. Now I'm not an obstetrician or whatever—"

"Right now, I can't tell."

"Ha! I've always taken daddy duty very seriously, you know that. Carl and I are always reading up on baby stuff and swapping information."

"And he's told you I can't work?"

"He shared with me how he and his wife were with their latest baby: reading to her, talking, singing, from the time they found out they were pregnant. They were conscientious about what type of atmosphere she was around, were careful to stay away from stress, negativity, things like that."

"And?"

"They said it's crazy, but their little Malinda is the happiest, most well-adjusted child they've ever met. And before she stopped working, Joan taught kindergarten. So I think she knows a little bit about what she's talking about.

"I'm going to admit something to you. Every time we drop Dax off at day care, it breaks my heart."

Jessica's face showed her surprise. "Why?"

"Call me old-fashioned, but I think a child that young belongs with at least one of its parents instead of with strangers all day. Maybe I feel that way because of how I wish my parents had been there for me. I thank God for my grandmother. She made all the difference. But there were times I longed to talk to my mom or hear from my dad. And they weren't always there. I know in today's world that's how things are done, but it would thrill me to know that Dax is here with you while you pursue some of the things you haven't been able to do."

"Like what?" Jessica still sulked, and part of her was still distracted, but there was a reason why Vincent was making a name for himself at the legal firm. He could mount a persuasive argument better than anybody.

"Whatever you want: go back to school, start an online business, become a socialite." She rolled her eyes. "I know why you're hesitant. But I'm not him, baby. I'm not your ex. I won't try and control you or force you into something you don't want to do. Once the kids get older, you can get back in the game."

Jessie looked out the window, her expression troubled.

"Baby, I know it's hard for you to trust."

She shook her head. "No, it's not that."

"What is it?"

She looked at him. "I got an e-mail today. From Sissy."

"Damn that woman. Why can't she leave you alone?"

"She wanted to apologize for showing up unannounced the way she did. And . . . for everything else." She nervously nibbled her bottom lip. "I told her I'd meet her."

Vincent stood and paced the room. "I don't like it, baby. Especially not now."

"I know you're being protective, but you don't understand. I've wanted to talk to Sissy for over fifteen years."

He returned to the love seat and sat beside her. "See, this is exactly the type of negative situation that you should steer clear of while pregnant. Tell her that something's come up and you'll see her in a year or two."

"Vincent, don't be silly."

"I'm serious."

"I know you are. And so am I. I'm going to meet her."

"Then I'm going with you. Aside from your going behind my back and sneaking, which I hope you'd never do, that's the only way you talking to Jacqueline is going to go down."

"Do you want me to go with you?" Kris looked nervously at Jacqueline, who was a pair of earrings and a spritz of cologne away from leaving the room.

"No. This moment is too important, and should only be shared by Jessie and myself."

"If I didn't know you better, I'd say you're actually looking forward to this. You almost look . . . happy."

Jacqueline turned to look at her longtime best friend. "Why wouldn't I be happy to see my sister after almost twenty years?"

"Because you can't stand her, that's why. Because you plan to—"

"Never mind about my plans. A woman can always change her mind." She eyed herself in the mirror, reached for a lock of hair, and began to twirl it around her finger. "Besides you, I've never had a close female friendship, never even fathomed a close family relationship. Aside from a group of girls in Toronto who used to meet for drinks every now and again, I've hardly socialized with women at all. Camaraderie always came easier with the opposite sex. I probably have my bastard of a stepfather to thank for that.

"The other day when I met Jessica, she ran over and hugged me, I mean really hugged me. For one split second, before she had time to remember all the crap that happened, she was really glad to see me. I don't know if I've ever had anyone react to me that way."

"And after she remembered?"

"Ran away like I had Ebola." Jacqueline laughed, but her face wasn't smiling.

"Can you blame her?"

Jacqueline paused, stared at herself in the mirror. "No."

"It sounds like you love your sister, Jack."

"Love? I think my childhood scars have left me devoid of that emotion, but my feelings for her probably come closest to it." Again, Jacqueline delayed her departure by joining Kris on the bed. "When she was brought home from the hospital, I was delighted. She was this perfect miniature creation, my own living doll. I had big plans for us."

Kris noticed Jacqueline's sad expression. "What happened?"

"I became invisible. Everyone doted on her. They forgot about me. I did everything to get attention. Only when I acted out did those assholes masquerading as parents realize I still breathed. Then and late at night when the monster found his way into our room and my bed." Jacqueline's mouth slid into a sneer. "From then on I hated her. When the fire happened, I almost . . ."

"You almost what?"

Shaking her head to dismiss her moment of reverie, she jumped off the bed. "I've got to go. See you later."

The place where Jessica had agreed to meet was

only ten minutes away from Jacqueline's hotel. On the way there, she began to feel good again, began to imagine the heartfelt conversation, the laughter and tears, and the deep bond that might come as a result of baring their souls to each other. *Maybe we really can be sisters.*

She parked her car and went inside. The dinner hour had begun, so the place was fairly crowded. Jacqueline sailed through the busy dining room to the private room she'd reserved just for her and her sister.

Smiling, she opened the door. "Sorry I'm late, Sis . . ." She looked from Vincent to Jessica. "Why is he here?"

"Because I'm her husband," Vincent interrupted. "And every time you show up this is where I'll be . . . by her side."

Ignoring him, Jacqueline looked at Jessica. "Can it be just the two of us?" she implored. "Some things I want to share are for your ears alone."

Jessica looked at Vincent. "Maybe you can wait out in the main dining room?"

He looked from his wife to Jacqueline and back again. "I'll leave for five minutes. That's as long as I can trust her alone with you. Then I'm coming back in."

"Baby, I think—"

"Jessie, sweetheart, it's the best I can do."

She nodded. "Okay. Five minutes."

Vincent gave her a quick kiss on the cheek, stood, and looked at Jacqueline. No words were spoken, but his message was clear.

I'm watching you.

CHAPTER 16

Jessica watched a myriad of emotions cross Jacqueline's face as Vincent walked out the door. By far, the most dominant one was anger. Her stomach clenched. She thought about the baby, and what Vincent had said about negativity while pregnant. Maybe this meeting hadn't been such a good idea after all.

Especially given the fact that as Vincent walked by her, Jacqueline turned to follow him, her hand in her purse.

"Sissy?"

Jacqueline stopped short and took a deep breath. When she turned back around, there was a smile on her face. But her eyes were troubled and for Jessica, troubling.

"I'm sorry about that." Jessica stood. "Don't take it personally. Vincent is being very overprotective of me right now."

"Oh?" Jacqueline walked to the table. "Why's that?"

Should I tell her? For the moment, Jessica decided

against it. There were too many other things that needed to be discussed first.

There was an awkward moment where the two sisters stared at each other. Finally, Jacqueline leaned in for a hug. "Thank you for seeing me."

"I had to. There are so many questions, so much that's happened . . ."

The women sat. Jacqueline reached for one of the three menus on the table. "What are you having?"

"Oh no, I'm not eating."

"Why not? Are you okay?"

"Actually, no. My, um, stomach's been bothering me."

Jacqueline scanned the menu. "They have soup. Maybe that will help."

"Okay, maybe I'll get that. But let's order later. We only have five minutes to talk about . . . the private stuff."

"Your husband is a jerk. He had absolutely no right to talk that way to me. I was two seconds away from macing his ass. I can't believe you left one controlling man only to marry another one."

"Vincent is nothing like my ex-husband. Like I said, he's just looking out for me."

"Is that what I've become to you, someone to fear and from whom you have to be protected?"

"Are you my sister?"

Jessica could tell the question caught Jacqueline off guard. "Of course I'm your sister. Why would you ask?"

"Because I was told you are my half sister, that we have the same father but different mothers."

"Who told you that?"

"Mrs. Hurley."

"It's true, we have different mothers, though for me that never mattered. You were always just my sister." Jacqueline's eyes narrowed. "What else did she tell you?"

Jessica took a deep breath. "That you killed our parents."

"What if I did?"

Jessica's brow raised in surprise. This was not the reaction she'd expected. "Did you?"

Jacqueline reached for the water glass and calmly took a sip. "They died in the house fire that you and I barely escaped. It's nosy bitches like Hurley with no lives of their own who would like to think otherwise, to create drama where there is none. She always was jealous of me, of any pretty girl, really, any of us who could turn the head of a man. That's something she's never experienced. It's made her miserable her whole life. A miserable, lonely, lie-spreading hag."

"She didn't come across to me that way at all."

"Of course she didn't." Jacqueline gave her the once-over. "She hasn't seen you lately. But trust me, if you showed up on her doorstep with that handsome asshole you call husband, she'd change her attitude real quick. She'd flip the script and spread lies on you too, because you have something she's never been able to get and keep—a man."

"She said there was money, lots of it, from an insurance policy that was in my name."

Jacqueline took a moment to answer. "That time in my life was such a blur, fresh out of the system with nowhere to go and no idea how to get there. An attorney contacted me and handed me a check. That's about it."

"From our parents' insurance policy, correct? A

policy that, if not made out to me, listed both of us as beneficiaries?"

Jacqueline crossed her arms, clearly defensive. "Is that what this meeting is about . . . you trying to get money?!"

Vincent walked in.

Jacqueline whirled on him. "Get the hell out of here!"

Vincent walked over to the table. "I think that's what you need to do."

"We're not finished talking." Jacqueline jumped in his face.

"I think you are!"

Jessica stood up. "Guys, please!" She forced her way between Jacqueline and Vincent, who were standing toe-to-toe. "Can we act like adults instead of kids?"

Vincent immediately capitulated. He put a hand on Jessica's shoulder. "I'm sorry, baby." And then to Jacqueline, "I apologize for coming at you so harshly. No matter that I felt differently, Jessica wanted to meet you. I'm here to support that. We may never be friends, but we don't have to be enemies. I'm down with trying if you are."

"I'm down with having a private conversation with the sister I haven't seen since I was thirteen years old."

Silence. Even the piped-in music seemed to pause.

Vincent slowly nodded. "I guess that's fair. Babe, are you all right with that?"

Jacqueline snorted. Both Vincent and Jessica ignored it.

Jessica turned to Vincent. "I'll be fine, baby, really. It's okay."

For the second time, Vincent left the room.

Jessica eyed Jacqueline apprehensively.

"Boo!"

Jessica jumped. Jacqueline's laughter filled the room. She laughed until tears came to her eyes, until she doubled over. She laughed until it became contagious, and Jessica laughed, too.

Jessica shook her head. "You're crazy."

"I believe the politically correct term is mentally ill."

The two sisters looked at each other and burst out laughing again. "See," Jacqueline began, picking up her menu, "we can get along without your bodyguard."

"He's really a good guy, Sissy."

"I'm glad you're happy." Jacqueline looked at Jessica, her expression unreadable. "It was a quarter million dollars."

"Huh?"

"The life insurance policy. I took half of that, gave it to a savvy investor, and now live well. I don't mind giving you half . . . of the original amount, that is . . . a hundred and twenty-five thousand."

This information was technically true. The initial policy was a quarter million dollars, but because their deaths had been ruled accidental, Jacqueline received twice that amount. Jacqueline didn't feel bad about not providing full disclosure. Had she not done what she did, there's a good chance their parents would still be living and neither of them would have the money right now.

"I didn't bring it up just to get the money."

"Sure you did. Why wouldn't you? After all, they were your parents, too. I can have the money transferred into your bank account within the next day or two. Consider it a parting gift."

"Where are you going?"

"Away from North America. I've had enough of the States yet have no desire to return to Canada. So I'm heading overseas."

"That's so far away."

"Just a plane ride or two."

"Where over there?"

Jacqueline shrugged. "Don't know yet. I'm going to take a few months and tour a few countries. Don't worry. I'll keep in touch so you know where I end up."

Jessica reached for the menu, her jumbled thoughts and previously queasy stomach settling the more Jacqueline talked. Maybe there was a little truth to what was said by both Jacqueline and Mrs. Hurley. Jacqueline was her half sister. But so what? Did that change anything about what had happened to them, or how Jessica felt about her? No. And perhaps Mrs. Hurley had drunk a glass of haterade where her sister was concerned, maybe she didn't want the two of them to get along. One thing for sure. Jacqueline couldn't be all bad. She could have lied about the money, could have said she never received it or that it was all gone. But she hadn't. She'd done the right thing and offered her a hundred and twenty-five thousand dollars! That was a lot of money, perfect timing with another child on the way. She could quit her job like Vincent wanted but still have her own funds. She might even take that trip to Canada that Vincent had reminded her of this morning. The money wasn't even in her account yet, but already the world seemed brighter.

"My stomach feels better now," she said to Jacqueline. "I think I will have a bowl of soup. Are you hungry?"

"I'm starved. I'm going to get a steak and all of the trimmings."

"Would you mind very much if I invited Vincent to join us? I'd love for the two of you to get to know each other a little bit."

Jacqueline sighed dramatically. "If you insist."

"Never mind. I just thought that—"

"Jessica, I'm kidding. How rude would it be of me to not want to include family?"

Jessica's smile reflected her joy. "Thanks, Sissy! I'll text him now. Better yet, let me just go get him."

Vincent joined them soon after. Anyone watching would have thought the diners good friends, enjoying a great meal. Jessica showed Jacqueline pictures of Dax and decided to announce her pregnancy. Jacqueline insisted that Jessica forward a picture of "her handsome little nephew" and congratulated them on the one on the way. Vincent confirmed everything that Jacqueline had discovered online. Vincent saw a side of Jacqueline that made him understand how his wife could love her. The earlier friction was seemingly forgotten, and when their late lunch was over there were hugs all around.

Jacqueline left the restaurant feeling especially happy. While oohing and aahing over the picture of their child, the one who to her looked like neither of them, she'd been able to attach an ultrathin wiretap on Jessica's phone, and later another one to the strap of her purse. Using the pretense that she'd forgotten her sunglasses, she'd also returned to their table and wrapped and pocketed silverware from both their plates. That and the pacifier she'd swiped from Jessica's purse when she'd gone out to get her husband, was all she needed for a DNA test that might come in

quite handy. Soon, she'd have Jessica's banking information, and now that Vincent wasn't treating her with
suspicion, there might even be a chance to electronically enter his world and eventually, should her curiosity and desire remain, his bed.

All in all, a very productive lunch. Tonight she'd
spend time with Nathan, her chocolate dessert, and
wiretap his world.

CHAPTER 17

"Keep me updated on what's happening, all right?" Nathan sat back in his office chair. "Absolutely. I want to know where she is at all times. All right, man. I appreciate it. Bye."

Nathan slowly returned the phone to the receiver, his spirit troubled by everything the detective had said. Jessica's sister had checked out of her D.C. hotel yesterday and later, someone closely resembling her had been spotted near Jessica's office building. Since he'd found no airline ticket, Ralph assumed she'd driven there. He was still checking the dozens of possible car rental companies she could have used. No matter how she'd arrived, the news was unsettling. Presumably the catalyst to his meeting Jessica in the first place, Jacqueline Tate, was in town. He swiveled his chair around and looked out the window. Was it his imagination or had the sky gotten darker, the clouds more gray? Either way, the skies weren't the only place a storm was brewing. The one in his mind had him pondering the timing of his getting a call from Alice yesterday and a call from Ralph about Jacqueline being in town today. A year ago this kind of *CSI* thinking wouldn't have crossed his mind. But a year ago he wouldn't have guessed he'd be poisoned, either. He sat back, remembering that fateful encounter.

"Hey, man, check that out."

Nathan followed where his friend Steve's gaze was directed and saw a cutie-pie lazily sipping a pomegranate martini and reading something on her phone. "That's a fine young lady."

"Yeah," one of the other two gentlemen at the table answered, "too fine for you."

They laughed, and then got into a debate about who was going to win the NFC title. Nathan sat back, let them go at it for a minute, then sat up in his chair and spelled it out. "It doesn't matter who wins it, to tell you the truth. Y'all know what I've said all season. My eyes and money are still on that team. They are a part of the AFC and they are the ones who are going to win it all."

"Excuse me."

The men had been so deep in discussion they hadn't noticed the pretty lady who now stood at Nathan's side. "I'm sorry to interrupt you, but after careful observation yet no idea what you're talking about"—she cocked her head in Nathan's direction—"I think he's right."

Shouts of protest hit her back as she walked away and reclaimed her stool at a table several feet away. After giving Nathan a flirty smile, she finished her drink and headed to the door.

Nathan was not about to let that much sexy get away so easily. He stopped her just as she was about to step outside.

"Excuse me. I didn't get your name."

She walked out the door. Nathan followed. "I didn't give it to you." Her eyes twinkled with a devilish glint. She held out her hand. "It's Jessica."

"Nice to meet you, Jessica. I'm Nathan. How did you know I was right?"

"I didn't. You have a look of someone who knows what he's talking about."

"You have the look of someone I'd like to take to dinner. May I have your number?"

The following evening, he took her to dinner. The week after that they enjoyed a concert. Soon after, they made love and began to date exclusively. He adored her, knew he had someone special. It would take him several months to realize that it was the kind of "special" that could kill you.

He turned back to his desk and tapped a computer key. His laptop came back to life. He typed in the name Jacqueline Tate and clicked on images. There were several pictures of the raven-haired beauty. There was no denying, the sistah was as fine as she was certifiable. But she looked nothing like the blond bombshell who'd rocked his world last week.

Wait a minute, Nate. Hair color can change. If there's a chance I've slept with the enemy . . . He snatched up his cell phone and hit redial.

"Ralph, look man, I have a question. Describe the

woman you're surveilling who you believe is Jacqueline Tate."

"I don't only believe it, I now know it for a fact." Ralph described a woman who fit one of the images Nathan stared at to a tee. "She had lunch with her sister this afternoon."

"What about her eyes? Did you get close enough to see those?"

"What's this about, Nate?"

"Perhaps I'm overthinking. But I met this chick a week or so ago. She's from London, or so she says, in town for a couple days. I get a call yesterday that she's unexpectedly back in town, and a call from you today saying Jacqueline's here."

"Does this woman look like Jacqueline?"

"No. Alice has blond hair and cat eyes, tiger eyes. But anyone can put on a wig and contacts, man."

"Do you know her last name?" Ralph asked. Nathan told him. "Did she tell you where she's staying?"

"No, but I can find out."

"Sit tight for now. I'll run the name through the database and see what comes up. Are you planning to see this woman anytime soon?"

"Tonight. Should I cancel?"

"Absolutely not. If it's Jacqueline, we can be on to her game from here on out. If it's not, then you'll have canceled a good time for nothing."

"Thanks, Ralph. I feel better having talked to you."

"No problem."

Nathan hung up the phone and for the rest of the afternoon was able to get some work done. Sherri called, but he decided against mentioning anything to her. Ever since last year when she'd jumped on a plane following a situation he was in that concerned her, he'd been careful about what he shared, and when. He loved his sister with all his heart, would do anything to protect her. She'd proven the feeling was mutual.

At a little past seven, he shut down his computer, picked up his briefcase, and headed out the door. Once in his car he tapped the wheel and initialized the car's Bluetooth.

"Hello, Alice Smith here."

"Nathan Carver over here."

"Nathan! I was just thinking about you!"

"Oh? What were you thinking?"

"Something quite naughty, I can assure you."

"Hey, are you at the same hotel as last time?"

"No."

"Where are you?"

She told him. "But honestly, I've spent the last week in hotels and was hoping that tonight could be a homier affair."

"You want to come to my house?"

"Unless you've something that hasn't been shared with me, such as a wife."

"No, darling, I'm very single, and equally private. It would make me uncomfortable to have you in my home."

"Even when you seem quite comfortable in my pussy?"

Dang, since you put it like that . . . But no, you might be her. I can't chance it. Finally he put it simply. "Even so."

"A bit annoying to be treated like a call girl, but

considering I'll probably never see you again, I guess it doesn't matter."

"What the hell does that mean?" For Nathan it conjured up visions of car trunks, syringes, and glasses of juice.

"I just ended a call with my boss. My work here is done."

"What do you do?"

"I'm one of several vanguards for a wealthy English businessman who researches businesses and/or people with whom he may want to invest. I thought a situation here had potential, but for him it's not a fit. What about you?"

"I'm a business consultant."

"What's your last name, Nathan? I don't remember."

"It's Carver."

"Carver. Ah yes. Do we have a date tonight, Mr. Carver?"

"I sure hope so."

"Where shall I meet you?"

"I thought we'd have a more traditional date tonight, beginning at a restaurant."

"I'm all for that."

"I know a nice place in Buckhead."

"Then Buckhead it is."

"Good." He gave her the name of a well-known restaurant there. "How does eight o'clock work for you?"

"Perfect."

"See you then."

* * *

A little past eight, Nathan strolled into Bones, an upscale steak and seafood restaurant on the city's north side. It was crowded, but due to a last-minute cancellation he'd been able to secure a reservation. At first glance it appeared that Alice hadn't yet arrived. Until his eyes landed on the bar area, where she sat partially hidden, looking more gorgeous than ever and, not surprisingly, holding the attention of two men. He spoke a quick word to the host and then walked over.

"Good evening, beautiful."

"Good evening, handsome." The men eyed him like an intruder until she added, "This is the date I've been waiting on, gentlemen." She slid off the bar stool. "Thanks for the company, and the drink."

Slipping her arm through Nathan's, she lowered her voice. "Your arrival is quite timely. A persistent bloke, that blond one."

"Can't blame a man for trying."

They reached the hostess and were quickly seated. Small talk about the restaurant's ambiance and reputation for good food ensued until drink orders were taken. Then Nathan sat back, staring openly at Alice.

She stared back, looking at him just as intently.

He slid his cell phone from his pocket and, without taking his eyes off her, tapped its face. She settled against the leather booth and continued to watch him watch her.

"You're a very beautiful woman."

"Thank you."

"I might get in trouble for asking, but is that your hair?"

"No, it belongs to the manager of the hotel where I'm staying. I promised to give it back upon my return."

Nathan chuckled. "I deserved that."

"You did, but no offense taken. It is a wig. Not long ago, I experienced a personal tragedy that was very stressful, and as a result developed alopecia areata, the sudden thinning or loss of hair. I'm taking medications to help it grow back, but it's still thin and patchy, hideous looking if I may be frank. For one whose job success and personal confidence are very much tied to how I look, that type of appearance in public—or privately, for that matter—is unacceptable."

"I'm sorry. I had no right to ask."

"That type of question would definitely be considered intrusive and uncouth in most circles, and totally unacceptable in polite company. However, as long as you promise to not make the mistake again, I'll consider it a small faux pas that is already forgotten."

Nathan nodded, his head down as if in deep thought when actually he was studying the picture of Jacqueline Tate he'd saved to his phone. "Does that mean I can't compliment you on features I find attractive, like the color of your eyes or that cute mole on the side of your lip?"

"I know few women who'd turn down a compliment."

"Right."

"Nathan, is there something you'd like to ask me?"

Yeah, are you the crazy bitch who tried to kill my sister? "No, why would you say that?"

"Because it appears that there is something on your mind, something regarding me perhaps, that you're trying to figure out. I find that the easiest way to gather information is forthrightly. For instance, I'd like to know if you were ever married, have any children, how old you are, and your annual income."

"Wow. That's pretty forthright. Could maybe even be considered rude in some circles."

The waiter delivered their drinks—a glass of sparkling wine for Jacqueline and a soda for Nathan.

Jacqueline held up her glass. "Here's to rude, uncouth, and intrusive questions asked among friends, but not always answered."

He held up his glass, nodded, and took a drink.

"So," Jacqueline said, leaning forward and revealing a generous amount of cleavage, "is there any part of my earlier query that is top secret information?"

"None of it is top secret. What I make is simply none of your business." Jacqueline smiled. "I've never been married, no kids, and I'm thirty-four."

"Do you think you'll ever get married?"

He nodded. "When the right woman comes along. What about you?"

"I married young, too young actually. Neither of us knew what we were doing. We divorced ten years later. Thankfully there were no children born of that union to be shuttled between households."

"Have you always lived in England?"

"Who says I've ever lived there?" Said with eyes twinkling.

"That's the same as someone with a distinctive drawl asking how one knows they're Southern."

"I was born and raised in England. I love it there. I live in the countryside, less than an hour from London with my best friend, two cats, and a parrot who refuses to say a word."

These words were uttered so effortlessly that for a minute even Jacqueline believed them.

"The next time I'm there I'll have to look you up."

"Do you often come across the pond?"

"I've never been to Europe."

"No!"

"True. I've been to several islands in the Caribbean, a couple Latin American countries and Canada, but never Europe. Always wanted to go, though. Now I have a reason."

Jacqueline laughed easily. "Really, Nathan, you don't have to use such duplicitous talk with me. We both know what this is, two sex-starved ships passing in the night, jumping on the chance to enjoy a good swiving. And for the record, you are very good. But I have no illusions for a continued relationship, and indeed no desire for one."

"Damn. Why don't you tell me how you really feel?"

"I just did."

Nathan chuckled, and tried to relax. There was some resemblance between the woman in front of him and the image on his phone. But lots of women had similar features. Didn't they? He put the phone away, and spent the next hour enjoying her company and the excellent cuisine. By the time they finished the entrée he was convinced that there was no way the delightful woman before him could be insane. While waiting for dessert, he went online and booked a room at a nearby hotel. They went to the room, screwed each other senseless, and after a hug and a handshake, wished each other well and drove off in different directions.

They'd both pretty much gotten what they wanted. Nathan felt he'd clarified for sure that Alice was not Jacqueline. Jacqueline had successfully placed a GPS device on Nathan's car, and after he opened the attach-

ment regarding London hotspots that she'd promised
to send him, she'd have a miked camera view into
whatever room his open laptop was placed. If he
opened it on his phone instead, there would probably
be less video, but the audio on his phone calls would be
priceless. In other words, he'd said good-bye to Alice,
but was still very much connected to the crazy "B."

CHAPTER 18

Two days before Thanksgiving, the Atwaters touched down in the Bahamas to clear blue skies, white sand beaches, and a balmy eighty degrees. Everyone was happy to be there. Randall and Sherri were excited because their good friends James and Debbie Sullivan, along with the younger of their two children, had accepted the invitation to join them. Nathan was happy because as soon as he placed the call, Dev would be on her way to get him. Mom Elaine and Aaron were happy because they'd talked the others into bringing along the dogs this time. Albany was ecstatic because she'd been given back her iPad and her phone.

Everyone entered the home that had been cleaned and stocked in preparation for their arrival. While the women went to consult with the chef and Randall joined the kids to take the dogs to the beach, Nathan went into his room, pulled out his cell phone, and called Develia. He placed the call on speaker and began to undress.

"Hey, baby!"

"Nathan! You're here?"

"I sure am. We just landed."

"And we're talking by phone instead of in person because . . ."

"Because I've not yet rented a car. Is there any way you can come get me?"

"I'll see you in fifteen minutes."

By the time Dev pulled up in her sturdy red Jeep, Nathan was showered, dressed, and waiting for her in the circular drive. He jumped up as the car came to rest in front of her, and ran to the driver's-side door.

She opened it and walked into his waiting arms. They enjoyed a warm embrace and a quick peck on the lips before she issued an order. "Get in."

He walked around and hopped into the open-air Jeep without opening the door.

She smiled. "I'm impressed. Looks like you've been working out."

"A little bit."

He had, but not in the way she meant. An image of Alice naked and sprawled against the hotel's white sheets caused a pang of guilt to assail him.

They engaged in small talk as Dev expertly drove the Jeep across the bumpy road, around hairpin turns, and over rough terrain. Nathan raised his arms, clasped his hands behind his head, and closed his eyes to the still bright sun. There was something about the laid-back energy and paradisial beauty of the island that made one relax upon arrival. Every concern he had, from the pressures at work to the whereabouts of Jacqueline Tate, all rolled away as easily as the tide flowed from the shore.

"Yes!" he shouted to the gulls and passing houses.

"I'm on vacation!" Dev's lyrical laugh further brightened his mood. "I needed this, baby. I didn't realize how badly I needed to get away until this very moment: being with you in paradise."

"What's going on? Work stuff?"

"That and something I'd rather not talk about on our first day together. What's happening with you?"

"You know my life, Nate. It's steady, peaceful, never changes. That can be both positive and negative, especially the 'never changes' part."

"I know this is the middle of your work day. Did you take the afternoon off?"

"Even better. I took off for the rest of the week."

He reached for her hand. "Then you'll be joining us for Thanksgiving dinner."

"I guess so, now that I've been invited."

"You're welcome whenever I am down here. I thought you knew."

"I had a feeling that was the case. But a woman should never assume where she stands with a man."

They reached her colorful yellow cottage with blue trim. She pulled the Jeep up to the front door and got out. Nathan followed suit.

"I didn't think to ask if you were hungry. Are you?"

"A little bit, but we can eat later. The way you were driving, I have a feeling that you brought me here to assuage a different type of appetite."

Once inside, Dev closed the door to the cottage and pulled him into a bedroom that, given the outside temperature, was surprisingly cool.

"I hope you don't mind," she began, her eyelids lowering to his mouth as she leaned into him. "I've missed you so much." She ran a hand down his crotch. "I've missed this, desperately. Make love to me, Nathan. I want to feel you inside me, now."

She lifted her head, pressed her lips against his. Her tongue sought and found entry into his mouth. The kiss was filled with all of the longing for him that she had expressed. She reached for the buttons on his shirt, working quickly to undo them. Stepping back so that he could undo his belt and remove his pants, she pulled the sundress she wore over her head to reveal the soft, voluptuous body that had helped him get over the life-threatening events he'd endured last year. Burying his head in her soft mounds and his shaft in her heat had helped him bury those painful memories, and after he went into a mild depression, start to live again. This is what he remembered as he removed his briefs and joined her in bed. This is what he kept in mind as he rolled on a condom and plunged inside her. Her loud moans and wet snatch pulled him deeper into the moment and pushed away memories made with another woman two nights ago. When she lovingly took him into her mouth and pleasured him orally, he imagined spending half the year in the Bahamas and the other half in the Peach State. By the time he lay on his back with her bouncy movements causing her juicy buttocks to flap up and down on his thighs, the last vestiges of Alice's nasty commands and twisted desires drifted away. Once they'd both released and Dev lay snuggled next to him, he was reminded of what it was about this woman he now held that had made him say no to all prior invitations save Alice, and why, even if he visited London, he'd never sleep with the freaky Brit again.

A short time later, Dev rustled beside him. "Nate, sweetheart?"

"Yes, baby."

"Did you wear a condom?"

He frowned. "You know I did. You saw me put it on."

"I'm not talking about just now. I'm wondering about the other woman you slept with recently. Did you practice safe sex with her?"

Even though it was true, her comment made him defensive. "What makes you assume I've been with someone?"

Dev's voice remained calm and casual. "It's not an assumption. I asked the question because of the fresh bite mark I saw while giving you pleasure. I know you work out and you might be quite limber, but even the best contortionist would be hard-pressed to bite his own ass."

Nathan couldn't come back to that type of logic with anything but the truth. "It was a spontaneous moment with a woman I met in a bar. She's from England, on a business trip. I'll never see her again." A sigh and then, "I'm sorry."

Dev sat up against the headboard. "Thank you for being honest. It doesn't feel good to know that you're not taking this relationship as seriously as I am, but it would have felt even worse had you lied."

Nathan rolled over. "I care about you, Dev, and this recent slipup aside, take you and me very seriously. In Atlanta, there are willing women everywhere I go, but that is the only time I was unfaithful."

"What made her different?"

"I don't know. Maybe it was the way she approached me, maybe it was the fact that she lives overseas. It was a bad decision." He sat up next to her. "I am truly sorry. Will you forgive me?"

"Sure." She kissed his temple, climbed out of bed, and went to take a shower.

Nathan sat in the middle of her white everything canopy bed feeling like a pile of crap. She said that she forgave him, but Nathan didn't believe her. And even if she had, could she ever forget?

Eventually he got out of bed and cleaned up, too. They left for a restaurant just down the street. Conversation flowed, laughter came easily. They even held hands as they walked along the beach. But as they returned to her home for a night of lovemaking, Nathan couldn't shake a growing sense of unease that the nights he spent with Alice would come back to haunt him.

CHAPTER 19

It was an American holiday, and Jacqueline planned to take full advantage of the fact that most people in the country were taking time to give thanks. The entirety of her plan hinged on whether or not she could pull off everything on her to-do list in the next several days. If she was successful, everyone who cared would believe that Jacqueline Tate was on her way to Australia, the country she'd chosen before she left jail, giving Kate, the big girl Jasmine, the gangster WaKeem, and any other persona she chose to employ, the ability to move around more freely. There was a lot on her plate, more than usual given the fact that Eric had gone home to North Carolina to spend time with his family before handling the job she had for him on Sunday afternoon. It worked out just as well. She'd given a lot of thought to what Kris had said about him knowing so much about her operation. Not that he had any real reason to snitch. So far, possessing forged documents and using fake IDs are about all she could be accused of, something that thanks to her he was now guilty of as well.

To implicate her in their future endeavors would be to incriminate himself. Plus, he was greedy. And she paid well. She wasn't worried about him doing anything foolish anytime soon. Still, handling this next item on the agenda was something she was glad to do alone.

Back at the Hay-Adams hotel, Jacqueline slowly walked back and forth in front of the closed closet door, viewing the pictures she'd taped there, pictures that had been e-mailed in response to an ad she'd placed on PremiereArtist.com, a classified advertisement website for those talented in all forms of art and for those seeking such talent. Forty-seven women had responded. The pictures now taped to the closet door represented the ten whom she'd see personally. From these, one lucky winner would get an all-expenses-paid vacation to Australia. Though this would come with a roundtrip ticket, Jacqueline doubted the return portion would ever be used. Chocolates and other decadent goodies laced with death-inducing poisons would hopefully inspire this Jacqueline Tate look-alike to stay abroad forever.

Reaching up, she pulled down the photos of the two women who she thought not only most captured her physical features but gave off the type of confident aura she would need to possess. She took them over to the desk and pulled up their résumés. One lived and worked in New York. The other was trying to get a foothold in the film industry by way of Louisiana, where Jacqueline was surprised to learn a lot of movies were made. She compared the two side by side. New York looked to be the type who could carry herself well, was probably older with more life experience. But she also seemed to be quite an accomplished actor, someone who would be missed by more than family if she didn't return home. Louisiana's credits were mainly independent films and commercials. She might need more training but be a better fit. Jacqueline huffed, stood up, and paced. *Where is Kris when I need her?*

Jacqueline walked to the window and looked out. She loved Kris, but felt her bestie was still upset that during her prison stint she hadn't kept in touch.

"Can I blame her?" she mumbled, leaving the picturesque view and returning to the closet door. *I'm a walking catastrophe. If possible, even I would have left me by now.*

She took a step closer to one of the pictures, eyeing it from various angles before standing back to fully take it in. While it would take cosmetic adjustments— dyed hair, lip injections, maybe a nose job—there was something about the look in the woman's eyes that Jacqueline had overlooked when she'd focused on the two actors. The average person wouldn't notice it at all. One would have had to live a similar life, one fraught with challenges, to recognize the pain behind the mascara and shadow.

Chirps from a burner phone interrupted her thoughts.

"Hey, Todd."

"Yeah, whatever. Do you miss me?"

"Obviously you've called for your ego to be stroked, but I can think of a part of your anatomy that would be much more fun."

"I can cut the trip short and come where you are. My mom's singing the same old song, trying to make her dream mine, and my dad wants to hunt and fish. I need to fly the coop."

"Spread your wings but don't come here. I'm busy. Our rendezvous is Sunday. My schedule is full until then."

"Whoa, the question I want to ask now could get my head bashed."

"Best keep it to yourself. Look, I'm not a chitchat chick, so I'm signing off."

"Wait a minute. I called for a reason."

"What?"

"Law enforcement is up in arms about a prison guard who got whacked a few weeks ago, around the same time that you were released. She worked at the women's prison and was one of my mom's best friends. The last name Stockton ring a bell?"

"Why would the name of a dead guard in North Carolina ring a bell with someone who's not spent a day behind bars?"

"Aw, man. Can we just have a straight conversation for two minutes?"

"We just did."

Click.

Jacqueline went back to the group of pictures, but Eric's phone call was like throwing a chunk of concrete into a placid stream. It made waves. That he'd mentioned the murder wasn't overly surprising. Law enforcement always gave more attention to crimes involving their own. That his mother used to be the warden of the prison she'd been released from made it even more probable that the topic would come up over turkey and dressing.

"But dammit, you're always sticking your nose where it doesn't belong!" She growled, walked over to the desk, and swiped everything off of it onto the floor. Looking around, she picked up the desk chair and tossed it toward the window. It fell mere inches from the intended target and bounced against the side of the bed. She reached for the lamp and caught a glimpse of herself in the mirror. Her eyes were wild and unfocused, lips twisted into a snarl. In that moment she looked just like . . . her mother. Memories rushed into her mind and flooded her soul. Her mom, drunk and screaming, fighting with her father, arguing with the neighbors, lashing out at her. The sounds of fists against flesh and beer bottles meeting paneled walls. Finally, her mother would grab an ever-present fifth of gin, retreat to her bedroom, and slam the door. Once the sound of her snoring echoed down the hallway, her father would leer at her. Then the true nightmare would begin.

"I hate you!" In her head, she screamed at the top of her lungs but in actuality the words came out in a hoarse whisper, from a throat closed tight with the strength it took not to hurl herself against the picture window and free-fall into eternity.

She hated them, both her mother and father, so much so that she wished they were alive just so she could kill them again.

Looking in the mirror once again, a shaking hand smoothed down her hair. She reached for a Kleenex, wiped the tears from her eyes and face. She straightened her clothes and slowed her breathing until she'd regained the self-control her parents never mastered. *You have work to do.* Looking around the room, she slowly retrieved everything from the floor and returned it to the desk, walked over and righted the desk chair, bringing it back to its rightful place. She walked over to the breakfast nook and poured herself a glass of water. By the time she'd drained it and set it down, she was ready to resume the planning process.

Over the course of the next two hours she secured information about Alexandria's prestigious Fairfax

First Preparatory Academy as well as the Fairfax First Step Middle School, and she also believed she'd found the alternative education organization that Sherri had mentioned to Randall at dinner the other night. After sending an e-mail to her sister requesting bank information, and texts regarding phone interviews to the ten women who'd made the final Jacqueline Tate look-alike cut, she was satisfied with the status of everything on her list. So after taking a quick shower and dressing casually, she decided to embrace the moment and find a restaurant where she could celebrate Thanksgiving.

One step out of the hotel doors, however, and she realized that she wasn't the only one working the holiday. The black SUV with the tinted windows was the same one she'd observed just before her trip to Atlanta, the one that had followed her first to the bank and then to a library down the street. She was glad she'd kept to her look of black wool coat, matching black hat, and dark glasses. That's exactly how her "twin" would dress when headed to the airport for her trip Down Under, giving Jacqueline the opportunity to travel to Baltimore in anonymous peace.

Everything was coming together. Within a week or two, Jacqueline would have left the country so the real work could begin.

CHAPTER 20

The day was glorious. It began with a Mom Elaine breakfast followed by several hours on a sailboat with a bunch of city men trying to fish. They returned to the house around two and spent the next three hours doing their own thing before all descending to the shore for a Thanksgiving feast. A long table, covered with a white tablecloth and laden with covered dishes, had been set up to offer a pristine view of the ocean. A shade cloth protected them from the sun and eased the heat factor of an eighty-five-degree day. Twenty people had gathered to feast on the best of American and Bahamian holiday traditions: turkey, dressing, and all of the trimmings alongside callaloo, pigeon peas, lobster tails, and conch done three ways. Conversation was lively and the champagne flowed. Dinner lasted three hours. Afterwards, everyone gathered near the water's edge, chilling and sharing stories as the sun went down.

"Dev, you should have seen your man trying to fish," Sherri said, more loosely than many ever saw her. Clearly, she'd enjoyed her champagne that afternoon. "I'm surprised his butt didn't fall into the ocean for the fish to eat him up!"

Dev smiled politely.

Mom Elaine was sitting on the other side of her. "He never was much for fishing or hunting, like the other boys would do when we visited North Carolina. You would be more likely to find him somewhere in a corner, his head bobbing and his ears covered with big headphones, ready to be the next hip-hop star."

Nathan reached over and gave Dev's shoulder a squeeze. "I still might give music a go, and Jay-Z a run for his money."

Randall laughed. "Man, you couldn't even beat Jay-Z in a race down the block."

"Look, New Edition, don't you start."

"Whoa."

A collective murmur went through the group as James spoke up.

"Remember that conference with the karaoke challenge?"

Randall buried his head. "Oh, man. Don't talk about what happened on that cruise."

"Debbie, get your man." Sherri laughingly tried to help her husband. "Doctors aren't supposed to reveal trade secrets."

Dev stood abruptly. "Sherri, everyone, thanks for making me feel so welcome. But I have an early day tomorrow so I'm going to bid you good night."

This was obviously a surprise to Nathan, who threw his legs over the lawn chair on which he was lounging and walked over to join Dev.

Sherri and Randall stood, too. "Always a pleasure to see you." Sherri gave her a heartfelt hug. "We're

going jet skiing and parasailing on Saturday. Hopefully you and Nate will be back and able to join us."

After saying good-bye to everyone, Dev and Nate
started up the walk.

Nathan placed a hand beneath her elbow to help
guide her up the rocky slope. "What's happening early
in the morning, babe? Do I need to bring over something special to wear?"

They reached the area where the ground leveled
off. Dev gently removed Nathan's hand from her arm.
"I've changed my mind and decided to work tomorrow.
I've tried to make light of your one-night stand but,
Nathan, I cannot. I just turned thirty-one last month.
We've been dating for over a year. This is partly my
fault because I never came straight out and told you
what I wanted. But now I will.

"I'm ready to get married, to be committed, to find
that person with whom to spend the rest of my life.
While I used to not think so, I now am even entertaining the idea of having a child. Having a long-distance
relationship isn't something I wanted. But I felt you
were worth the distance. I still think you're a good
man, but I'm no longer willing to spend most nights in
bed alone, suppressing my sexual needs and desires,
when I'm the only one doing so."

"Dev, that's not fair. I messed up, but this was the
only time." He lowered his voice, stepped closer to
her. "You know, when I looked up and first saw you on
what for me was going to be a lonely New Year's Eve,
I could not have imagined that fun night would grow
into what we have, or that I would feel this way about
someone I only see once every couple months. Neither
you nor I planned for this to turn into what it is. Long-
distance relationships call for true sacrifice."

"Then it's time for us to discuss a solution to the distance. Because this is no longer working for me." She put up a hand to stop his protest. "The timing makes it appear so, but this isn't solely about your cheating. I've been thinking more about this as we've become closer; how long being this far apart could work and what alternatives we could discuss to solve the problem. I realize now the timing for such thoughts was perfect. If we're going to stay together and make what we're building something that lasts, we can't keep doing it from a distance."

She gave him a hug. "Go back to your family. I'll call you tomorrow once I get off work."

"Are you sure you don't want me to come with you, and for you to take off work tomorrow as you'd planned?"

"No, I need time and space to think and resolve my feelings of hurt and anger. Work relaxes me and will give me that time. I'll call you tomorrow."

Nathan watched her until she rounded the bend that led to the drive where her car was parked. When he turned to walk back down the beach, he saw Sherri walking toward him.

From her look, he could tell that she hadn't expected to see him. "Where's Dev?"

"She left."

"And you didn't go with her? What's up with that?"

"We had a little, um, disagreement."

Sherri hooked her arm through her brother's, bringing him up the walk beside her. "What about?"

"Do I ask you about your and Randall's arguments?"

"If you were around when they happened, you would. Plus, you two don't see each other enough to have time to get mad. She was quiet all night. What happened?"

Nathan opened the door for his sister to enter the house. "What'd you come up here to get?"

"Mama's medication. Wait for me, and don't think I'm going to forget what I asked you."

Nathan placed his hands in his pockets, looking out the front door while he waited on his sis. On one hand, he didn't want to hear Sherri's mouth about his cheating. No doubt she'd have a thing or two to say about it. He didn't need anyone to tell him that what he did was wrong. On the other hand, she might have some helpful advice on how to handle the situation.

A couple minutes later, Sherri bounded down the stairs. "Okay, let's go."

They'd barely left the porch before Nathan blurted out his news. "I cheated on Dev."

Sherri looked at him in surprise. "Cheated? I didn't know the two of you were exclusive."

He nodded. "When I came down for the Fourth we had a long conversation and decided to make the relationship official."

"Yet here it is just four months later and you've been unfaithful? From the few long-term relationships I've known about, that doesn't sound like you. How'd she find out?"

"I don't want to get into all that. The point is, she did."

"No wonder she was so quiet tonight." They reached the bottom step that led to the beach and stopped. It was dark, the night punctuated with light from the insect repellant torches set up around the group by the shore. Snatches of conversation and laughter reached their ears, having traveled on the wind. "Did she break up with you?"

"No, but she's upset."

"Can you blame her?"

"No."

"Who was this woman so tempting that you took a chance on losing a very good woman?"

"Just some chick I met at a bar."

"Nathan! Come on, now. You're almost thirty-five years old!"

"Look, Sis. I don't need any help feeling bad."

"I know you don't. I'm sorry. What are you going to do?"

"Give her a day to cool off, then start trying to make it up to her."

"How?"

"I know what she'd like—either for me to move here or relocate her to Atlanta."

"Are you ready for that? It's a big step. The obvious one after that is marriage."

They began walking toward the festive sounds of their family and friends. "I don't know if I'm ready. But Dev is a good woman. I know I'm not ready to lose her."

Later that evening, Randall and Sherri lay side by side, enjoying the breeze coming in from the open patio doors in their master suite.

Randall reached for Sherri's hand. "Did I detect a little trouble in paradise?"

"With Nate and Dev?"

"Uh-huh."

"Yes, you did."

"What happened to upset the lovebird nest? I can't remember ever hearing that those two even argued."

"The same thing that happens far too often: Nate couldn't keep his penis to himself."

Randall was silent a moment before responding. "They've been together for what, a year or so?"

"Right at . . . a little over a year."

"Shoot. I'm surprised he lasted this long."

"Babe!"

"Hey, I'm just being honest. How realistic is it to expect a young, virile man to be satisfied sexually when he sees his woman every month or two, especially a man living in Atlanta, surrounded by all of that chocolate-covered goodness? There's no way I'd commit to someone who lived so far away."

"Weren't James and Debbie long-distance lovers before they got married? They met online, right?"

"He was in New York and she was in Texas. But the minute they decided it was serious, she relocated. That's what either Nate or Dev is going to have to do if they want the relationship to work."

Sherri nestled her head against Randall's shoulder. He ran a hand up and down her arm. "I was so glad to hear that James's father pulled through. While watching him today I saw relief all over his face."

"Wasn't for Debbie, they wouldn't be here. James was reluctant to leave his father, but Debbie knew he needed the break. It was good for them to get away."

"It was good for us, too."

"You'd better believe it."

"No calls from Ralph, huh?"

"Nope."

"I wonder what that means?"

"It probably means that whatever she's doing is none of our business. Let's hope it stays that way."

CHAPTER 21

Jessica walked into the room where Vincent and Dax were watching a Disney film. "Can you watch him for an hour or so, Vincent? I'm going out."

He turned and looked at her. "Where are you going?"

"Not sure, just feel like getting out for a minute, maybe go to the mall."

"Then you must be feeling better."

"Yeah, a little."

He lifted himself off the floor. "Little man and I haven't been out, either. Why don't we all go, and maybe include a movie or something."

"No, I don't feel like doing all of that. I just want to go walk around, maybe find a bargain and maybe even do a little early Christmas shopping, which I can't do with my two favorite men around."

He put his arms around her. "Well, in that case . . . go on out and enjoy yourself."

"Thanks, baby. Bye, Dax."

Dax didn't even bother turning around. "Bye."

Jessica got into her car and didn't truly breathe until she'd rounded the corner. Even though it was a small one, she hated lying to Vincent. After her business at the bank, she'd go by the mall just to make that part true.

She'd grappled with how to handle her share of her parents' estate ever since Jacqueline had offered it to her. A hundred-twenty-five-thousand dollars was a lot of money, definitely more than she'd ever had at one time. Getting a separate bank account for this money seemed to be the easiest way to handle it all the way around. She wouldn't divulge her and Vincent's joint checking account information. She'd be able to keep the spending from that account totally separate from her employment income and household expenses and she'd have a private little nest egg to fall back on in case she and Vincent ever split up. After the money had been successfully deposited in her bank account, she'd tell Vincent of her plans to quit working at the law firm, as he'd requested.

Maybe focusing more on her family would help her take her mind off Nathan. She'd tried to forget him, to ignore the love that lingered and the guilt she felt at his not knowing about Dax, but it seemed the harder she tried the more he stayed on her mind. Like now, when she had a more pressing issue that deserved her complete focus.

Thirty minutes later, she arrived in Lithonia, Georgia, a community of around twenty thousand citizens located east of Atlanta. She figured doing business here would lessen her chances of being seen by someone who knew her or Vincent. After securing a small post office box, she pulled into the branch parking lot of a national bank.

"Good afternoon. May I help you?"

"Yes. I'm here to open a checking account."

"Right this way, please. Toni, sitting at that first desk, will be happy to assist you."

Jessica sat in front of a fresh-faced redhead who looked all of eighteen. "Good afternoon. May I get your name, please?" Jessica told her. "Mrs. Givens, you're wanting to open up an account with us?"

"Yes."

"Do you have another checking account with us somewhere else, or is this your first account with our bank?"

"This will be the only account I have with you."

"But you do have another checking account?"

"I have a joint account with my husband, but I would like to open this without using that information. I don't want them to be connected in any way."

"All right. We have several types of checking accounts for you to choose from. Will this be a household account, one that you use often, or if not, would a savings account be a better option?"

"My parents died."

"Oh, I'm so sorry."

"My sister and I received money from their estate. My part of that check is what will be deposited. I won't use the account a lot, but I will need to be able to access it with a debit card. I don't know if that can happen with a savings account."

"It can, but if you feel there may be several withdrawals within a thirty-day period, then a checking account might be best. Why don't you tell me how much you plan to deposit? Then I'll better be able to choose the option that works best for you."

It took longer than she'd anticipated, but an hour and a half after leaving her home she had interest-bearing checking and savings accounts solely in her name. Dax Givens had been listed as the beneficiary. It made her feel good to know that if anything happened to her, she'd be able to leave something for her son. She had no doubt that Vincent would take care of him, but he'd know that his mom loved him, too.

She pulled out her phone and sent Jacqueline a text, giving her the account number where the money could be deposited. Once she was on the highway, she called home. "Are you guys hungry? I'll be home in about an hour and can get us something to eat."

"Where are you?"

"At a mall. I haven't seen anything I like, so I'm going to try at least one more. Do you want something?"

"I always want something."

"Ha, ha. Do you want something to *eat*?" Realizing the slip, she further clarified, "Food."

He laughed. "Baby, we still have a ton of leftovers from the delicious turkey dinner I made us yesterday."

It was true. Vincent's grandmother had taught him how to cook, and yesterday's dinner had been delicious. "Yeah, but we just had that yesterday. I thought you might want something different."

"I was going to cut up some of the turkey and make turkey salad sandwiches. But if you don't want that, I'd rather we go out and eat. It's Friday night. We should do something fun."

"Okay, I'll be home in a little bit."

She stopped by a mall, bought something for herself and her men and headed home, happy that she'd been able to handle her business in an out-of-the-way place where nobody who knew her could try and get all up in her business. Where no one she knew had seen her.

But someone had.

CHAPTER 22

She'd instructed them to come into the hotel in disguise, looking as different from their actual selves as possible. The two candidates chosen from the phone interviews to be seen in person had definitely accomplished that goal. The girl who'd flown in from Louisiana had come wearing an auburn wig and had darkened her face and skin with makeup. Bonita, the ambitious frontrunner whom Jaqueline had almost overlooked, had embraced the challenge with enthusiasm. When she knocked on Jacqueline's door dressed as housekeeping, Jacqueline was ready to let her clean the room. She'd been ready to make up her mind right then, but in her judicious fashion had put both women through a series of paces to see which one of them most embodied her, the one who could get through hotel and airport security with everyone having absolutely no doubt that she was Jacqueline Tate.

That moment came fifteen minutes into Louisiana's audition.

"Why am I trying to act like you?" she asked, totally

unaware that asking one question was one too many, and had just cost her the lucrative job.

"What better way for me to test your observation skills, the ability to embody someone else's persona, and to adapt based on character qualities."

"Interesting. I've been on tons of auditions and have never been asked to play the casting director."

Jacqueline stood. "I'll be in touch."

Louisiana was taken aback. "Oh, that's it? Would it be possible for me to do a monologue or two? I flew all the way from—"

"No," Jacqueline said, ushering her toward the door. "It will not be possible."

Frowning, she walked over to the desk, retrieved her cell phone, and called the second candidate, who arrived ten minutes later.

"Thanks for coming back so quickly," she said once they were back in the room sitting on the couch. "You got the job."

"Wow, this is fantastic. Thank you!"

"Well, maybe. Let me first describe what the job entails to see if you're still interested." Jacqueline laid out her plans to fly the woman to Australia under her identification, and the circuitous route the woman would then have to take to make sure she'd traveled without being followed. She would have to live there for at least three months and totally change her look to a new identity, which Jacqueline would provide her, should she decide to come home. "So . . . do you still think this is such a fantastic offer?"

The woman's beautiful face scrunched up into ugly. She tried to talk but couldn't. Instead she buried her face in her hands and sobbed.

Jacqueline wasn't expecting this outburst. Maybe

the woman wasn't emotionally strong or sound enough to do this job. Then again, it could be a result of the pain Jacqueline had seen behind the makeup after taking a second look. "Are you all right?"

"I don't mean to be so emotional, but you don't know how much I need this right now. I just broke up with my boyfriend. He was physically and emotionally abusive for seven years. This is the third time I've tried to leave him. He always gets me to come back by threatening to kill me or to hurt my family. But the last time . . . it was the worst. He made me do things sexually, made me . . ." She shook her head as if trying to rid herself of the memory. "I couldn't take it anymore. I knew that if I stayed with him I'd be dead anyway. But I had no money, not the kind it would take to move somewhere else and start over. Not somewhere far enough where he wouldn't come find me like he did all the other times."

She reached out and tentatively touched Jacqueline's arm. "Are you the angel I've been praying for?"

Jacqueline had every intention of laughing. Then she looked into Bonita's eyes. The sincerity, gratitude, and sheer relief reflected in her big black eyes totally pierced Jacqueline's heart. In that moment she knew two things: that she would spend more money on this trip than she'd expected and that she would not kill this girl.

The two women spent the rest of the afternoon holed up in Jacqueline's hotel room with Bonita soaking up every ounce of the Jacqueline Tate that was to be presented to the world. By that night, Bonita was well-versed on enough of Jacqueline's history so that, were she questioned, she would pass most basic questions, and a few more probing ones. She was drilled for eight hours, but as midnight neared, Jacqueline was still pushing. They took a break to eat a room service meal, then Jacqueline took her through the paces again.

. "Okay," she said, picking up her bottle of water and settling back as though she were about to watch a film. "Tell me who I am."

Bonita took a deep breath, and in that instant transformed from a somewhat shy and basically reserved human being to a woman who could kick butt, take names, and drive a stake through the heart of Satan.

She flipped her hair in a manner she'd observed Jacqueline do several times. Jacqueline's face remained neutral, but her lips turned up the slightest bit.

"My name is Jacqueline Tate. I'm from a small village just outside Toronto. Mine was a difficult childhood, framed by alcoholic parents, physical and sexual abuse, and feelings of not being good enough and not being seen. I have a younger sister who was adored from the time she was born. I loved and hated her at the same time, but when I was ten and our house caught on fire, there was never a doubt about saving her life. To this day, getting her out of the house is still my finest hour.

"I spent the years between ten and eighteen in foster care. After that I received money from an insurance policy. Learning had always come easy, especially math and science, so once out of the system with money in the bank, I began writing freelance articles for the medical and science community, which parlayed into several prestigious assignments including a paper that was reviewed at Harvard University. I developed a circle of associates, loosely defined as friends, with whom I'd share dinner or drinks now and then. Out of these I was closest to Kaitlyn, though I haven't seen her in a while."

Bonita looked questioningly at Jacqueline, who nodded. "Go on."

She took a breath, pacing slowly as she thought about what to say next.

"A few years ago an assignment with *Science Today* brought me to the United States, where I met and began an affair with award-winning biologist Randall Atwater. To say it didn't work out is putting it mildly. I did some things I am not proud of, was accused of several egregious crimes, including murder, and wound up in prison. Recently, my attorney was able to get the murder charge against me thrown out, a decision made easier when I told the judge I'd leave the country. So that's what I'm doing, leaving the States.

"Why Australia? Because I know absolutely no one there and thankfully, no one knows me." She stopped, flipping her hair again without even realizing it. "How'd I do?"

Time seemed to stand still as she awaited the answer, which came in one word. "Fantastic. I have every confidence that you'll sail through the airport and customs with absolutely no problem. After our cosmetic procedures, you won't be playing me . . . you will be Jacqueline Tate."

In order not to be conspicuous, Bonita spent the night in Jacqueline's room and left at eight the next morning. She returned to New York but not the Bronx, where she lived. Instead, Jacqueline put enough money into Bonita's checking account for a roundtrip ticket to Rochester, New York, a ten-day hotel stay, and other travel expenses. During Bonita's flight, Jacqueline was busy scheduling her outpatient lip augmentation and Botox procedures and found a doctor hungry enough to perform rhinoplasty tomorrow night. Jacqueline didn't want anyone but the doctor to know that this procedure had been done.

Ten days. Jacqueline had ten days to dot every *i* and cross every *t* regarding Operation Revenge, beginning with the oh-so-perfect Atwater family. She'd made some headway. Eric was able to wire and place surveillance cameras throughout PSI. The one place that mattered most had been locked tight though. Jacqueline was convinced that the way to rock Randall Atwater's world was hidden in that lab.

Plans of destruction were underway for Randall, Sherri, and that spoiled brat Albany. Aaron would get his just due, too. She'd not yet figured out how. She had somewhat of an in into Nathan's world, although so far the GPS charted a life that was fairly routine, and she still hadn't decided whether or not to take his life. She wouldn't touch the mom, Elaine Carver. Even when Jacqueline had threatened her life, she'd continued to be kind. Mrs. Carver reminded Jacqueline of her grandmother, who died when she was seven. Jessica was in her palm and for right now would remain alive.

Jacqueline took the night off and watched a movie. It was supposed to be a comedy, but Jacqueline found it more stupid than funny. Maybe it's because of all of the thoughts running around in her head, all of the strategic parts to the greater plan that had to come out just so. Or maybe it was because the dream of getting rid of the people who'd helped put her away would start to become reality in just ten days.

CHAPTER 23

Sherri arrived at the Fairfax First Preparatory Academy and instead of getting stuck in the roundabout with other parents dropping off their non-driving teens, pulled up to the curb just beyond it. She put the car in park and turned to face her daughter.

"Okay, Albany. You are no longer on punishment and again have your phone. You'll only get one opportunity to let your dad and I know we've made the right decision in reducing the original time we'd planned to keep you in the house, off the computer except for homework, and without a phone."

"You did, Mom."

"Time will tell."

"I already told y'all. I'm going to stop spending so much time with . . . my friends . . . and focus on school."

"Uh-huh. Tell Corvales I said hello."

Albany and Sherri shared a laugh as she opened the door, already waving at one of her classmates. "Bye, Mom."

"Bye."

Sherri watched her daughter hook up with a friend and then pulled away from the curb. They'd had a glorious five days in the Bahamas, but everyone was ready to get back to what was happening at home. Randall was chomping at the bit to get back in the lab. First up on her agenda was going home and wading through the dozens of e-mails she'd glanced at when they arrived home. She'd been too tired to do more than a quick scan but was pretty sure she'd seen something from Capitol Alternative Education. The more she thought about the possibility of heading up an organization that could reach young adults who most needed assistance to change their lives, the more she knew that this type of position was why she'd obtained a master's in higher education.

After enjoying a cup of tea with Mom Elaine, Sherri walked into her office and turned on the laptop. Rather than wading through all her unopened e-mails, she typed Capitol Alternative Education in the inbox search engine. Two e-mails came up. The first one was an e-blast announcing plans for a Christmas event. The second, with About Your Meeting in the subject line, was more intriguing. She clicked on the e-mail. As it opened, her computer blinked and then froze.

"That's weird." She hit Control-Alt-Delete and brought up the task manager. Everything seemed to be running, so she canceled the action and went back to the e-mail. Whatever had caused the blip had righted itself as she was able to read the e-mail with no problem. Its contents gave her a measure of both relief and frustration. Her meeting with the board had been rescheduled, pushed back a bit to the third week in December. Frustration because she felt in her heart this job was hers, and couldn't wait to get started. The sooner the interview process began, the sooner she could implement her plans to change lives. Relief because she had more time to do research and fine-tune her presentation. She knew that several other applicants were being considered, so even with a solid résumé and a semi-celeb husband, having this job was nowhere near in the bag.

She changed the date on her electronic calendar and was just about to click Reply to respond to the e-mail, when her phone rang. She tapped the speaker button.

"Hey, Nay!"

"Hey, girl."

Sherri's brow creased. It was a rare moment when her friend Renee wasn't firing on all cylinders: loud, proud, and full of energy. Today it definitely didn't sound like this was the case.

"What's the matter?"

Renee sighed. "I think I drank too much wine last night."

"Nay! Is that all? The way you sounded I thought someone had died."

"Someone did."

"Who?"

"My single self."

"Who? What did you just say? Renee, you are not making any sense."

"I got engaged last night."

"You are kidding me! Kenneth finally popped the question, huh?"

"Oh, he's been popping it. I've just always said no."

"What changed this time?"

"That damned second bottle of Krug."

"You're blaming a bottle of champagne?"

"Yes. See, what had happened was . . ."

Sherri laughed. "Go on."

"He called me yesterday, asked if I wanted to take a helicopter ride. I told him, you know I don't go up in nothing smaller than the car I drive, and that's a big-ass Escalade. He has a way of being quite persuasive, especially when it involves promises of gifts and pledges of what he plans to do with his tongue."

"I remember you telling me that he knew how to use it."

"Girl! Anyway, he finally talked me into it. When he arrived at my house in a limo, I should have known something was up then. But sometimes Ken likes to flash, so I didn't think much of it. We get to the helicopter hangar, I take one look at that contraption that looked the size of one of those carnival rides, and requested my first drink right then. Ken knows me well, because don't you know one of the workers came walking over with an open bottle of champagne and a flute?"

"So how was the ride?"

"What I saw of it out of the one eye I had open was beautiful."

"Oh, Lord."

"Honey, I was hanging on to Kenneth like he had wings and if something happened he could fly us to safety!"

"That's how he proposed . . . in the helicopter?"

"No, what happened next is how he really showed out. We were out in the middle of nowhere, it looked like a big field surrounded by trees. When we land, I'm like, uh, what are you doing because I don't have a country bone in my body, couldn't care less about nature, and am not about to step my brand-new suede boots in grass and mud. But after more convincing, which involved promises to buy me a new pair of boots, I walked with him around this grove of trees, and, Sherri, the man had somehow arranged for a dinner for two in the middle of nowhere. It was so pretty. There were these miniature fire pits surrounding a linen-covered table with candles, and this white, billowy fabric that had been strung between two trees. There was a man there playing a guitar."

"Oh, Renee. That sounds so romantic."

"It was, girl. I almost cried. By then I was on that second bottle and we were dancing and the cool wind played against the warm fire and his wet lips were on my neck and we started grinding, making something else wet. He was whispering in my ear—and that man's the best dirty talker I've ever met—and the next thing I know he's on his knees. I'm thinking he's about to throw down in front of the guitar player and I wasn't even going to stop him."

Sherri whooped.

"I was thinking, go 'head, big daddy, let's give him a show!"

"Girl, you're a fool!"

"But he got down there and proposed, and I said yes."

"I think that's wonderful. Why are you sounding unhappy?"

"Because he's not the type of man I thought I'd marry."

"Given your taste for the young ones, that's probably a good thing." Sherri looked at her watch, jumped up, and headed out of her office. "Oh shoot! Nay, I have to run. I promised Randall I'd pick up his order at the cleaners. He needs some of the items for his trip and he's leaving town tomorrow. Can I call you later?"

"Sure."

"In the meantime . . . congratulations! You need to stop tripping about some fantasy man that doesn't exist and count your blessings. Kenneth is a good man!"

"He's an old man."

"He's what, fifty-eight? That's not old."

"That's thirty-two years older than my last boy-friend."

"Yes, a boy. Kenneth's a man. And a good one. Don't mess around and lose him by being ungrateful and letting another woman show you what I'm talking about." Silence. "There's no need to respond. I know you're listening. You can thank me later."

"Bye, girl."

"Ha! Bye, Nay. Love you."

"Love you, too."

Sherri entered the second floor sitting room where her mother was watching television. "Mom, I'm about to run some errands. Do you want to come with me, maybe have lunch and walk around a bit so you can get some fresh air?"

"Child, my stories are getting ready to come on."

Sherri walked over and picked up the remote. "We can tape your shows for you to watch later. It'll be even better because you can skip the commercials." She programmed the DVR and turned off the television. "Come on, woman. Let's go!"

Miss Elaine gave Sherri the side eye as she rose

from the couch. "You're acting like you're forgetting who the mama is around here."

"We both are," Sherri countered. "But I'm the boss." She stepped to the side and avoided the swat intended for the back of her head.

"You'd better duck."

"Mom, you've been thunking our heads since I could walk. You know I'd anticipate that move!"

The two women walked out of the house and into bright sunshine. After picking up Randall's clothing and having lunch, Sherri and Miss Elaine, in a totally rare and spontaneous move, decided to take in a movie. It starred Idris Elba, a man who both ladies agreed was worth staring at for two hours. It was the first time they'd hung out like this in a while, just the two of them. Sherri enjoyed every minute of it.

Once they returned home, normal life returned. There was dinner, followed by homework and Sherri tending to Aaron, who'd complained of a headache accompanying his sore throat. She and Randall retired early, to spend some alone time before the trip that would take Randall away from the house for the rest of the week. As soon as the door closed, Randall made it very clear what was on his mind. His tenacity quickly placed making love at the top of her list. Ten minutes in and she forgot all about responding to the alternative education memo, talking to Aaron about the computer blip, and pretty much everything else save the delicious things Randall was doing to her body. The next day presented a whole new set of things to do. Some things that would later prove very important, for now remained forgotten.

* * *

Jacqueline sat in front of the brand-new computer she'd purchased yesterday. It was a sleek, top-of-the-line, fully-loaded model that could be used as either a laptop or tablet with lightning-fast processing and eight gigs of RAM. The seventeen-inch screen would allow her to easily view video feeds from up to four source points, and a special gadget that Phillip's computer-whiz boyfriend had created would send messages to her targets from four false IP addresses. She'd learned valuable lessons from what had happened following her arrest and the confiscation of a roomful of computers that had been used in her underhanded dealings. And thankfully, technology had grown by leaps and bounds, too. A bulky desktop and eight monitors had been replaced by two sleek laptops, with a self-destruct mechanism that could be activated from her cell phone. No paper trail. No electronic stamp that could lead to her doorstep.

Which is why she'd spent the last hour browsing through Fairfax First's student roster on the school's employee website she'd just hacked into without a care in the world. As she clicked on various links to the student who'd caught her eye, she began to believe that the hour had been time well-spent. Corvales Mitchell was a standout athlete at the upscale school, which meant he was confident, probably cocky as well. His social media pages were filled with pictures and posts that gave the impression that he thought of himself as a star. In many of them he was surrounded by females. Which probably meant he was persuasive and good with the ladies. He'd survived a rough childhood and still lived in a challenging neighborhood. Which meant a large amount of money would probably appeal to him. All of this together made this young man very appealing to Jacqueline for what she had planned.

"Looking forward to meeting you, Corvales," Jacqueline murmured, picking up a glass of sparkling wine and taking a sip. "I have a job for which I think you'll be perfect."

CHAPTER 24

On December sixteenth at 12:17, a Monday afternoon, "Jacqueline Tate" strolled out of the Hay-Adams Hotel looking confident and fabulous. Hanging off her shoulder was an oversized red-and-black leopard print designer bag. Behind her, a porter rolled a cart holding two suitcases and a carry-on bag. Her black leather coat was cinched at the waist. A red wool scarf kept the frigid air away from her throat. A stylish black felt hat and black leather gloves protected head and hands from the twenty-degree wind gusts and gently falling snow. Oversized black sunglasses added just the right amount of panache. Before getting into the idling black town car waiting to transport her to the airport, she pulled out her wallet and tipped the porter. He commented on the size of her tip. She laughed, delivered a witty response that left him smiling, and entered the vehicle. The porter stood and waved, watching the town car until it was out of sight.

Seconds later, a black SUV with tinted windows pulled away from the curb and followed the town car.

Inside the hotel room, Jacqueline paced and waited. She was more than ready to leave the place she'd called home for a little more than a month, ever since her ill-timed phone calls to Randall and Sherri's room, placed from one of the hotel's courtesy phones, had forced her departure from the Liaison. Soon, if everything went as planned, she'd have the ability to move about freely without being seen, or worse, followed.

But that's only if they take the bait and follow that car! What if they don't? And what if something happens at the airport and Bonita gets questioned? Can she handle it? Can she be me? The questions unnerved her and sent her heart racing. Jacqueline wasn't really a drinker, a glass of sparkling wine every now and then or a flute of champagne to celebrate. At the moment, however, a double shot of vodka like the one her sister had ordered sounded pretty darn good. She needed something to help her calm down. She needed to get her nerves and her thoughts and her rapidly beating heart under control.

On her way to the bar, her phone beeped. She raced back over to the desk and picked it up.

So far, so good.

Jacqueline breathed a sigh of relief as she replied to the text. Are you sure they're following you?

Absolutely.

Good. Keep me posted at every step.

Will do. Thanks again.

Don't thank me yet.

☺

Jacqueline put down the phone and walked to the bar. Her near panic attack passed, she reached for water instead of wine and poured a glass. She held her emotions in check and staved off any thought of celebrating. That the SUV was following the town car was a good thing. But this plan had a long way to go before it could be classified as successful.

Needing to keep her mind busy, she walked back over to the desk and fired up the laptop. There were any number of directions she could have gone to check her revenge plan's progress. The first unsuspecting critter in her complicated web who came to mind was Sherri. She logged on to Sherri's computer. Silly that in this day and age some people still felt a log-on ID and a password was adequate protection against hackers. Getting on probably took a minute longer than it did the owner of the device.

She did a quick scroll down Sherri's in-box. *Nothing too exciting here.* Just as she was about to log off, a subject line caught her eye. She clicked on the e-mail and laughed with delight. "The minions must be on my side." After pondering the situation, she deleted the e-mail, scrolled down to a few weeks prior and deleted the first e-mail she'd sent.

"Let's see what else you're up to, Sherri Atwater."

Two things kept her from getting that chance. Her phone's message ringtone went off, and she heard Sherri returning to her computer. It took her less than a second to shut down, but that was too close a call. Another lesson was learned in that moment. During the day at least, she'd need to use this link solely as her eyes and ears into wherever that computer was located in the Atwater household. Once again, her sheer hatred for that woman combined with her nerves being stretched to the limit had her, a woman used to handling each and every project with pinpoint precision, making elementary mistakes.

She gritted her teeth to tamp down her anger. "I can't wait until Kris shows up." Everything seemed easier when working with her partner in crime.

She read the screen. *Yes!* A knock at the door made her sense of relief short-lived. A thousand thoughts exploded in her head. Bonita had been forced to send that text and was in fact on the other side of the door handcuffed to a cop. Or Eric, with his ex-warden mother and a bailiff ready to take her to jail. Perhaps it was the man behind the tinted windows of the SUV. For the first time since being released, Jacqueline wished for a gun.

Instead of tiptoeing to the peephole as she'd first thought to do, she marched to the door and yanked it open. Whoever was on the other side was headed for a kick in the groin. She would go down fighting if she went down at all.

"Kris! Thank God it's you. I was hoping you'd get here soon."

"Why, did something happen?"

"No, I just need your advice."

Kris walked over to the bed and plopped down. "What's going on, chick?"

"Check this out." Jacqueline typed something into the computer and then stared at the screen.

Kris bent down to peer more closely. "Oh. My. God. Is that . . . you?"

Jacqueline wheeled her chair around. "I'm in the process of leaving the country."

"When?"

"If all goes according to plan"—she looked at her watch—"in about two hours."

"Um, shouldn't you be at the airport?"

Jacqueline's eyes sparkled. "I am."

"Okay, Jack. Back up and come again and this time lose the histrionics and just tell me what the heck you've gotten us into this time."

"Remember what I told you when I was in Atlanta, the plans for the Atwaters and my sister?"

"Yes. So, what, you've started implementing them?"

Jacqueline gave Kris a quick rundown of what had happened since Kris had left, shortly after Jacqueline returned from Atlanta. She showed her the computer lab that was being developed, one that was much less bulky, more mobile and more sophisticated than the one Jacqueline had configured when she lived in D.C. before. It was incredibly advantageous for her to be able to lay out her complete plans to someone else, to get them out of her head, and to review their likelihood of success with someone in whom she had ultimate trust.

"The last and most important piece is happening now." Jacqueline reached into the bag beside her chair and pulled out a folder. She took a picture from inside it and placed it on the bed for Kris to examine.

"Pretty girl," Kris said, picking up the picture and looking from it to Jacqueline and back again. "She could be your sister."

Jacqueline smiled and showed Kris a picture on her phone. Kris said nothing.

"Well?"

Kris was looking at the picture on the bed again. "Well, what?"

"What do you think about the pic on the phone?"

"Why would I think anything about you showing me a selfie? I'm more interested in this woman, and how she . . . no."

Jacqueline slowly nodded.

"No. Way. You did that crazy shit I said you'd never get away with."

Jacqueline laughed heartily at Kris's stunned expression. "Yep, though the story of whether or not I get away with it is still being told."

Jacqueline tossed the burner phone on the bed. Kris picked it up, tapped it on, and went to the picture. She looked from the phone to Jacqueline and back again. "I cannot believe this, Jack. She looks just like you in this picture."

"It took a little cosmetic surgery to make us exact but—"

"She went under the knife for your ass?"

"Turns out, it worked in her favor." She told Kris about Bonita's domestic violence past. "Pretty crazy, huh?"

"No, you are what's crazy. I mean, who gets out of prison after killing someone—"

"Allegedly—"

"Through some hotshot attorney savvy enough to get the case thrown out on a technicality, finds someone who not only looks just like you—"

"With the help of a couple doctors and a needle or two."

"This is just ridiculousness on top of insanity. God only knows how you talked this woman into literally taking on your persona for how long? Forever?" Jacqueline shrugged. Clearly, she was enjoying hearing her exquisite plot recited back to her. "All of this and I haven't even gotten to the one-woman war you're waging against the Atwaters. I'm going to change your name from Jack to Joan of Arc."

"That's a fairly apropos comparison actually. Except my horse"—Jacqueline rubbed her fingers across the computer keys—"is right here."

"You know what? This sounds like the kind of mess you'd see on Lifetime or read in one of those contemporary fiction novels. Wait a minute, this is even crazier. If someone read this in a book they'd swear it's unrealistic."

"That's why it's so brilliant, Kris. That's what is going to make all of this work. I'm taking this so far beyond what anyone would dare imagine, much less do, that my plan will be carried out and I will have left America for parts unknown before the first piece of the J. T. puzzle gets put into place. I'm not going to take chances, though. I'm going to work quickly, have all of this done and be out of the country in thirty days, max."

"Whoa, Jack. That's a pretty aggressive timeline."

"But very necessary. The Atwaters haven't forgotten for a minute what I'm capable of. Once the shit starts hitting the fan, you can best believe they and the authorities will be triple-checking on me."

The phone buzzed. Jacqueline looked at Kris. "This is it. She was in the security line before, so let's see." She read the text, took a breath, stood, and looked in the mirror.

"Jacqueline Tate, have fun in Australia. You are one bad bee-atchi."

CHAPTER 25

Nathan had been hitting the gym hard, no less than three nights a week. He'd stepped up his game for two reasons. One, he was determined to get through the holidays without a tire around his middle, and two, he was trying to tamp down a libido that, ever since his nights with Alice, was out of control. She'd awakened something that had been asleep since his teen years. Basically, he was either thinking about work, working out, or working it with a sexy mama. Considering his sexy mama was not only not in Georgia but not in America, things were . . . complicated.

He bypassed the gym showers, preferring his own. After a rendezvous with a drive-through, he headed home, jamming so hard to his neo-soul track that he almost missed a phone call.

He turned down the music and tapped his steering wheel. "Hello?"

"Nate. Ralph."

"Ralph, what's going on, man? I looked for you at the gym."

"Turns out, I got tied up on some work for a client."

"I know how that can be. I've been grinding pretty hard myself."

"Yeah, well, I've been grinding pretty hard for you, and it's paid off." The music was low, but Nathan turned it off. "What do you have for me?"

"Good news. There actually was a British citizen named Alice Smith here on business last week. But even better? Jacqueline Tate has left the States."

"How could that happen when she's on parole?"

"She's not on parole. Her case was thrown out, which means she was treated as though the crime never occurred. Since the conviction was thrown out and not overturned, however, it can be appealed. Hopefully your lawyers are working on that."

"Yes, they are."

"Well, until that happens, I would recommend that you have your attorney present a special circumstance case to the judge where if and when she returns to the States, your family is informed."

"Man . . . that is the best news I've heard in a while. Have you called Ran and Sherri?"

"No, I wanted to call you first."

"Do you mind if I give them the news, and pass along your recommendation as well?"

"Not at all. Be sure and let them know they can call me if they have any questions or need more details."

"Knowing how my sister is, I need to get more now. How are you sure that Jacqueline left?"

"My man followed her from the hotel to the airport."

"That's not going to reassure Sherri."

"I'm not done. His partner had gone on ahead and was inside the airport. He confirmed beyond a shadow of a doubt that the person who went through security was Jacqueline. I had him wait around the area an extra twenty minutes to make sure she didn't double back and exit the terminal area. Even still, because I know what your family's been through, I called an associate in North Carolina and they said the airline confirmed that she indeed boarded a flight headed to Australia. And there's one more thing."

"What's that?"

"While you didn't ask me, I kept the tail on your personal nightmare going, even after her sister left."

"You continued to track Jessica?"

"Yes."

The news hit Nathan in a way he wasn't expecting. How could one be protective of and still have feelings for someone who tried to do him harm? "I appreciate your looking out for me, Ralph, but don't know if that was necessary."

"As it turns out, it doesn't look like it was. She and her husband seem to be happy, focused on each other and their son. Looks like the nightmare your family has endured for years is finally over."

"Man, you don't know what this phone call is going to mean for my sister, for my entire family. Thanks so much, Ralph. I can't tell you how much I appreciate it."

Nathan reached his condo and pulled alongside the curb. His relief was so profound that he was overcome with a surprisingly intense wave of emotion that almost produced tears. After another moment or two he'd gotten himself together enough to park his car in the garage and head to his house. While walking, he dialed Sherri.

*   *   *

It was thirty-nine degrees, but Sherri didn't notice as she stood in the solitude of her magnificently landscaped backyard. For the past hour, she'd been wracking her mind for a plausible explanation for the day's events. So far, she couldn't come up with one. To say she was troubled was putting it mildly. She was actually afraid.

Her phone buzzed and snapped her out of the daze that had made her impervious to the weather. Her body shivered from the cold as she turned and went back inside, greeted by the fire that burned every night in the room that was accessible from the French doors she'd just entered as well as the garage.

Walking over to the fire, she tapped her phone. "Hey, Nate."

"Sis! I've got great news!"

"Oh yeah? I could use some."

"Jacqueline Tate is out of our lives for good."

"What makes you say that?"

Nate relayed the information he'd just received from Ralph. "He suggests that we get some type of order that mandates we be contacted if she ever returns to the States. With all the trouble she's gotten into, I don't think she'll be back at all."

"Hmm."

"What? Is that all the reaction I'm going to get after basically telling you that the wicked witch is dead?"

"Something happened with my computer."

"What?"

"Something weird happened with my computer. A few weeks ago I received an e-mail about the alternative education director position I've been so excited about. In it I was informed that my first meeting with the board had been moved from the first week in this month to the nineteenth. So I use the time this morning I'd already taken off for that meeting to go to the spa and get a full treatment: facial, body rub, manicure and pedicure, the works. I was in there for over four hours. When I retrieved my personal belongings and turned on my phone, it was to several missed calls and messages about the meeting with the board that I'd also missed!"

"Are you saying the meeting hadn't been moved?"

"Not only was the meeting this morning, as had been originally planned, but the coordinator said no one from their office had sent a second memo. All this, and that's not even what has me most upset. When I went back and tried to find that e-mail, the one about the meeting being moved, I couldn't find it anywhere. I looked in my spam, in my deleted messages. I searched by topic and by sender. Nothing. It's like it was never there. But it was! I vividly remember reading the message just before Thanksgiving! Now, I feel like I'm losing my mind.

"I can't wait to talk to Randall. I'm terrified that what happened to Mom may be happening to me, that I might have an infection in my brain that's affecting my memory!"

"Sis, I'm sorry this happened to you, but I think you might be overreacting."

"Overreacting? I missed a very important meeting, the first step in the interview process for a job I'm passionate about, one that I want very badly. I remember reading an e-mail that the organization says was never sent, and now I can't find it in my inbox. And you say I'm overreacting? I can't talk to you right now."

Sherri couldn't remember the last time she'd hung up on her brother, or anyone for that matter. Yet she felt not one ounce of guilt. No one could judge how she was reacting unless they'd worn her size eights.

Said size eights stomped up the stairs and reached Aaron's room. As she suspected, he was knee-deep in a video game, with schoolbooks strewn across his bed.

"Aaron, come talk to me. I've got a question for you."

Aaron paused the game and came over to where his mother sat on his bed.

"What is it, Mom?"

Gauging from his reaction, Sherri knew that the fear and panic she felt inside was written on her face. She relaxed her shoulders and attempted a smile. "Oh, nothing for you to get concerned about. I just have a question for the computer whiz."

"Oh." Aaron visibly relaxed as he nodded. "What's your question?"

"How can I find an e-mail that I'm sure was on my computer but isn't there now, not in the delete folder or trash."

"Where's your computer?"

Sherri stood. "In the office. Do you want to go get it or work from there?"

"Let's go down there."

They started downstairs. "Is your homework finished?"

"All but one chapter of reading."

"Then why were you playing a video game?"

"I was just giving my mind a five-minute break so that it could more adequately receive more data."

"Good answer. How many of y'all did it take to come up with it?"

Aaron laughed. "Mom!"

They reached the office. Sherri opened her e-mails and then moved so Aaron could sit down. That's where Randall found them when he arrived home ten minutes later.

She looked up when he entered the room. "Hey, baby."

He walked over to where she stood next to Aaron and kissed her cheek. "Hey. What's going on here?"

"I'm recovering Mom's deleted e-mails," Aaron responded, his fingers flying across the keys. Soon, a large batch of e-mails appeared on the screen. "Okay, here are all the ones you've deleted lately that were still on the hard drive."

"Okay. Search for one that says CAE or Capitol Alternative Education."

Randall and Sherri looked at the screen as Aaron typed in the request. He shook his head. "Nothing comes up, Mom."

"You're sure those are all of the files on the computer?"

He nodded. "Yep, these are all of your deleted e-mails." He looked at her. "Do you want me to check under a different name or subject?"

"Yes." She gave him the name of the coordinator. He checked under that and also under the word *meeting*. This produced several responses. None were the e-mail for which Sherri searched.

"Okay, Son. Thanks for your help."

"But I didn't find it."

"You helped me look."

"Oh, okay." He started toward the door.

"Finish your homework before you get back on that game."

"Okay!"

Sherri's brave veneer followed Aaron out of the room. Randall immediately noticed the change. He walked to the door and closed it. "Okay, out with it. What's really going on?"

Back in Atlanta, Nathan sat in his home office, still tripping because Sherri had hung up on him. His first inclination had been to call her back, but he'd quickly changed his mind. When Nathan was in a mood like that he didn't feel like talking. In this respect he and his sister were very much alike. Still, he wondered why something like a missed meeting, even an important one, would put his sister in such a mood.

Figuring he'd spent enough time trying to figure it out, he decided to check his own e-mails real quick before calling Dev. They'd ended up spending Thanksgiving weekend in the Caribbean together, but the relationship had shifted since discovering his indiscretion and her wish to marry. Neither was ready to throw in the towel on the relationship, but Nathan wasn't quite ready to buy a ring either.

Seeing nothing exciting, Nathan reached for his cell phone. He continued to scroll while the dial tone sounded. The call went to voice mail. "Hello, beautiful. When you get this, hit me back."

A click to the next page of e-mails and Nathan was glad Dev hadn't picked up. It would have felt uncomfortable to be talking to her while reading an e-mail from Alice.

He clicked on the link.

Hello, Nathan.
I trust this e-mail finds you well. As
promised, I've attached information
regarding my lovely country and all you can
do here. There's one activity I did not put
on the list but with which you're quite familiar and one I can't wait to do with you
again. When are you coming over?
Alice

Nathan read the note once, and again. He thought
of various responses: professional, witty, nasty. Finally
he decided to speak truth from the heart.

Alice:
Thanks for the information. I most certainly
enjoyed meeting you and won't easily forget the time we had together. As you said,
we were two passing ships who took advantage of a situation. It was fun, but because of where I am in my life, I choose not
to continue contact. I wish you well.
Nathan

After rereading the letter, he confidently pushed
SEND. With Jacqueline Tate out of the country, and Jessica off and married to another man, he felt he and his
family had dodged several major bullets. For right now
he'd see where things went with Dev. There was no
need to tempt fate.

CHAPTER 26

Jacqueline looked around her new residence, the two-bedroom, two-bath apartment in Baltimore's thriving downtown that Eric, using the name Bruce Clarke, had rented the month before. Hard to imagine that yesterday afternoon the place had been empty. Today it was minimally yet tastefully furnished with items she'd swooped up at an inventory clearance sale. Her most important purchase had been the long rectangular desk flush against the back wall of the bedroom that would serve as her office, the one that now housed the laptop, tablet, three phone lines, four burner phones, and a plethora of other electronic devices all stashed behind two locked drawers. She'd decided to take the entire day and get caught up on everything that had happened, since working with Bonita had used up much of her time. She needed to get everything set up electronically so that monitoring her various projects could be done simultaneously, without switching screens. Now that she had her freedom, it was time to speed up her timetable.

Spending time with Jessica and Bonita reminded her of time with her girls back in Toronto. The nights with Nathan and even with Eric had her entertaining thoughts of a real relationship. The Atwaters had taken up enough of her thought process. Once she executed this payback, she was going to turn the page on the past five or so years, move to London, and start a new life.

While munching a slice of pizza, she pulled up her split-screen command station. It was the first time she'd paid any real attention to the cameras that had been placed at Randall's company, PSI. Since the Thanksgiving holiday, his travel schedule had ramped back up. The good news was that Eric had finally gotten inside the laboratory and mounted a camera over the door, a camera that basically allowed one to scope the entire room, entirely discreetly.

She looked at the bottom right of her screen and watched Sherri walk into her home office with her son in tow. "Oh crap."

She tossed down the slice of pizza and engaged the volume for that screen just as Randall walked into the shot.

"I'm recovering Mom's deleted e-mails."

Hearing Aaron's words, Jacqueline whipped around to her tablet, quickly accessing Sherri's screen so she could see what the boy was doing.

"Okay, here are all the ones you've deleted lately that were still on the hard drive."

She watched his keystrokes with grudging admiration. *He's pretty good, excellent actually.* When he got up from the computer, she relaxed. But only for a moment. When Randall asked Sherri what was going on and she told him about the deleted e-mail, Jacqueline knew that in-depth snooping into what was on Sherri's computer might blow her cover.

No one was in front of the computer screen. Jacqueline waited until she heard their voices coming from some distance away. She took a chance, went into Sherri's startup menu, and checked the running programs. Her icon remained successfully hidden. It would take a computer expert of the highest level to be able to find it. Rapping her fingers across the base of her computer, she pondered her options.

"Penny for your thoughts."

She turned to see Kris lounging against the door-jamb. "I didn't hear you come in."

"You were too focused on whatever's on that computer screen to hear anything." Kris entered the room. "The starship is back in action."

Jacqueline smiled. "One that, had an astute engineer been at Sherri's computer right now, might have been discovered."

"Really? And you're smiling?"

Jacqueline nodded. "I sent Sherri an e-mail and switched the dates of an important appointment, and then deleted the e-mail. She thinks she's going crazy."

"That's scandalous."

"It's just the beginning. I'm thinking about whether to stay linked to her computer. They must use another one to store financial and other important documents. Besides her e-mails and family calendar, there's not much pertinent information."

"What were you hoping to get?"

"Anything to help me make her life hell but mostly access to their conversations, like the one I just heard. But mostly she's alone in the office and rarely takes the computer into other rooms." She sat back against the office chair, swirled it this way and that. "But that's not worth getting discovered and having my whole scheme unravel."

"Exactly. Missing an interview might cost her the job. But that's not guaranteed. And with so many people you've targeted to get back at, you need to—"

"Shh!" Jacqueline turned up the volume on the feed into the Atwater computer.

". . . take any chances. I want to go through with the appeal. And I want to do as Ralph suggested and put a protective order in place. That way, if for some reason she steps one foot back into the country, we'll be notified."

"All right, baby." Randall's voice was lower. Jacqueline increased the volume a little more. "With the Christmas holidays approaching it might not be easy, but I'll ask the attorney to try and get us before the judge within the next two weeks."

The two women waited, their breath held, to hear more information. But the voices receded. Randall and Sherri had obviously walked out of the room.

Jacqueline stood and began to pace. She walked the length of the room and back, then stopped in front of Kris. "Damn that woman. She just can't leave well enough alone. Now do you understand why everything has to happen so quickly?" Kris nodded. "I'm going to work on implementing all I've planned while everyone is distracted and celebrating; eff up all of their holidays and then get the hell out of town."

Kris settled against the back of the couch. "How?"

Jacqueline sat back down in front of the computer. "Very publicly. Randall's working on something important. I'm going to steal the information and send it to his competitor, a nemesis of his in the science world who I once interviewed and who was very impressed with my skills." Jacqueline winked. Kris rolled her eyes. "Todd's working on getting inside the lab, where Randall does his experiments."

"And his brother-in-law, Nathan?"

Jacqueline tapped a key to bring the computer out of sleep. "Well, speak of the devil. An e-mail from my Hershey bar."

Smiling, she opened the e-mail. A piece of that grin melted away with each word she read. By the time she got to the end, that smile had flipped and turned ugly.

"Uh-oh. Looks like you're not too happy with what Mr. Chocolate wrote you."

"Looks like he's dumped me. Thanked me for the good time"—she used air quotes—"and wished me well. Men are so stupid, always thinking they're in control." She pressed a few keys. "Dangit. He didn't open my attachment. Very bad move. He's just helped me decide how to rock his world and has no idea how out of control things are going to get. I'm going to send a message to my sister, let her know that I've safely arrived in Sydney."

"That was an unexpected segue. Considering what went down between them, what does your sister have to do with Nathan?"

"A lot, if my hunch is right about her little brown-skinned baby."

"You think your sister's baby is Nathan's, not Vincent's child?"

"He's a shade darker than both my sister and Vincent, which I find suspicious. Stirring that same suspicion in Nathan will not only rock his world but Jessica's marriage, too."

"Is that what you want? I mean, what did Jessica really ever do to you?"

"Besides abandon me when I needed her most? Nothing."

"Um, trying to kill someone isn't exactly small potatoes."

"Who's to say she ever really tried? I was behind bars, with only her word to go on. She could have told me anything. How could I prove it was true?"

"Fair enough. Maybe she lied and didn't try at all. But is that any reason to stir the pot in a way that could end her marriage?"

"Some days I think yes, and on others, no. Since texting me a thank-you for depositing the money, she hasn't made any effort to keep in touch."

"Did you tell her you were leaving?" Jacqueline nodded. "Well, maybe that's it. Maybe she thinks you're out of the country."

"I guess you have a point. So here's what I'll do. I'll shoot her a brief e-mail about arriving in Australia, see if that stirs up any talk about me with her husband. If it does, and she talks about me in a positive way, I'll entertain other options for ruining Sherri's brother."

"And if she says something negative?"

Jacqueline opened one of the desk drawers, pulled out a baggie containing two forks and the pacifier she'd swiped from Jessica's purse, and swung it back and forth. "Then it will be time to order a home DNA test. See how dismissively Nathan reacts to the news that he has a son."

CHAPTER 27

"What is this I smell cooking in my kitchen?" Vincent came up behind Jessica and wrapped his arms around her. "Did you make this food, or are you heating up something you bought from the store?"

"Ha ha, my attorney husband wants to moonlight as a comedian." She turned around and gifted his lips with hers.

"What's for dinner?"

"Baked chicken with mashed potatoes and green beans. I used a spice mix that I put together from an online recipe."

"Baby, Suzy Homemaker looks good on you. Do you know how happy it made me when you agreed to quit the firm?"

"I'm happy that you're happy."

"Where's Dax?"

"Next door with the neighbor."

"What?"

Jessica laughed. "I knew you'd act like that. Since I quit my job, I've met the neighbors on both sides.

Sally, she's the one on the left, has a son who's a year older than Dax. I told Dax he could play with his friend for an hour while Mommy cooked."

"I'll go get him."

"Wait, I want to talk to you first."

Vincent turned back around. "What about?"

"I got an e-mail from Jacqueline. She wanted me to know she's arrived safely in Australia."

"I say good riddance."

"Vince!"

"I'm sorry, baby, but I never trusted your sister."

"When we had lunch together we all ended up getting along."

"Anybody can fake it for a couple hours. I never said anything because I know how much having your sister around meant to you. But I paid serious attention to your sister during that luncheon. I looked into her eyes, baby, and I have to tell you. I didn't like what I saw."

Vincent had Jessica's total attention. She turned off the fire from the potatoes and green beans. "What did you see?"

"Nothing."

"What do you mean, nothing?"

"I saw nothing behind her eyes. It's like her mind was blank, or like the lights were on but nobody was home: no feeling, no humanity, no life." Vincent reached over and ate a piece of lettuce from a nearby bowl of salad. "Classic signs of a sociopath, baby. The best thing that could have happened is that she left America."

"She's my sister, Vincent. What harm can come from simply keeping in touch?"

"I don't know, and don't want you to find out. Be careful. Drop her a line, engage in casual chitchat. But don't let down your guard with her, Jessie. She's not to be trusted at all." Vincent walked over and hugged his wife. "Your sister is a part of your past. Dax and I, and the baby growing inside you, are your present. Okay?"

Jessica wrapped her arms around his slender waist. "Okay. Don't worry. I've learned that Jacqueline only truly cares for herself. You, Dax, and the baby that's coming are all I need. You're my family now."

The conversation shifted from Vincent winning his latest case to Jessica slowly getting over morning sickness. Dax came home from his playdate with the neighbor. Dinner was pleasant and the night even better. The next morning, Jessica strapped Dax in the car seat, took a trip to Lithonia, closed the account she'd opened less than two months ago, the one where Jacqueline knew the account number, and redeposited the money in a bank ten miles away. There was no doubt that she loved her sister. But Jessica also loved her husband and believed his words held truth. Jacqueline in Australia might be best for all of them.

A myriad of emotions tore through Jacqueline as she listened in on the conversation via the wire she'd attached to Jessica's cell phone. Unfortunately for the couple, while they were discussing Jacqueline, the phone was lying on the kitchen island right beside them, making their voices as clear as bells. For Jacqueline, Jessica's last comment had sealed her fate. Her next move was clear. But first, she had to pacify Eric, who with all that had been happening for the past few weeks was feeling sorely neglected. After a quick look around, she entered the modest apartment building on the outskirts of D.C. Eric answered the door. Jacqueline hiked up her leather skirt and brought the man to orgasm before she'd even removed her gloves.

With the scent of sex still floating in the air, she got down to business. "We need to wire Randall's office. Everywhere possible, I need camera and sound."

Eric fell back against the couch. "No problem."

"Do you interact with him often?"

"Not really. That's because our patrol is primarily after-hours, when all personnel are gone. Should I step up my attempts to be friends with him?"

"No. I'm glad your association has been casual. I have another job I need you to focus on and the less the two of you interact, the better."

Eric raised up on an elbow. "What is it?"

Naked, Jacqueline walked to her bag and pulled out her phone. She came to sit beside him. "I need you to befriend this kid."

Eric took the phone. "Who is he?"

"The star basketball player at Fairfield First."

"How am I supposed to do this and why?"

"Approach him as a college basketball scout. Wave money in his face. Gain his confidence. Become his friend. Since you've only used it once, I think using the Bruce Clarke alias will be fine."

"And then?"

"Do that, and I'll tell you what comes next." She rose and began putting on her clothes.

"Where are you going?" Eric reached for his jeans and slid them on.

"Sorry I can't stay longer. Busy day ahead."

Eric walked over to where she was refreshing her makeup. "How long do I have to do this?"

"Really, Todd?"

"I know it's a question, but I need to know. That

job is boring as hell and I'm going stir-crazy cooped up in this place."

Jacqueline slid into her coat, picked up her bag, and put on her glasses. "That girl you've been messing with the past week or so seems to be pretty good company."

This stopped Eric in his tracks. "What the hell? You're spying on me?"

She laughed at his incredulity. "Do you think that magic wand between your legs makes you exempt from my distrust? I know more about you than you think I know." She stepped toward him. Her tone turned cold. "Never again bring extracurricular to this location. If you must fuck substandard, do it at their place, not the apartment I pay for."

"Jac . . . Al, I'm sorry. Damn, it just happened."

"I know it did."

"I miss you."

"I know you do." She reached up and cupped his jaw. "I tell you what. I'm going to trust you with part of my enterprise, bring you into my secret world a little bit. Think you can handle it?"

"Hell, yeah!" Eric was clearly excited to gain her trust.

"Rumor has it that Randall Atwater is working on a highly confidential experiment that could change how infections and some common contagious diseases are treated. Get your hands on files, documentation, or something like that with more information, and we'll take the weekend off, just the two of us." She reached into her bag. "And find a way to attach this to his laptop."

Eric looked at the thin rectangular piece that she'd placed in his palm.

"Slide it into one of his USB ports. It is magnetic and will attach itself to the top of the port. The port can still be used, so Randall will have no idea that it's there." At Eric's raised brow, she answered, "It will allow me to see everything that is on his computer, and give me access to every file."

"Where do you get this stuff, and who taught you how to use it?"

Ignoring the questions, Jacqueline walked to the door. "Put that on his computer as soon as possible and text me when it's done. We've got a lot to do and have to work fast. Time's a-wastin'."

CHAPTER 28

Randall left the break room and headed back to his office with coffee in hand. Given the conversation he'd had and the document he was expecting, it was going to be a long night. He rounded the corner just in time to see Eric, aka Todd, standing by his office door.

"Oh, um, hey, Doctor."

"Hello, Todd."

"We had a blip on the screen downstairs, an image of movement. The cameras are sensitive and can often be affected by something as minor as a blast of heat through the air duct. It looks like that's what it was, but I still have to come check, just in case. I'll get out of your way, let you get back to work."

"No, that's okay, man. I feel better knowing the security company is doing their job. Why don't you come into my office for a few minutes? We've never had the chance to talk."

"Oh, um, well, sure."

"No need to be nervous. Whatever story about me that has reached you has probably been inflated."

"Actually, sir, there is a story that has me curious about you. It involves a woman . . . Jacqueline Tate?"

Randall frowned. "What about her?"

"In reading the history of the building, I came across a restraining order against her. Naturally I wanted to be aware if she still poses a threat, so I did a search on the name and learned she was in prison. This is my first security job and I must admit"—he gave a sheepish grin—"I didn't expect to find any convicted murderer stories while guarding office buildings."

"Jacqueline Tate was an unfortunate incident that is over, and best forgotten. I appreciate your diligence, and your curiosity is natural. But she is out of our lives and in fact, the country. There's nothing there to worry about." Randall's friendly mood was over. He reached for a folder. "Thanks for your time, Todd. I'm going to get back to work."

Todd left, but it took a while for Randall to get back into the swing of things. Though Todd's explanation for asking about Jacqueline made perfect sense, it was unsettling. He went online and typed her name in the search engine. Information regarding her arrest was readily available. Randall scrolled through a few pages but found nothing mentioned about her release.

His in-box indicator dinged, taking him away from a memory that was best forgotten, as he'd suggested to the guard. He switched to his in-box and saw the e-mail he'd been waiting for. Rubbing his hands together in excitement, he smiled.

"This is what you've been waiting for, Randall," he said to himself. "This is the information that can potentially take me and my partner straight to the top."

He opened the e-mail and began reading its contents voraciously. He wasn't the only one reading the documents. Within seconds they were downloaded to another computer and quickly printed out. Randall had no idea his breakthrough research had fallen into a pair of French-manicured hands, hands that right now were typing an e-mail to his cross-country rival, in hopes of making a deal.

At a little past eleven p.m., after turning off the security office cameras monitoring the floor where PSI was located, Eric took the stairs to the PSI offices. He was disappointed that Randall had left work with his laptop but was still able to place cameras throughout the room, including a microscopic one on the top of Randall's paperweight, sure to pick up every word uttered from anyone sitting at that desk. Another camera was above the conference table and the third one had been placed on the table lamp that separated two chairs in a sitting area. Additionally, microphones had been taped under seats and tables. It was while performing this task that he struck gold. In a magnetic key box stuck to the underside of Randall's office desk, was the key to the lab.

"Yeah, baby!"

Eric punched the air with his fist. He pulled out his phone, as giddy as a school boy hoping to impress his teacher. "Al."

"Hey, Todd."

"You won't believe what I'm holding in my hand."

"Your dick?"

"Haha. The key to the lab."

"You're bullshitting me."

"You think so? Hold on." He took a picture of the key and sent it to Jacqueline. "I just sent you the pic."

"Haven't you retained anything I've taught you? Delete that picture off of your cell phone. Now!"

"Okay."

"Are you even sure it's the lab key?"

"No, but—"

"Go check it out. Right now. Hurry."

Eric did as ordered, the joy he'd felt at finding the key fading fast. He reached the lab, took a quick look around and opened the door. "It's the key."

"You're inside?"

"Yeah."

Jacqueline squealed. "Excellent work, big guy. I knew you could do it. You are the man."

A little of Eric's joy returned.

"Okay, here's what I want you to do. Take pictures of everything you can get your hands on: labels, petri dishes, files, whatever is in that room. How many mini-cameras do you have left?" Eric told her. "Good. Place four of them in that room. Cover every possible angle. Place a couple microphone strips in there as well so that I can monitor conversation. Lastly, get a copy of that key."

Eric examined the key in his hand. "Can't. It's one that can't be duplicated."

"The word *can't* is for losers. I want you to meet me in half an hour. Bring the key. I know where I can get it duplicated."

"But what if Randall discovers it missing?"

"Are you expecting him back at the office tonight?"

"No."

"Good, because a couple of hours is all I'll need. We've got a lot of work to do. So get busy. Meet me in thirty. And Todd?"

"Yes, Al?"

"You've just earned yourself a bonus."

The click in his ear served as Jacqueline's good-bye. Eric didn't mind the rudeness. He was used to it by now. He smiled, snapping pictures of every inch of the lab and its contents. Jacqueline was a bitch on wheels but the things she did to him in bed, and the things she allowed him to do to her was worth every ounce of frustration.

CHAPTER 29

As she left the newly renovated building in central D.C., Sherri was smiling. She'd just met with the board for the alternative education director position and knew she'd left an impression that would be hard to beat. While coming in strong on her own merits, that her husband was the award-winning Dr. Randall Atwater, who'd developed the Atwater Achievement Model, a science and math program for inner-city youth, had been a huge plus. Her formal one-on-one interview with the coordinator was slated for the first of the year, but the board had all but told her that the job was hers.

She got into her car for the ride back to Alexandria. Humming a Dru Hill throwback, she tapped her car's Bluetooth and waited for Renee to answer. Once she did, Sherri bypassed hello, choosing instead to jump right into conversation. "It's not yet official, but I can pretty much bet that you are talking to the Executive Director of Capitol Alternative Education, a position that comes with a very nice salary!"

"Congratulations, Sherri! I'm so happy for you!"

"I keep telling myself to calm down and not count chickens before they're hatched, but if you'd heard me in with the board just now, you'd know why I'm so excited."

"I have no doubt that you're the one for the job. You can relate to the way many of these kids live, yet can give them real insight and assistance into bettering their lives. You'll be perfect."

"It's funny how excited I am. I didn't know how much I'd missed being in the workplace and having a career until I started teaching part-time again last year. What I give to the students is often mentioned, but in truth they give me so much more. This is just the type of news I needed right before the holidays. I don't even need to wait for Santa. Getting this job is my Christmas gift."

Renee's laughter trickled through the phone. "What are you guys doing for Christmas?"

"Would you believe staying at home for a change? Randall's been traveling and we were just in the Bahamas last month. For the first time in what, almost three years, we have Jacqueline totally and completely out of our lives. So we decided to have a quiet Christmas here at home."

"What, is she back in jail?"

"Oh my gosh, girl, I can't believe I didn't tell you. A lot's been going on. Jacqueline has left the United States and is now in Australia . . . hopefully for good."

"Whoa! No, you didn't tell me and I can't believe it either. How'd that happen? Isn't she on probation?"

"That's what I thought. Turns out that because her case was thrown out, she's free unless or until we can win an appeal and have her re-tried. A week ago, she flew to Australia. And before you ask, yes, it was confirmed through her photo ID. She absolutely, positively got on that plane."

"Did her crazy-ass sister go with her?"

"No, but according to the detective, she's totally into her marriage and family. Nathan and I believe there's no way Jessica would have tried to hurt anyone, had it not been for the witch's spell."

"I'd imagine Nathan is coming up from Atlanta to spend the holidays with you?"

"Actually, no. He's going back to the island and spending Christmas with Dev and her family."

"Is that heifah getting ready to marry my man?"

Sherri laughed. "If I remember correctly, *your* man is the one who put those two carats on your finger and is making it possible for you to spend Christmas on an island yourself."

"Yeah, Big Daddy K knows how to spoil me, that's for sure."

"When's the big day?"

"Probably June. He'd rather we drive to the strip and get married by Elvis, but you know I've got to have the cake and all the trimmings. Which reminds me. You need to get your butt in the gym because you're going to be my matron of honor and our dresses are going to fit like gloves."

"Me? Are you serious? I'd love to stand beside you! As for the gym, that particular date is long overdue. After the holidays, I'm going to get serious. These pounds I lost and put back on have got to go."

"You'll be by my side no matter what. But Nathan might not get invited."

"Why not? Y'all have been friends forever."

"Because when the preacher asks for anyone to speak now or forever hold their peace, I might be the one who shouts 'hold up,' before walking over to grab Nate's fine ass and pulling him to the altar."

"Ha! Girl, you have no sense at all."

"I have a little bit. I might talk crazy, but I heard what you said and took it to heart. I know men like Kenneth don't come along every day. He's a good man, and I'm not going to give another woman the chance to find that out and leave you saying 'I told you so.'"

"I'd never do that."

"Sure you would."

"Thank goodness I don't have to." Sherri looked at her dash and saw another call coming in. "Nay, it's Randall calling. I'll talk to you later."

"It's going to be busy before we leave for Tahiti, so if I don't get another chance, Merry Christmas to you and your family."

"Absolutely, Nay, to you and Kenneth as well."

CHAPTER 30

"Merry Christmas, Develia."

"Merry Christmas, Nathan."

It was early morning, 12:01 to be exact. The two lovebirds had just enjoyed a round of "welcome back" lovemaking. Mere hours into Nathan's return to the island, they had foregone the parties and island festivities in exchange for the chance to be alone.

"I'm glad you're here."

Nathan gently placed a lock of Dev's damp hair behind her ear. "Me too."

"Are you sure you're not wishing you were with your family? How close you all are is a beautiful thing to behold."

"We were all just here for Thanksgiving and I'll see them again in February, when we all get together to watch the Super Bowl. Right now I'm where I want to be, with my favorite lady, in my favorite place."

Develia turned on her side and propped herself up on an elbow. "Nathan."

"Yes?"

"Could you see yourself ever moving here?"

He rolled over to face her. "I could definitely see myself splitting time between here and Georgia. Because of the work I do, a good amount of time has to be spent with my clients in the States. But technology has made it possible for a good deal of work to be done via the Internet. Freeing me up"—he tugged her earlobe between his lips—"to spend more time"—he licked his way to her cheek—"with you."

They shared a kiss. He pulled back and propped a pillow behind his head. "What about you? Would you be willing to move to Georgia?"

"If I were to become your wife, I would."

"Hmm."

"Can you envision that, Nathan? Can you see us together for the long term: ten, twenty, fifty years?"

"It's taken me thirty-some years to see myself married, period. The concept of spending my life with one person, having sex with only that person for the rest of my life, was one I couldn't grasp. I think if men were honest, few can. But then I look at my sis and Randall, and my boss, Broderick, and his wife, and I see the type of bond that can only happen when there is true commitment, and I realize that marriage is more about the mental and emotional than the physical. It's about how that person makes you feel, what the two of you can build together that couldn't be forged alone. It's about partnership, and legacies, and being best friends. And when I think of those things, yes, Dev, I can see all of those possibilities with me and you."

"Then where's my flippin' ring, man?"

The two of them laughed, rolled out of bed, and took showers. It was time to open gifts.

* * *

Back in the States, Jacqueline, dressed in her Kate Freeman getup and Eric-slash-Todd, now working his Bruce Clarke alias, sat in front of a rundown project in southeast Washington, D.C.

"What do you think? Should we just go to the door and knock?"

Jacqueline glanced around them, then in the back-seat at the gifts they'd purchased. "Yeah, I'd say hit them with the element of surprise. It's Christmas. We're play-ing Santa. What's not to like?" She took a deep breath. "Let's do this."

The two exited the car, grabbed the bags from the back, and walked up the stairs to the complex of large, drab red buildings. A blanket of snow covered trash and cracked sidewalks, and softened the harsh realities of the people who lived beyond these concrete walls. Eric and Jacqueline checked the doors for apartment numbers. Many were missing a digit or two. Others showed no number at all. Walking by a particular win-dow, Jacqueline noticed a window blind sway slightly. Though neither had any doubt it had been happening since they entered the complex, this was the first obvi-ous sign that they were being watched.

They reached an end apartment. The blinds next to the door and on the facing window were tightly closed. No light escaped. Jacqueline looked at her watch. It was ten o'clock, but could they still be sleeping? She'd not thought to come later. Even on this holiday, there was too much to do. She gave Eric a nod. He knocked on the door. They waited a second. Two. Five. He knocked again, harder this time. Still no sound or sign of movement.

Eric walked to the window and knocked there. He placed his mouth close to the window. "Corvales, are you in there? It's Bruce."

The frigid air turned his breath into puffs of steam as he talked. He clasped the bag tighter. Next to him, Jacqueline shivered. Eric knocked on the door again. Jacqueline saw the blinds move, and breathed a sigh of relief. If they were looking, they'd see gifts and open the door.

Sure enough, it opened seconds later. Though only eighteen, Corvales's bulk filled the doorway. "What's up, Bruce? How'd you find me?"

"We sports agents are pretty ingenious and can find most anybody when we put our mind to it." He increased the Southern twang in his voice, as Jacqueline had suggested. He held up the bag. "I hope you don't mind that my assistant Kate, and I have brought these over for you and your family. Merry Christmas."

"Who is it?" The question was asked in a gruff voice from behind the door.

Corvales turned to answer. "It's that agent dude I told you about. He has some Christmas presents."

A female voice yelled from within the apartment. "Well, what are you standing there for, letting in that cold-ass air? We don't have enough heat to warm up the whole neighborhood. Let them in and shut the door!"

Jacqueline and Eric entered the dark, dank, two-bedroom abode. A silver Christmas tree adorned with red bulbs was perched in a corner. A few scraggly Christmas gifts were under the tree. A girl who looked to be around ten or so lay on the couch, which, if the scrunched-up sheets were any indication, had obviously served as her bed last night. Next to her was a box containing clothing, and beneath it, hastily torn gift wrap paper. Two young boys sat eating cereal at a small dining table in the corner of the room. Next to one boy's elbow was a board game, and on top of it, a couple of shirts. Beyond the table was the kitchen, where a teenage girl in a fluffy pink robe stood stirring something in a skillet on the stove. Pieces of bacon sat on a towel next to the skillet. The place reeked of fried pork and the cigarette smoke swirling from between a woman's fingers as she leaned against a living room wall. Jacqueline assumed this was Corvales's mother, and the one who'd yelled.

"I'm sorry to barge in on you like this," Eric said. "But my assistant here thought it best. That way, you wouldn't have a chance to turn me down."

Corvales strolled over to the couch and plopped down. "It's all good."

Eric reached into his bag. "I remember you telling me about your siblings and bought some stuff I hope you all will enjoy."

The first gift he pulled out was a Nintendo Wii U. The party was pretty much on after that. Later, when Eric asked Corvales to take a walk and discuss business, Jacqueline stayed behind and chatted with the high school star's now-much-friendlier mom. She liked the gutsy woman raising five kids in the hood without a man and without apology. It felt good to know that not only would she be sticking it to Randall and his horse-faced wife, but that she'd be helping out a sistah in the process. When she spontaneously decided to gift the mother with the recently purchased designer bag she carried, placing her personal belongings in a recycle bag, she slipped two one-hundred-dollar bills into the zippered compartment. She wouldn't be there when the woman found the bounty. But given the hour that they'd just spent together, she could hear what had to be the woman's favorite comment. "Well, I'll be diddly damned."

Nathan stepped out onto Develia's back porch, which offered a glimpse of the ocean. She was talking with a girlfriend who lived in New York, and had called with holiday greetings. He left not only to give her privacy but to take advantage of the opportunity to check his e-mails and return texts. They'd spent the afternoon with her family, so he knew he'd missed a few.

He reclined in a hammock that was tied between a hook on her house and a large tree, and after getting settled in a way that ensured he wouldn't fall out, pulled out his iPhone. As suspected, there were a few texts. He responded to those from his good friend Steve; the detective, Ralph; his boss; and Sherri's crazy friend, Renee, before switching over to his e-mail account and doing a casual scroll. There were several e-mails with holiday greetings in the subject line. It drove his sister crazy, but for him it wasn't a problem that so many people sent e-cards instead of real ones these days. He settled back against the hammock, enjoying its sway as he read. Toward the end was one from a company he didn't recognize, but that wasn't a big deal. For businesses, the holidays were as much about networking as anything else. Having given his assistant a Christmas card list of people he'd not communicated with all year, Nathan knew this firsthand.

He clicked on the link.

Merry Christmas, Nathan! May this be
the happiest of holidays for you and your
son.

The message shot him straight up and sent the
hammock wobbling. He tried to right himself but too
late. His body slammed into the hard dirt.

Pain raced through the shoulder that had taken the
brunt of his fall. "Dammit!"

The thud was loud enough to bring out Develia,
who raced to his side. "Nathan! What happened? Are
you okay?"

He nodded and said he was. But the truth of the
matter was anything but. The sentence he'd read and
the picture that had accompanied it had convinced him
that things weren't all right. They weren't okay at all.

CHAPTER 31

The day after Christmas, Jessica and Vincent sat in their bed with Dax between them, watching him play with one of his new video toys.

"Times have changed," Vincent said, his eyes shining with love as he watched his son. "Back in the day, if this were my old block, not one child would be inside. We'd be out on bikes, skating on boards, bouncing new balls, showing off our presents."

"That's probably still happening in some parts of town, but I agree, not as much as when we were kids. All of them are tied to their game controls now, and stuck inside."

"That's not going to be you, Dax. Matter of fact—" Vincent hopped out of bed. "Come on, Dax. We're getting ready to go outside and soak up sunshine."

"Where we going, Daddy?"

"To have fun." He picked up Dax. "Let's go put clothes on." With a one-handed pillow toss at Jessica, he added, "You too."

"No, I'm good. You two go on, though. It looks nice outside."

"Come on, Mommy!"

"Maybe I'll join you after a quick shower. Give Mommy a kiss."

Dax ran back to comply with her wishes, then was off to his room with Vincent to change out of his pajamas.

Jessica stretched as she watched them leave the room. *I probably should join them and get some exercise. Just because I'm pregnant doesn't mean I have to get fat.* She hopped out of bed and into the shower.

When she came out, Vincent was coming out of their walk-in closet dressed in shorts and a long-sleeved tee. "Are you coming with us?"

She nodded. "Just let me throw on a pair of sweats."

"You'd better hurry up and throw on something. You know what happens when I see you naked."

"Yes, baby, you show me over and over again."

Dax waddled into the room, sending a still naked Jessica dashing into the closet. Ten minutes later, they entered the park two blocks from their home. The unseasonably warm December weather had brought out the neighborhood. Some women chatted on benches while others strolled with their children in tow. A pickup game of basketball was in full swing on the court while kids rode skateboards, bicycles, tricycles, and other wheeled devices on the square chunk of asphalt in the center of the park. Jessica's neighbor was there with her son. As soon as Dax saw his friend, he squirmed away from his parents and joined the kid in the sandbox.

"Let's jog around the perimeter," Vincent suggested, placing his leg on a bench to get a good stretch.

"Let's walk around it a couple times and then jog."

"Okay."

"Don't worry about Dax," the neighbor said. "I'll keep an eye on him."

"Thanks, Sally." Jessica tightened her shoelace and fell into step beside her husband. "I didn't feel sick this morning."

"Maybe the morning sickness has passed."

"I sure hope so. With Dax, I was sick for almost six months, and it wasn't limited to mornings."

"Yeah, boys are obnoxious like that. My daughter is much more thoughtful."

"You really think it's a girl, huh?"

"I know it is."

"Oh, and how's that?"

"I directed the X and Y chromosomes to do what I wanted, just like I sent that soldier sperm and told it to go grab that egg."

"Ha!" They met another couple running toward them and waved as they all moved into single-file to pass on the narrow path. "What are you going to do if it's a boy?"

"Love him as much as I love Dax. And start working on number three."

"You'll also need to start working on who's going to carry that baby because this girl right here is two and through."

"Why? I told you I want a big family."

"And you can have one, as soon as you figure out how to carry to term." They laughed. He reached for her hand. "So, if it is a girl, what should we name her?" she asked.

"Valencia."

She immediately looked over, surprised at his quick response. "Something you've already thought about, I see."

"Yes."

"I like that name. It almost sounds like a combination of ours, Vincent and Jessica."

He nodded. "Right."

"And if it's a boy?"

"Vincent, Jr."

"I do not want my son called Junior. To me, that sounds old-fashioned."

"Then we won't call him Junior. We'll call him Vincent."

"But other people might call him Junior."

"Then we'll have to teach him how to make the correction."

They'd made the first lap around the asphalt square, all the while keeping an eye on Dax. Upon starting the second lap, they picked up the pace. Vincent easily took the lead.

"That's not fair! Your legs are longer."

He threw a retort back over his shoulder. "They're not the only thing long on me."

"Ha!"

He slowed so she could catch him. She clung to a piece of his T-shirt to keep him beside her. "Do you wish I'd named Dax after you?"

He shrugged. "It would have been nice. But I'm not tripping off that. Our son looks like a Dax. And I like the name. It's original and unique, a lot like him. But Valencia? She's going to be a daddy's girl all the way. A chip off my block."

"Oh, really. Nothing to do with me, huh?"

"Nope. She's going to look just like me. And she's going to be an attorney, just like her dad."

"I'm sure she'll appreciate that you've got her future all planned out."

"Yes, and I'm going to plan yours next, starting with changing your mind about having babies and getting you on board with creating a basketball team."

"Like I said, as soon as you can carry one to term, I'll be right there to rub your back."

The trip to the park turned out to be the perfect family outing and the start to a perfect day. They came home, changed, and went to the movies. Back home, Vincent and Jessica made love while their son napped. That evening, Vincent volunteered to take Dax out to see the remaining Christmas lights while Jessica enjoyed an hour of time alone. She kissed her two men, plopped on the couch, and reached for the remote.

She settled on a channel but didn't watch it. Instead she lay back against the couch and watched the movie of her life play across her mental screen. Where she was now was much different than where she was ten years ago—heck, even two years ago. Being this happy was something she thought was for other people, not her. Yet here she was in a beautiful home with a stunning Christmas tree, three stockings taped to the fireplace mantel, representing the three people who resided in the home. The happy family living the American dream. Her family.

Clutching a throw pillow against her, she couldn't help but ponder. *How did I get so lucky?*

Her phone rang. "Hey, baby."

"Babe, you want us to pick up something to eat?"

"Sure."

"What do you want?"

"Whatever you guys get is fine with me."

"If your son chooses, that might be chicken nuggets and fries."

"Then nuggets and fries it is."

Ending the call, she noted several unread e-mails and tapped on the in-box. One name jumped out and took her totally by surprise. But it was the holidays when people often made a special effort to reach out.

She clicked on the e-mail sent by Nathan Carver. The picture in the e-mail caused her heart to leap to her throat. It was a picture of Dax, and one single line:

Is there something you need to tell me?

CHAPTER 32

It was almost midnight when Sherri's phone rang. She and Randall were sitting by one of five fireplaces their home boasted, this one in the master suite's sitting room, enjoying a glass of wine and recapping the day.

Randall looked at his watch and then at her. "Who is it?"

Sherri smiled. "It's just Nate." A tap and then, "Hey, baby brother!" At the first word spoken, she knew something was wrong. Rising from the chair, she asked him, "What's the matter?"

Hearing the worry in his wife's voice, Randall was attentive as well.

"But that's crazy."

What is it? Randall mouthed.

Sherri gave a quick head shake, put up a "hold on a minute" finger. "Okay, Nate. Send me the picture and try and calm down." Walking back over to where Randall sat and sitting beside him, she put the call on speaker so that she could talk to Nathan and check her e-mails. "Ran's here with me. I've got you on speaker so we both can take a look."

"Is it there yet? I'm calling while Dev is in the shower and don't have much time."

"I'm refreshing, but it's not here . . . oh, wait, here it is." Sherri tapped on the attachment icon and watched the picture download. Ran leaned forward. They studied the picture together. "Someone sent a picture saying this was your son?"

"Yes, wishing us a happy holiday."

"It came anonymously."

"Yes."

"Okay, so you get an anonymous e-mail with a picture of a little boy. You don't even know who sent it? Why are you jumping to the conclusion that he's yours?"

"Really look at the picture, Sherri. He favors me. His skin is lighter than ours, but think back to Mom's brother. He was lighter than us, too. And Jessica's fair-skinned."

Sherri enlarged the picture on the screen. Upon careful consideration, there were traits similar to other members of her family, but none that couldn't also be attributed to thousands of other Black families.

"When I learned Jessica was pregnant, a part of me believed it was mine. It wasn't just the timing. It was a feeling. But she spoke so surely of it being Vincent's that I didn't question it. Her saying that helped me make a clean break from a dirty situation. At the time, that's all I wanted. Look, I have to run. I'll call you back as soon as I can."

The call abruptly ended.

For a second or two neither Randall nor Sherri

spoke. When he did, it was the question that both were thinking. "What the hell just happened?"

Sherri stood. "I'll be right back." She walked out of the room and returned a short time later with two large photo albums. Sitting next to Randall, she turned on the lamp beside them. "These belong to Mom. There are several pictures in here of when Nate was a baby." She quickly flipped through the album, stopping at a section that showed several pictures of a little boy, from newborn to around the age of five.

She reached for her phone and brought back the picture Nathan had sent to her and placed it down with the other pictures. "Well?"

Randall slowly shook his head. "I don't know."

Sherri sighed. "I don't either. But there is a resemblance. Look at their eyes, and mouth. They're exactly alike."

"He doesn't have Nate's big nose."

"That's probably from Jessica's side of the family."

"Sounds like you think that's Nate's son."

"I think he should be finding out. God knows I hope it isn't true. Because that would mean . . ." She shuddered.

"It would mean that you and Jacqueline would be aunts to the same child."

"Sweet baby Jesus. Please never again say that out loud."

Randall picked up the phone with the picture of the little boy. He looked between it and the photo album. "Then you probably don't want me to say what I'm thinking right now either."

"What's that?"

"That the more I look at this picture, the more it looks like this boy could be Nate's."

Back in the Bahamas, Nathan tried his best to act nonchalant and stay in the romantic groove he and Dev had enjoyed all day, one that had them discussing a future together. But it wasn't easy. His thoughts kept going back to Jessica. *Why hasn't she answered my e-mail?* That's what Nathan had expected when he sent it, a quick response flatly denying the possibility and maybe a reason why someone would have sent him the pic. He tried to tell himself that maybe she hadn't read it. But the Jessica he knew constantly checked her texts and e-mails; she was always scrolling her phone. If she'd responded and said the boy wasn't his, the matter would have been over. Instead, her silence increased his curiosity and made him think that Dax might actually be his son.

He remembered the day he found out Jessica was pregnant, the absolute shock mixed with another feeling that he never defined. When she told him the child was Vincent's, he remembered feeling a sadness and type of loss. No matter what had eventually happened between them, once Jessica had been his world. So much so that he'd wanted her to become his wife. It took him a long time to get over her and what happened. Feeling the way he did in this moment made him acknowledge that he never totally had.

"There you are!" Dev came out of the house and joined him on the porch. She wrapped her arms around his waist. "It's a beautiful night, isn't it?"

"Yes, it is."

"It's nights like these that make it hard for me to ever picture myself leaving the island. If we get married, do you think it would be possible to conduct your work from here, with frequent trips to the States?" She waited for a response that never came. "Nate?"

He looked down into eyes filled with love and excitement, and knew that what he anguished over was something Dev needed to know.

"Come over here, baby. Let's sit down."

Dev immediately noticed his change of mood. "What is it, sweetheart? What could have happened in the ten minutes it took for me to shower?"

"Earlier today, I received news so shocking that I fell out of the hammock."

Dev's mouth dropped open. "You received shocking news back then and have been holding it all day?"

"I didn't want to spoil our day, your Christmas."

"What type of news would spoil it, especially concerning you?"

Nathan pulled out his phone and took a breath, knowing there was no easy way to say what he had to tell her. "Somebody sent me this picture today."

He watched as she studied the picture. "Whose little boy is this?"

"According to the person who sent the e-mail, he may be mine."

CHAPTER 33

Jessica checked her watch for the umpteenth time. It was nine o'clock, three hours past the time Vincent usually left work and an hour past the time he said via text that he'd be home. They'd decided to ring in the New Year quietly, at a restaurant, choosing the late seating at nine p.m. The neighbor had agreed to watch Dax for the night. It was a night that would belong to just Vincent and her. But the last two calls to him had gone to voice mail. She was beginning to worry. No, that's not quite right. She'd been worrying for days now, ever since getting the e-mail from Nathan and having her subsequent ones to Jacqueline go unanswered. Her biggest fear was that whoever sent the e-mail to him would send one to Vincent. It felt bad to admit it, but she'd rather her husband had been in an accident than find out that Dax was not his son.

Keys in the lock. *Finally, he's home!* The heels of her stilettos click-clacked against the hardwood as she briskly walked from the bedroom to the living room, arriving there just as Vincent closed the door.

"There you are!"

He brushed past her and threw his keys on a side table. Removing his coat, he answered without facing her. "Yes, here I am."

"I tried phoning you. The calls went to voice mail."

He walked to the hall closet and hung up his coat.

"You'll need to hurry, baby. Our reservations are for nine thirty."

Vincent eyed her with a strange expression, turned and walked toward their bedroom.

"Vincent, what is it? Why are you acting so strangely?"

He gave her a half smile while removing his cuff links. "Is that how I'm acting?"

"Yes. Did something happen at work?"

"Yes, it did." He sat on the bed and removed his shoes, tossing them, almost throwing them toward the closet.

She joined him on the bed. "With one of your clients?"

Vincent jumped up, walked over to the closet. "No, not with one of my clients."

Jessica crossed her arms. She was beginning to get annoyed. "Well, am I supposed to sit here and guess why you're acting so funky?"

Removing his shirt, he answered almost casually. "I guess that would be fair enough, since I've spent the better part of this afternoon and evening trying to guess whether or not Dax is my biological son."

The words were like a dagger in her gut. She held her stomach as it clenched, almost cramped, at the hard tone of his voice. In mere seconds, a torrent of questions assailed her. *Should I act angry, denying all pos-*

sibility? Maybe ignorant, as though I don't know what he's talking about? Laugh, as though the thought is so ludicrous it's funny?

In shock that this was even happening, she did nothing. Said nothing.

"What, no blatant denial, no gasp of shock at my making such a statement? That almost leads me to believe it's true."

Jessica found her voice. "You come home, obviously pissed, asking no questions and spouting crazy accusations, and I'm supposed to defend myself?"

"Oh, my bad. I guess I should have come in here calmly, and lovingly asked you whether or not Dax is my biological son. I guess it's the DNA test results forwarded to my in-box that has me standing here forgetting how to be a gentleman. The test results that said the likelihood of his being mine was zero, while the chance that he was the son of Nathan Carver was 99.9. So beg my motherfuckin' pardon for being upset that my wife is sitting here all innocent like she doesn't know this shit is true!"

"Vincent!" Jessica jumped up and ran to him. "I don't know what you're talking about. Why would I have a DNA test done on Dax when I know he's yours?"

"Why would someone send me information to the contrary?"

"I don't know! Probably so that this would happen, to put doubt in your mind and disrupt our happy home."

He placed his hands on her shoulders. "You don't know how much I want to believe you."

"Then do it. Believe me! Anyone can make up a document to look like something it's not and send it in an e-mail. Did it come directly from a DNA company or from some weird e-mail address that you've never seen before?"

Vincent sighed, reaching for Jessica's hand as he led them over to the bed and sat. "It came from a Yahoo account."

"Oh my God, Vincent, and you think that's legit?"

"I didn't know what to think. I wracked my brain for the name of anyone who would do this, an angry client or someone from a case I won. I couldn't think of anybody. Can you?"

"Yes."

"Who?"

"My sister. She hates you, and probably the fact that I'm with you. That we're in love and happy and expecting another child." She turned to Vincent. "It's the only possibility that makes sense. And would explain why she hasn't responded to my e-mails."

"You've been e-mailing her? I thought we'd decided to put her behind us, especially after finding out she's left the States."

"We had, but, um, it's the holidays, baby. I just reached out to wish her a merry Christmas and happy New Year." *And to find out why she sent Dax's picture to Nathan!*

"And she didn't respond?" Jessica shook her head. "Then maybe you're right. Maybe this was her way of trying to get back at us. She knows that I don't like her, and she had to know how much news like this would bother me." He hugged her. "I'm sorry for assuming the worst without talking to you first."

"I understand, babe. Getting an e-mail like that would probably have led me to do the same thing." She stood. "It's almost nine thirty. Think you can be dressed in fifteen minutes?"

"Yes, but I have one more question."

"What's that?"

He stood and eyed her keenly. "What were you doing in Lithonia?"

Jessica's eyes widened in surprise. "Lithonia?"

"Yes. I was talking to Carl earlier and he mentioned that a month or so ago he saw you coming out of a bank."

"Oh, that. Why don't you get ready, baby, and I'll tell you over dinner."

"No, Jessica. I think I'd rather hear the explanation right now."

She sat down, feeling defeated, her eyes filling with tears. "I should have told you earlier. This is all Sissy, and with what else you've heard tonight, you're going to be mad."

He leaned against the wall and crossed his arms. "I'm listening."

"I went there to open a bank account."

"What? I didn't hear you."

"I went to open a bank account, a separate one just for me."

"Why?"

"Vincent, you know why. Because of what happened in my last marriage, how money was used to control me and make me feel trapped."

"Have I ever made you feel that way?"

"No, but . . . it makes a woman, it makes *me* feel more secure in the relationship, knowing that I'm not totally dependent on you."

"That makes no sense, Jessie. We both have separate accounts, and each contributes to the joint one for the household. So I'm going to try this one more time, and if you continue lying to me then you're right, I'm going to get upset. Why were you in a town thirty miles from Atlanta opening up a bank account?"

"Sissy gave me some money." She waited for a reaction, but when there was none, when he continued to stand there, arms crossed, expression unreadable, she went on. "Remember the insurance policy Mrs. Hurley told me about, the one she said my sister took and kept for her own?"

"Yes, I remember that."

"It was true. I asked Jacqueline about it when we had lunch. She admitted receiving money and said it was only fair that I get half."

"That's what you deposited in Lithonia?"

"Yes."

"How much?"

"A hundred and twenty-five thousand."

"You got a hundred and twenty-five thousand dollars and didn't say a word?" She didn't say one now. "Were you ever planning to tell me? Or were you just going to wait around for me to mess up, and then run off with the kids?"

"You know that's not true, Vincent. I love you. I love the life we're building. I love our family. I've never felt as safe and secure as I have since marrying you."

"Then why be so secretive? That's a lot of money, Jessie. There are ways to handle an amount like that to make it grow. If you felt so safe, why not share that you got it?"

"I don't know. At the time it just felt like the thing to do."

Vincent pushed off the wall and paced the floor, thinking. "Now I'm understanding how we were able to have such a wonderful Christmas, how you found all of these—what did you call them?—inventory clearance and discontinued items, how you were able to afford to buy me that diamond stud. It wasn't eBay, was it?"

"No."

"Damn, Jessie, the more we talk, I uncover lie after lie. And I'm supposed to just take your word that Dax is my son?"

"I'm sorry, Vincent. At the time I felt I was doing what was best. Now, I wish I'd told you everything."

Vincent walked over to her, squatted down to eye level. "Then look in my eyes and tell me for sure that Dax Givens is my son."

CHAPTER 34

Jacqueline and Eric sat in a car she'd rented and parked in a busy mall a couple of miles down from his security job. It was his lunch hour. He sat munching on a chicken dinner picked up at a drive-through. She sipped a bottle of water, clearly annoyed.

"Look," Eric said around a spicy drumstick, "I told you everything was taken care of. You need to chill."

"How can I relax when you don't have anything concrete to tell me about how this is going to be pulled off?"

"I did tell you. There's a party tonight."

"A party? He's going to try and do this at a party, where dozens of witnesses can identify him if something goes down?"

"Not just any party. This is a New Year's Eve party at the swanky home of one of his friends. He said the house is a mansion, something like twenty rooms. He's going to get her into one of them and do what we asked him, in order for him to get the rest of the money. He knows how important it is to work alone and not be seen. With a scholarship at stake and his athletic future on the line, trust me, he's got too much to lose to take this lightly. He's more determined than we are not to be connected to this in any way."

"And he's sure she's coming to the party?"

"It's supposed to be a big deal to have been invited. Plus, he kind of gave her the impression that if she came to the party, you know, they'd be able to hang out a little bit."

"Hmm."

"It's going to be easy, Al. I don't know why you're so worried that something could go wrong."

"Because the daughter is only part of an overall plan to bring down this family, that's why."

Eric stopped eating. He looked at Jacqueline. "What did this family do to you?"

"Their lies put me behind bars."

He nodded, picked up a fry. "They're going to wish they hadn't done that in less than twenty-four hours."

Randall and Sherri walked with their hosts to the front door. Sherri turned and hugged her neighbor. "The party was lovely, Caroline. Thanks again for inviting us."

Next to her, Randall was shaking the husband's hand and voicing his appreciation of a fun-filled evening.

"Which is all the more reason you should stay," Caroline joked. "It's New Year's! Even our children get to stay up past their bedtime."

"That's why we're heading home," Randall said. "Aaron is spending the night with a friend but Albany is due home at one o'clock We want to be there to make sure she arrives safely."

"I understand." The two women hugged again. "Remember, the party continues with brunch at eleven: Bloody Marys and mimosas, and a menu boasting some of the country's finest dishes. From Maryland crab cakes to California salad with strawberries and avocados."

"Sounds delicious. We'll more than likely be over."

Hand in hand, Randall and Sherri walked the short distance from their neighbor's home to theirs. The air was crisp, the sky filled with what looked like a thousand stars. "It's beautiful out here," Randall remarked.

"I was just thinking the same thing."

"Want to go home and make love on the balcony, under the stars?"

"And freeze our you-know-whats off?"

"We could bring out a blanket. Plus, I have a few ideas to take your mind off the cold."

"Oh, really? Such as?"

He leaned over and whispered in her ear.

"Ooh, Ran, that's nasty! Promise you'll do it?"

"Ha!"

"Hurry up. We have an hour before Albany gets home."

They reached their manse and hurried upstairs, giggling like teenagers. They stripped off their clothes and went outside on their balcony, where Randall kept his promise to keep her warm. Something about making love outside was exhilarating: cold air all around them while under the blanket Randall did things with his fingers, tongue, and penis that had Sherri stuffing her mouth with a pillow to not scream out loud. Finally, shivering and satiated, they went back inside and straight to the master bath. A warm shower removed most of the chill.

Sherri knew how to remove it completely. "I'm going downstairs for tea. Would you like some?"

"Yes. That sounds good. Thanks."

She'd only been in the kitchen five minutes when she heard footsteps, looked up, and saw Randall rounding the corner. "Miss me already?"

He came up behind her and wrapped his arms around her waist. "Do you know how happy you make me?"

"Yes, because you make me feel the exact same way." She opened a cabinet and pulled out a canister. "What type of tea would you like?"

"I think I'll go for chamomile, something that will totally relax me and help me sleep in tomorrow."

"That sounds good. I think I'll have that, too." They continued casual chitchat while she made their tea, adding lemon and agave to both mugs before handing one to Randall. "Should we go back upstairs?"

"Why don't we stay down here, drive Albany crazy by waiting up for her and pouncing as soon as she enters the house, like our parents used to do?"

Sherri laughed. "That sounds perfect."

They went to the great room just off from the entrance they thought Albany would use. Sherri reached for the remote as she sat and turned on the TV. Randall cuddled beside her. He watched as she flipped through channels.

"Crazy that there are over a hundred channels and still nothing good on TV."

"I was just thinking the very same thing!" Sherri looked at him. "There used to be so many good shows like the *Cosby Show*, *A Different World*, *Family Matters*, *Sister, Sister* . . ."

"*The Fresh Prince*."

Sherri laughed. "You loved that show. I loved *Living Single*."

"*In Living Color* . . . now that was some good TV! Now all we've got are reality shows that are far from reality."

"There's still a few good ones out there, thanks to Shonda Rhimes."

"Yeah, thank her for giving our women scandalous ideas."

"You don't even watch it to know what it's about!"

"Hell, it's called *Scandal*. Thinking that it's scandalous isn't much of a stretch." He looked at his watch and then at Sherri. "Uh-oh. She's late."

"What time is it?"

"One minute past one."

Sherri gave his arm a playful slap. "Thank goodness you're my husband and not my father. Let's give her five minutes for goodness' sake."

"Okay."

"Ooh, look, honey." Sherri turned up the volume and placed down the remote. "*Boyz n the Hood*!"

They watched silently for a few minutes, with Randall periodically checking his watch.

"What time is it?" Sherri finally asked.

"One fifteen." He raised a brow. "Is she still in the grace period?"

"No. Let me call her."

She got up, retrieved the cordless phone, and rejoined Randall on the couch. After dialing the number, she placed the call on speaker. It went to voice mail.

"Albany, it's your mom."

"And Dad."

"I told you to keep your phone handy so that we

could reach you, which is what we're trying to do right now."

"Because you're late!" Randall growled. Sherri looked at him and laughed. "So if you don't want to get grounded until you turn eighteen, you'd better be walking through the front door in the next five minutes."

"You heard your father. Call us back."

They cuddled and laughed at some of their favorite scenes from an African-American movie classic. But when one thirty rolled around with still no word or sight of Albany, neither were smiling.

"Call her again," Randall demanded, looking anything but relaxed after a cup of supposedly calming chamomile tea.

Sherri picked up the phone, tapped redial and then the speaker button. "Hey, what's up, this is your mom, Albany." She ended the call. "Should we call the house?"

"No." Randall stood. "I'm going over there."

"I'm coming with you."

The two went upstairs, dressed quickly, and left for the ten-minute drive to an even tonier neighborhood in Fairfax County, one where each house could have had its own zip code. Randall reached the gate and hit the buzzer. He hit it again, and a third time before someone finally answered.

"Williams residence."

"Yes, this is Dr. Atwater. I'm here to pick up my daughter."

"One moment, Dr. Atwater." A few seconds later, the heavy iron gate swung open. Randall drove down a tree- and car-lined drive that opened up to a large parking area that looked as though it could hold at least twenty cars. Currently, there were only seven cars parked there. The front was lit up with holiday lights, as well as several lights shining from rooms facing them. Randall pulled into a space closest to the home's massive double-door entrance. He and Sherri quickly walked to the door.

A maid answered. "Come in, Dr. Atwater." She nodded at Sherri. "Mrs. Atwater. Mr. Williams is on his way." After ushering them into a smartly designed sitting room, the uniformed house worker quietly retreated out of sight.

Randall and Sherri were too keyed up to sit. Talk was minimal as they looked around the room. Randall stared out the window. Sherri ran her hand over a table decoration.

"Randall! Sherri! Happy New Year!"

The booming voice of Daniel Williams, a shrewd businessman known for his cutthroat deals as well as his charisma, filled the room. Randall approached him. "Happy New Year, Daniel."

Sherri walked over and gave Daniel a light hug. "Happy New Year. Where's Joan?"

"She's gone to bed already and will hate that she missed you."

"Well, we weren't planning on picking up Albany, but it's past her curfew and we couldn't get her on the phone so . . . here we are."

Daniel frowned slightly. "I was just in the den, where it looks like the remaining revelers have gathered. Don't remember seeing her. But that doesn't mean anything. Joan and I could be in this house for a month and not see each other."

"It's probably rivaling the square footage of Buckingham Palace," Sherri admitted, as the three of them began to walk down a wide hall with marble floors.

"No." Daniel shook his head. "It's bigger."

The three laughed, sharing small talk until they reached the room where the Williams's daughter and some of her friends gathered around a grand piano. Portia, their daughter and a talented pianist, was playing a song that was popular with her age group.

She stopped playing when the adults walked in and over to the piano. "Portia, you remember the Atwaters."

"Of course. Hello, Dr. and Mrs. Atwater."

The Atwaters returned her greeting. Sherri continued, "We're here to get Albany."

Portia frowned. "She's not home?"

This comment elicited a frown from the Atwaters. "No," Randall answered. "She isn't."

Portia looked around the room. "Have any of y'all seen Albany?"

Various replies abounded, all to the negative.

Portia rose from the piano. "I thought she was gone already, but I guess not. There are a few people watching a movie in the theater, and several others in the game room or the indoor pool. Don't worry, guys. We'll find her."

A young man joined Portia. The five of them went in search of Albany. After checking all of the places that Portia had mentioned, they still hadn't found her.

"That's strange." Portia put a finger to her chin, in thought. "The only other place I can think of is in a guest room, but I can't think of a reason why she'd go there."

"Hold on a moment." Daniel walked over to a phone on the wall. "Yes, I need you to perform a full house check. Seems that one of our revelers has gotten lost in our maze of rooms. Yes, a young lady named Albany Atwater. Call me the moment you find her."

Daniel gave the Atwaters a reassuring smile. "My security detail will handle this matter. Come, let's share a spot of brandy while we wait."

Ten minutes later, Daniel's phone beeped. "Yes." He nodded. "Good." He looked at the Atwaters. "They found her." And into the receiver, "Is she okay? Fine, no, don't worry about that. Just bring her to the library."

Moments later, one of the security guards walked in with Albany in his arms.

Randall and Sherri jumped up at once.

"Albany!" Sherri's panicked voice was an octave higher than normal.

She raced over to the large leather recliner where the guard had set her daughter down. Randall was right behind her. "Albany!" He reached her and immediately put a hand to her forehead, felt her pulse. "Albany!"

"What?"

"Albany," Sherri said, kneeling beside her. "Baby, what's the matter with you?"

"Sleepy," Albany croaked.

Randall leaned over and forced open an eyelid. He watched as Albany's eye rolled to the back of her head. He checked the other eye, tested her pulse again. He reached for his phone. "I think she's going to be okay, but she's taken something."

Sherri gasped. "What?"

Randall spoke into his cell phone. "Sorry to bother you, but I have an emergency. Can you meet me at my house in ten minutes?"

Daniel joined the Atwaters. "You think she's taken a drug?"

Randall nodded. "I'm almost sure of it."

Daniel shook his head. "My daughter doesn't do drugs."

"Maybe not," Randall said as he picked up his unresponsive daughter, "but somebody she invited here brought them to your house."

The commotion had awakened Joan, who met them as they raced toward the front door. "Oh my goodness! What on earth is the matter with Albany?"

"I'll call you later," Sherri assured her. "Don't worry. We're not blaming you guys. We're sure that whatever happened is not your fault."

CHAPTER 35

Randall and Sherri stood at the foot of their daughter's bed, watching her as she peacefully slept. In this state, she looked like their straight-A, precocious little fashionista, not the drugged-out, disheveled teenager they picked up last night.

Randall's rage was immense. Yet its only outward sign was a continued clenching and unclenching of his jaw and a scowl that hadn't left his face for the past eight hours.

"What do you think happened?"

Sherri ran nervous hands up and down her arms, fighting off a chill that had nothing to do with the temperature in the room. "I'm almost afraid to think about what happened."

The fear was warranted. When Sherri had undressed her baby for bed, Albany had on no panties.

"You do everything you can to keep your child safe, try to keep them away from harm. You get an education, work hard, move far away from the drugs and violence prevalent in the hood." He looked at Sherri, tears in his eyes. "And the stench of those common catastrophes reaches us still. I didn't keep her safe, Sherri. I didn't . . ."

She quickly walked over and put her arms around him. "Don't do this, Ran. Don't blame yourself. Drugs are everywhere and every kid is a potential target. Think about the calls we made today. Her friends swore up and down that she's never done drugs, at least not consciously, and I believe them. I know it's hard, but let's wait until she wakes up and can tell us what happened before passing judgment. And let's be thankful that she's only sleeping and can wake up. Every parent isn't so lucky."

It had been almost two a.m. when Randall had carried a knocked-out Albany to the car and placed her in the backseat. The doctor friend Randall had called while still at the Williams's house had broken speed limits to meet them at their house, run the necessary diagnostics, and then convinced Sherri, mainly, but Randall too, that once their daughter woke up she'd be fine. It was now almost two in the afternoon.

Finally, at four o'clock, she woke up, hungry, thirsty, groggy, but able to talk. Her parents' faces were the first thing she saw.

She looked around, clearly confused. "Mom?"

"Albany!" Sherri, who'd been sitting on the side of the bed, leaned over to hug her daughter. She looked deep into her eyes, continued to brush the hair away from her face. "Baby, how are you feeling? Are you okay? Are you hurting?"

Randall, who'd been sitting in an oversized furry pink chair, walked over to the bed. "Albany, what happened last night?"

"Randall, can you get her some water first?" Randall's mind was that of a detective. Sherri was in full mommy mode.

He walked over to a mini fridge, pulled out a bottle of water and another one of juice. Walking back to the bed, he unscrewed the bottle of water and handed it to Albany.

"Careful, baby," Sherri warned her. "Just small sips at first."

Albany did as her mother instructed, looking around the room, down at her favorite princess pj's and then from one parent to another. Tears formed in her eyes as she blurted out, "What happened to me?"

Sherri took the lead, forcing her voice to remain calm and reassuring. It was clear her daughter was just as confused as they were. "That's what we're hoping you can help us figure out. When you weren't home at one, I called you. The call went to voice mail."

Albany's eyes widened. "Where's my phone?"

Randall took long strides and picked up the purse the security guard had brought with him and gave it to Albany, who hurriedly searched around inside it before emptying out its contents. "My phone is gone!"

"Let's not worry about that right now," Randall said. "We need to know what happened to you, who you were around, and what exactly you remember."

Albany put down the water and picked up the apple juice. Rubbing her head, she began. "A few of us were in the theater watching a movie. One of my friends had . . . they had . . ."

"Had what, Albany?" Sherri's patience was wearing thin.

"Some alcohol."

Randall blew up. "You were drinking?"

"It didn't even taste like alcohol. It was more like orange soda."

"Who had the alcohol and who fixed your drink?"

Albany slunk down, as if trying to disappear into the bed.

"Albany," Randall said, his tone as somber as that of a funeral director. "I swear I will talk to every single person who was at that party, along with their parents, if you don't come clean."

"I don't know who had it, really, I don't! Somebody just started passing cans down the row and . . . I took one."

"This drink was in a can?" Sherri asked. Albany nodded. "Did you set the can down, maybe leave it somewhere and then return and drink the rest of it?"

"No. I was drinking it and then I felt a little dizzy. So Corvales walked me outside for some air."

"Corvales?" Randall could barely contain himself. "Who the hell is that?"

"He's a friend from school, Daddy, but he didn't have anything to do with what happened. He would never do anything to hurt me."

Sherri snorted. "You are so naïve."

"He wouldn't, Mommy!"

Sherri's look was skeptical. "What did your *friend* Corvales do next?"

"He told me that maybe I should lie down." Randall and Sherri exchanged a look. "But he didn't go in the room with me! You guys are thinking the worst about someone you don't even know!"

"Who took you to lie down, Albany?"

Albany looked at her mother. "The twins, Cara and Sarah."

Sherri crossed her arms. "Oh, really."

"Mom, I swear I'm not lying. Cara and Sarah helped me get to a room because I was so dizzy I could hardly walk. I don't even remember walking, really. I just remember seeing them when we went back in and they are the last ones I remember talking to until just now. Until waking up and seeing you guys."

Fresh tears sprang up as Albany struggled with the reality of what had happened.

Sherri placed her arms around her. "Randall, can you give us a moment, please?" He got ready to protest. "Please?"

He huffed and puffed but finally left the room. A few seconds after the door closed, Sherri reached for Albany's hand and held it in her own. "Albany, I'm afraid that something may have happened to you last night that you are not at all aware of, something besides the drugs that were obviously slipped into your drink, and something besides your phone being stolen."

Albany's voice was almost a whisper. "What?"

"Were you wearing underwear when you left for the party?"

"Of course."

"Well, you were not wearing any when you came home."

Albany's eyes widened, tears fell anew. "Mommy, no!"

Sherri worked hard not to cry too, but couldn't stop the tears that flowed and blended with her daughter's. "Shh, baby. No matter what happened, we will get through this."

She grabbed Albany's arms and gave her a little shake. "Albany, pull yourself together." Albany's cries became whimpers, then sniffles before stopping altogether. Sherri reached for a nearby box of Kleenex and placed it on Albany's lap.

"We need to go to the hospital, today, right now in fact."

"Why, Mom? Whatever might have happened, I don't want my friends to know!"

"I'm sorry, baby. But you may have been raped, and if so, it needs to be documented. Samples need to be taken. The hospital will ensure your privacy."

"A lot of my friends have parents who are doctors."

"What takes place at the hospital will be confidential. I promise you, Albany, no one outside our family will know."

"You promise?"

"I promise."

When Sherri said this, she believed it, having no idea that there were secrets lurking outside of her control, just waiting to be revealed.

CHAPTER 36

Jacqueline released a string of expletives as she slammed her phone down on the desk. For hours she'd tried to reach Eric, with no response. It wasn't the first time. In fact, it was the third time in the past two weeks. More and more, Kris's words were resounding in her head. *I don't like him. I don't trust him.* Jacqueline was beginning to feel that way, as well.

Deciding she needed a break to calm down, she donned a coat, hat, and glasses and headed outside. For a city in various stages of redevelopment, Baltimore, Maryland, wasn't too bad. Her neighborhood was especially lively. Parts of it reminded her of Toronto: the culture and entertainment, shows and concerts almost every night. The restaurants were plentiful too, with good food. She entered a cozy little bistro with great sandwiches.

She'd just placed her order and sat down when she heard something that was most unexpected.

"Jacqueline?"

It was all she could do not to respond, to keep

scrolling her phone without a care in the world. *Thank God I didn't take off my sunglasses. Now if I can just convince this person that I am not me.*

A nice-looking young man came up to the table. "Jacqueline Tate?"

She looked up. Her face, that which was visible beyond the oversized sunglasses, was as still as stone, her voice a honeyed Southern drawl. "Excuse me?"

"Oh." The man put both hands up, and backed away. "I'm really sorry. You look just like a friend of mine. I swear, the two of you could be twins."

She offered the slightest of smiles. "They say everybody has one."

"No kidding. I was across the street when you walked in, and couldn't believe it. I'd heard she'd gone to prison and—"

"Forgive my rudeness, but I really don't want to talk to you. I hope you find your friend."

"Oh, sure thing. I'm sorry to go on like that. I'm just in shock." He continued backing away. "You look just like her."

Finally Evan, an ambitious journalist she'd met on several occasions while attending conferences on science and medicine, turned and left the restaurant. Only sheer will kept her from bolting herself. She forced her body to stay calm, and took several deep breaths until her heartbeat returned to a more normal pace, though it still beat somewhat erratically. That was the closest call she'd ever had, and one she never expected. Even though she'd grabbed a hat, she now realized the mistake of not wearing a wig, too.

Relax, Jacqueline, it's over. There's no way he can prove it's you.

She told herself this, and tried hard to believe it. But the truth of the matter was the close call rattled every one of her nerves. She needed to do what was necessary and then get out of town. Pronto. Immediately. ASAP.

She stood and walked over to the register. "I've changed my mind. Can you make my order to go?"

"Certainly."

While the worker walked into the kitchen to change the ticket, Jacqueline pulled out her phone and sent Eric a text.

IF YOU WANT TO BE LIVING BY THIS TIME TOMORROW, YOU'D BETTER HAVE WHAT I NEED BY TONIGHT.

She paid for her food, then left the restaurant and walked the opposite way from where she lived. She walked to Penn Station, took a train to the next stop, and paid for a circuitous sight-seeing journey by taxi back to her apartment. On the way she ate her sandwich and contemplated moves. Forty-five minutes later, she was back in the apartment, sure she hadn't been followed and even more certain that she wouldn't be here much longer. During the ride back, two messages she'd received assured her she wouldn't need to: a video from inside Randall's lab, and several photos taken New Year's Eve.

A light tap sounded on Randall's open office door. He waved in his perky administrative assistant.

"I've finished revising the report, Dr. Atwater. Would you like it printed, e-mailed, or both?"

"E-mail it, Cassandra, and then remove it from your computer and place it on the thumb drive."

She nodded. "I'll take care of that right now!"

"Thank you. And close the door on your way out."

He watched his computer screen, a myriad of thoughts running through his mind as he waited on the report to show up in his mail. Until the scare with Albany on New Year's Eve, the holidays had been wonderful. From their time in the Bahamas over Thanksgiving to spending quality time with the neighbors next door, Randall had been able to step back and appreciate the rewards of his hard work and the blessings of family. Now that the worst regarding Albany was over, and the doctor had confirmed there'd been no sexual assault, he could refocus on bolstering his research in contagious diseases and developing a type of mold that showed great promise in tests on lab animals. He'd promised himself and Sherri that in a year or so, when this project was truly up and running, he'd take a month off just to relax and enjoy life.

His intercom sounded. "Yes, Cassandra."

"Evan is on line two, Doctor."

"Okay, thanks." He clicked over and placed the call on speaker while opening the file his assistant had sent. "Evan! This is a pleasant surprise. I was just thinking about you the other day, and wondering how life is treating you in the city of Baltimore."

"Things are good, sir. I'm enjoying my stint at Johns Hopkins, learning a lot and making some great contacts."

"Sounds like you're headed toward sure success."

"I couldn't have done it without you, Doctor. I'm sure that interning at your company, along with your recommendation, helped pave the way for me."

"I helped a little, but if I didn't think you were the man for the job, I never would have given a reference. You do good research and reporting, with an eye for detail that this community appreciates. That's why you're there."

"Well . . . that eye for detail, Doctor, is why I'm calling. I had the weirdest encounter this afternoon."

"Oh?"

"Yes. I was in downtown Baltimore, about, oh, a ten- to fifteen-minute walk from the university, when I see a woman who I'd swear on the Hippocratic Oath was Jacqueline Tate."

This got Randall's immediate attention. He sat up straight, all attention now focused on the phone call. "Did you talk to her?"

"I tried, but it wasn't her. I mean, she said it wasn't her and it didn't sound like her, but the resemblance was uncanny."

"What did she sound like?"

"She had a Southern accent, and wore these big round sunglasses. I couldn't see all of her face but it still looked like Jacqueline. But I thought she was in prison."

"Actually, Evan, she's out of prison, and I have it on pretty good authority that she's out of the country as well."

"Okay, so that wasn't her. I'm glad you're telling me this, because all afternoon I've been driving myself crazy thinking that it was her."

"You mentioned an eye for detail. Did you see a characteristic or trait that you're sure belonged to her and no one else? A mole, for instance, or a birthmark? Because I don't recall her having any."

"I'm almost embarrassed to say. Knowing it will

sound pretty weird, but I'm a sucker for fragrances, especially when worn by a beautiful woman like Jacqueline Tate. When I first met her, at that conference in Los Angeles, we were sitting by each other. She was wearing this citrusy, flowery perfume that drove me crazy. It smelled so good on her. Unlike a lot of women whose cologne overpowers, this was a subtle fragrance that kind of hit you as an afterthought. I remember asking about it and she said it was from a perfumer in Toronto. I've never smelled it on any other woman. When I followed Jacqueline, or this woman I thought was her, into a restaurant and walked over to her, I caught a whiff of that exact same smell. That's why the incident like to have drove me crazy, because I kept smelling that scent."

"They say that all of us have a twin."

Evan laughed. "Yes, that's what she told me. I'm really glad I called you and found out she's left the country. Now I can stop thinking it really was Jacqueline just blowing me off."

"Not a problem, Evan. It was good talking to you."

"Hey, will you be at the conference in Atlanta next week?"

"No, I've pared back my travel schedule. Working on another project; trying to stay focused."

"Well, I'll leave you to it, Doctor. Thanks again."

When the call ended, so did Randall's smile. He knew that Jacqueline was in Australia. Nathan's friend, Ralph, had confirmed documentation showing that she'd definitely gotten on that plane. *But could she have slipped back into the country undetected?* Only one way to find out.

He reached for his cell phone. "Ralph, this is Randall Atwater. You got a minute?"

* * *

Back in Baltimore, Jacqueline and Kris were commiserating over the Evan incident. Jacqueline was drinking a rare glass of wine. It was four hours later and she still hadn't totally calmed down. "Three hundred million people, fifty states, and I have to run into someone I know."

"Yeah, but from the sounds of it, you handled things quite nicely. I mean, sure you saw the guy at a conference or two, but it isn't like you screwed him or saw him every day."

"I know. But Evan had a crush on me. He studied me. I caught him staring often enough to know he has a pretty good idea of how I look, especially since I wasn't disguised."

"Except for your sun shades."

"Thank goodness I had those puppies on or I would have been caught dead to rights. Seeing him spooked me, and now I'm on edge. Plus, I've learned to pay attention to paranoia. Sometimes it shows up for a reason."

"So . . . what now?"

"I'm going to stay here one more week. With what I received this afternoon, I think it's all the time I'll need."

"Then we're off to London?"

Jacqueline gave Kris a genuine smile. "Then we're putting this nightmare behind us to live our dreams."

CHAPTER 37

Jessica eyed herself in the mirror. She'd just returned from a visit to the gynecologist and was living life without nausea for the first time in days. According to the doctor, she was between twelve to fourteen weeks. But not according to the mirror. Except for the tiniest of belly bumps, Jessica didn't look pregnant at all.

The sound of the doorbell scared her. She looked over at Dax, who played beside her. "Who could that be, Daxton? Who's coming to visit you and Mommy in the middle of the day? Come on, let's go see."

Her son jumped up quickly, always ready to go on an adventure. Jessica continued a running dialogue as they walked down the hall. Glimpsing the distorted image through the front door's beveled glass cutouts, however, her words faded. Her steps slowed. It looked to be someone who could not possibly be at her front door.

"Who is it?"

"Jessica, it's Nathan."

Yet there he was.

She swallowed a jolt of fear and, noting that her son was watching every move, put a smile on her face as she opened the door. "Nathan. What are you doing here?"

He spoke to her but his eyes drank in the little boy by her side. "You've changed your phone number and didn't answer my e-mails. I had to come."

"How did you know where I live?"

"When a person is determined, finding an address isn't too hard." He looked at her. "May I come in?"

"Nathan, I don't know who sent you that picture but—"

"Are we really going to have this conversation through a screen door?"

Dax looked up at her. "Are you going to let the man in, Mommy?"

"Yes, Mommy," Nathan said, smiling. "Are you going to let the man in?"

Grudgingly, she opened the door. "Come on in."

He walked in, looking around. "Nice place." They reached the living room before he knelt down to almost eye level with Dax. "Hey there, young man."

Dax stepped behind his mother's leg.

"He acts shy until he knows you."

"I used to be shy."

Nathan and Jessica looked at each other. The wind of past happiness swirled around them. At one time, they'd been very much in love.

She moved and broke the spell-like moment. "Please, have a seat. And make this quick. Vincent sometimes . . . comes home unexpectedly."

"I wouldn't have a problem with that."

Jessica chuckled. "He definitely would."

"Why didn't you answer my e-mails?"

"Because it's so ludicrous that this has even happened. I said I don't know who sent the picture, but I do. It was Jacqueline."

"Are you sure?"

Jessica nodded. "Before she left for Australia, she came here, met Vincent and Dax. To say she and my husband don't get along is putting it mildly. They hated each other almost on sight. I hate to think this, but she seemed jealous over the fact that I'm married and happy, with a good man, a healthy son, and another child on the way."

"You're pregnant?"

"Yes, almost three months."

"I guess congratulations are in order."

"Thank you." An awkward silence ensued, during which time Dax and Nathan stared at each other.

Nathan smiled. "Are you protecting your mama, little man?" Dax nodded. "That's a good boy." He looked from the child to Jessica. "I see a little of you in his face, but I don't see Vincent at all."

"Vincent says he takes after his mother, while Vincent looks more like his dad."

"So you wouldn't have a problem giving me something of Dax's as a DNA sample, a piece of hair or some of his dribble on a cotton swab?"

"I wouldn't have a problem with it, but it's not going to happen."

"Why not?"

"Because I'm not going to be a part of my sister's . . . craziness. This is exactly the kind of mess that she wanted to get started. And for what? I'm married, and you've probably moved on. What's to be gained by stirring up stuff? She's miserable, and wants the world to join her."

"Does Vincent know about what she did?"

"Yes. She e-mailed him, too."

"And he was cool with it, just believed what you said and that was it, huh?"

"Pretty much."

"That doesn't sound like an attorney; they normally won't quit until they get the facts."

Truer words had never been spoken, because at this exact moment, in an office building downtown, Vincent was opening an envelope containing the results of the packet he'd sent in to quell the doubts inside himself, the packet he'd sent to test his and Dax's DNA.

Later that evening Jessica lay in bed, riding the waves of nausea that had set in shortly after Nathan departed and hadn't left since. Dax, who'd missed his nap, was thankfully sleeping. She hoped that within minutes she'd be asleep, too. Anything to stop the thoughts that were running through her head. Anything to ease the fear that gripped her heart.

That doesn't sound like an attorney. Jessica flopped from her back to her stomach. *They normally won't quit until they get the facts.* She repositioned the pillow, once and then again. *I used to be shy.* She squeezed her eyes tightly, gritted her teeth against screaming. *Yes, Mommy, are you going to let the man in?*

"Stop it!" She bolted upright, her head in her hands. "Just . . . please . . . stop." Her pleas turned to tears as she rocked back and forth.

"Is it the lies, Jessica?"

She jumped, clutched her chest, and stared at Vincent

as though he were an apparition. "Vincent," she stuttered, wiping her tears. "I didn't hear you come in."

"I can imagine that with everything running through your head these days, it's hard to hear or think at all."

Attempting a smile, she patted the bed beside her. "The nausea returned, baby. I think your daughter misses you when you're gone."

"Is that so?"

Jessica nodded.

"Yes, well I'm going to miss her, too."

"What do you mean? Do you have a trip out of town?"

Vincent walked to the closet, pulled out a carry-on bag, and began throwing things into it. "I have a trip out of this house."

She was out of bed now. "I don't understand."

"I'm leaving you, Jessica. Before I do something that you and I will both regret."

"Leaving . . . why?"

"Because you lied to me," he bellowed before remembering Dax and lowering his voice. "You looked me dead in the eyes, swore before God, and lied."

"Honey, baby, I don't know what you're talking about."

Vincent snatched an envelope from the inside pocket of his suit coat. He thrust it into her hands. "I'm talking about this."

With shaky hands, she pulled the correspondence out of the envelope. One look and her worst fears were confirmed.

"I wanted to believe you, but I had to know for sure. So I sent in samples to get tested. Dax is not my son."

Jessica latched on to Vincent's arm. "Yes, he is, baby. He's your son and you're his father, in every sense of the word."

Vincent pulled out a leather garment bag and placed a couple suits in it. "Why couldn't you have just been honest with me when I asked you? Why couldn't you believe that my love was enough, that even if the baby wasn't mine, I loved you enough to take care of both of you?"

"I do believe it!"

"No, you don't. That's why you were there shaking and crying. Your lies are driving you crazy, along with the fear that what just happened would occur." He pushed past her, walked into the bathroom, and began throwing toiletries in a bag.

"Vincent, where are you going?"

"Tonight, a hotel. Tomorrow, we'll see. I just know I need some space to think, someplace I don't have to look at you."

"I'm sorry, Vincent. Please don't leave."

"Where are you going, Daddy?"

They both turned around, surprised that Dax had entered. Rubbing his eyes, he walked to Vincent, who lifted him up and hugged him.

"Daddy's going on a trip."

"Can I come with you?"

"Not this time, Daxton. You need to stay here and take care of Mommy, okay?"

"That's what the other man told me, too."

Vincent froze. "What other man, Son?"

Even babies can sense when something's amiss. Dax clammed up tighter than a man with lockjaw. Vincent cast Jessica a questioning glance. When she didn't answer, he put Dax down, threw the toiletry bag into the carry-on, and zipped it up.

Jessica panicked. "Baby," she said to Dax, "go play in your room while I talk to Daddy. I'll be there in just a minute, okay?"

"Okay."

Vincent stopped him. "Come here, Son." The boy complied. Vincent kneeled down and wrapped his arms around him. When he spoke, his voice was hoarse with emotion. "Remember Daddy loves you, okay?"

"I love you too, Daddy."

Jessica knelt to try and make it a group hug. Vincent wasn't having it. He shook her off, picked up the garment bag and carry-on, and headed for the door.

"Vincent, wait!"

She followed Dax out of their master suite and into his room, then pulled the door closed so that he wouldn't hear her. She ran back to the room. Vincent held a garment bag in one hand and clutched the handle of his suitcase with the other.

"Please, Vincent, don't leave me. I'll do anything you say."

"Really? Then tell me what man came by the house?" Silence. His eyes narrowed. "Was it Nathan? Answer me!"

"Yes but I didn't invite him."

"Did you let him in?"

"Yes, but—"

"Forget it, Jessica. I'm out of here."

"Vincent, no! I was wrong to lie to you. I was scared, baby. I didn't want to lose you and thought that if you knew, then you wouldn't stay. Please, Vincent. Think of our baby, the one that's on the way."

He turned sharply. "How do I know that it's even mine?"

Her hand flew to her face as if she'd been slapped. "I guess I deserved that."

"No, you didn't. I'm sorry. I love you, Jessica. But I've got to go."

That night, Jessica cried herself to sleep. Between Nathan's surprise visit and Vincent's testing Dax's DNA, it had been too much. When she woke to severe cramps at four in the morning, there was a wet spot on her gown. She ran to the bathroom. Blood trickled down her leg.

"No, please, no." She ran to the phone and dialed 9-1-1. "Please, get here quickly. I think I'm losing my baby!"

CHAPTER 38

"Sis, you can do this. You've got to do it."

Almost a week had passed since Sherri had watched her husband carry their limp, unconscious child out of the Williams's home. It seemed no time had passed since their daughter had awakened, groggy and clueless as to what had happened and how she'd gotten home, haggard and confused but otherwise no worse for wear.

A week later, and still the incident consumed her, along with bouts of anger and guilt. They'd spoken to several kids from the party. Conveniently, none of them could remember who bought the alcohol, how it ended up in the house or got into Albany's hands. She understood the code of silence. Once she too had been a teenager. It didn't make what had happened to Albany any easier. The what-ifs had almost driven her mad.

"Sherri."

"I'm sorry, Nathan. I heard you, and you're absolutely right. The last thing I need to do is cancel this interview. Getting this job will help me move on from what happened with Albany."

"Still no information on who spiked her drink?"

"No. There's a very good chance we'll never know what happened. It could have been so much worse. I need to get over it and just move on!"

"I understand it's not easy, Sis. What time is your interview?"

"In a little over an hour, and I'm already dressed. In fact, I think I'll leave the house right now. I always think better while driving, and the fresh air will do me good."

She grabbed her keys and oversized Coach bag and headed to her car. "What about you? Anything new since you paid Jessica an unexpected visit?"

"I contacted a lawyer who handles paternity cases. I didn't want it to, but it looks like this might play out in court."

"She still insists that it's Vincent's child?"

"Pretty much. But I don't know, Sis. Something happened when I saw that little boy. I don't know if it's my imagination or what, but it's like I could see myself in him."

"Could be your imagination; could be instinct. I think in getting a definite answer you're doing the right thing." Sherri reached the car and was soon heading out the gates and down the street. "How's Dev handling all this?"

"I don't know if there's ever a good time to find out you might have a son who's a couple years old. But this news has added a wrinkle to an already tenuous situation. We're both still feeling our way and trying to work it out. All we can do is take one day at a time. What about Aaron? Y'all didn't tell him, did you?"

"No, but he's too astute to believe our flu story. I think Albany may have shared something with him. It's taken all I have to not share it with Mom."

"She already worries so much about us."

"I know, which is why I'm holding it in."

"Did you tell Renee?"

"Yes, and she's been my sanity. Really, I'm not sure if I would have even gotten out of bed the day after, if not for her."

"She's good people. I'm glad she found a man."

"Nobody's happier than Renee is about that!"

Sherri ended the call with her brother, feeling lighter than she had in days. She found her favorite Internet radio channel and grooved to a nineties mix. It was a crisp and sunny January afternoon. By the time she arrived in D.C., she felt almost like her old self again, definitely ready to do the interview and get this job.

It was only her second time in the building that housed the alternative education program. Built in the eighteen hundreds, the large former home of a wealthy businessman had been fully renovated to house several not-for-profit organizations. She appreciated its homey feel and could definitely see herself looking forward to coming here every day.

She reached the second floor and lightly tapped on the door at the top of the stairs before entering. The same woman who'd greeted her when she met the board was at the desk this morning. Her eyes didn't seem as bright or her smile as cheery, but Sherri tried not to read too much into it. Most likely it was her nerves making the difference and not the woman at all.

"Good afternoon. I'm here to see the director."

The receptionist nodded and announced her arrival. "Please, have a seat. She'll be with you soon."

Soon became ten and then twenty minutes. After a half hour waiting, Sherri's nervousness had been replaced with a bit of chagrin. Several people had come and gone since she'd been waiting. While there was no way to know if they'd seen the director, she still felt she was being ignored. She understood being busy and having to handle unexpected matters, but she'd had an appointment! This was borderline rude.

Walking up to the receptionist, she reined in her ire. "Excuse me, but do you know how much longer the director will be tied up?" Sherri had nothing pressing afterward but checked her watch anyway. "I'll understand if she's busy and needs to reschedule."

The door opened just as she was finishing the sentence. "No need for that, Mrs. Atwater. Right this way." The director, a mature, stout woman who Sherri felt could have played the role of Mary Bethune, Ms. Powell wore the same tight smile and no-nonsense attitude that had been there since the day they'd met.

They walked through the door and down a short hallway to Ms. Powell's office. It was a sizeable room made smaller by large, clunky furniture and a wall filled floor to ceiling with books. Mrs. Powell pointed to one of two chairs facing her desk and the windows. She sat down behind the desk, her expression pinched.

"I'm sorry for keeping you waiting," Ms. Powell began. "But I, we, were all taken aback at this new development with you and your family. I was actually as surprised to hear that you were keeping this appointment as I was to see the pictures that were leaked on the Web."

Sherri's heart jumped from her chest to her throat.

She felt if she coughed, it would pop out of her mouth and hit Ms. Powell in the face. "I beg your pardon?"

Sherri's confusion was clearly etched on her face. So much so that Ms. Powell sat back and really looked at her as if for the first time.

"Oh, dear Lord."

"Ms. Powell, what is it? You're making me nervous."

"The pictures of your daughter, Sherri. You truly don't know?"

A chill swept through the room. Sherri held on to the chair, feeling that she might tumble to the floor. Though she'd not had one before, she imagined what she felt was close to a panic attack. Visions of her daughter disheveled, unable to walk on her own to the car. In her bedroom, removing her leather pants and finding no panties. When her hymen was found to be intact, she and Randall knew they'd dodged a bullet. Now it appeared there may have been another one in the gun.

"There's no easy way to show you this. Come here, dear."

Sherri stood on shaky legs and walked around the large oak table to view the clunky desktop monitor. She grabbed the back of Ms. Powell's chair for support as the woman clicked on an e-mail, then on the attachment icon.

Albany, naked, laying on the bed.

Her precious daughter, lying on her stomach with packets of condoms all over her back.

Randall and Sherri's straight-A student propped up in a chair, fully exposed.

Sherri's legs gave out beneath her. She worked to stay conscious.

Ms. Powell reached for a bottle of water, splashed some on her hand, and began to pat Sherri's face. The cold liquid pierced through the daze of shock. From somewhere seemingly far in the distance, she heard a voice.

"Mrs. Atwater, breathe, dear. You've got to breathe."

Sherri stumbled to her feet. "I'm sorry, Ms. Powell. I've got to go."

"Are you sure that you're okay to drive?"

Sherri didn't bother to answer her. She raced down the steps and crossed the gravel parking lot. Inside her car, she let out the primal scream that had been suppressed ever since seeing Albany in the security guard's arms. She managed to call Randall and tell him where she was. He told her he'd be there in ten minutes.

He made it in seven.

"Sherri!" He tapped the glass. "Sherri, unlock the door." She sat dazed, as if made of stone. He found the key to her car on his key ring and opened the door. Taking her in his arms, he asked her, "What happened in there, Sherri? Baby, it's just a job. You'll get another one."

Her eyes were glazed over as she looked at him. "There are pictures, Randall. Oh my God, I wonder if Albany knows. We need to call her. Get her out of the school. Get . . . where's Blair . . . I can't . . ."

Randall grabbed Sherri's shoulders and gave her a firm shake. "Sherri. Tell me what happened."

She broke down and sobbed for several minutes. Randall held her, not caring if anyone saw them like this. Sometimes what other people thought was none of his business. Now was one of those times.

Finally, Sherri lifted her head and reached for a Kleenex. She blew her nose, wiped her eyes, and moved over to the passenger seat. Staring straight ahead, her voice monotone, she told him.

"There are naked pictures of our daughter on the Internet. I don't know where on the Internet, but someone sent copies to Ms. Powell, who showed them to me. There was no interview about any position. Just pictures of Albany . . . of our baby . . . and she doesn't know. And there's no way I can stop her from knowing, from seeing them, or get them off before they're seen by someone she goes to school with . . . some of her . . . friends." The tears fell anew.

Randall reached for his phone. "Yes, this is Dr. Atwater. There's been a bit of a family emergency. I need someone to find Albany and bring her to the office." He listened to something the school employee was saying. "No, everyone's fine, assure her of that. But she needs to be taken out of class and brought to the office. I'll explain everything once I get there, but it's imperative that she be separated from the student body."

Again he listened. "No, this isn't about a sickness or disease. Please, just do as I ask. My wife and I are on the way."

They locked Sherri's car and left it parked at the building, jumped in Randall's sports car, and flew down the highway.

Halfway there, Albany called and she was screaming.

She'd seen the pictures, too.

CHAPTER 39

By the next morning, it was as though the whole world knew about Albany Atwater and had seen the pictures. Randall wouldn't have been surprised had it been on CNN. Thankfully, it wasn't, but that seemed to be the only place. The news had traveled within the circles of the elite faster than a California wildfire. Albany's and Aaron's schools, Randall's work, the teachers at Sherri's part-time job and those in her business groups, social circles, the neighbors, even the pastor at the church they rarely attended had all gotten wind of it.

He watched his weary wife walk into their master bedroom and collapse on a chair. "How is she?"

"Sedated."

"Where's Aaron?"

"In his room."

"I'll go and talk with him in a minute. But right now, I'm worried about you. You haven't eaten or slept since it happened."

"I can't."

"Sherri, you can't help any of us if you're sick."

"I just keep wracking my mind for who could have done this, who could harness so much anger and hatred to try and ruin a young girl's life. She said there was no one with whom she was angry, nobody with whom she was having a beef."

"What about that dude, Corvales?"

"I'm going to call the school tomorrow and arrange a meeting."

"Nathan and his detective friend are flying in to-night."

Sherri's head shot up. "You called Ralph?"

"Absolutely. I want to get to the bottom of who did this. And when I find out, some heads are going to roll."

Sherri rubbed her eyes and yawned. "There's something we're missing, some piece of this puzzle is being left out."

"What's there to figure, baby? Some asshole wanted to embarrass our daughter and did."

"But it's not just that, Randall. It's that e-mail on my computer, the one that contained a new date for my meeting with the board and then disappeared. Then it's Nathan, a couple weeks later, who finds out he might have a son. And now this, with Albany. No one family can be this unlucky. It's just too crazy. It doesn't add up. Things have been weird ever since . . ." She stopped, slowly leaning back against the chair. "Ever since Jacqueline got out of prison."

"Baby, Jacqueline's in . . ."

"What?"

"I don't want to believe it's possible."

"What, Randall?"

"I got a call the other day from a colleague, Evan.

He's a young man who interned in my office for several months before landing a research assignment at Johns Hopkins."

"What does this have to do with us right now?"

"He thought he saw Jacqueline."

Sherri jumped up. "Where? Tell me where, Randall. I want to know where he saw that bitch."

Jacqueline prowled her apartment like a restless tiger, gripping the phone so hard it could break. "What do you mean, you're quitting, Todd?"

"Just that, I'm getting out of this sneaky, sticky, insane situation. What you did to that girl, man, it's just messed up."

"What I did to what girl?"

"Come off it, Jacqueline. You don't think I haven't put two and two together and figured this all out? I'm bugging a man's office, basically stealing confidential information, and around the same time his daughter, who I've talked a student into slipping a mickey to, finds naked pictures of herself all over the Net. I know you told me this family put you in jail and all, but . . . messing with the kid that way? That's just too much."

"I hear you, Todd. Can you hold on a moment?"

"I'm done with that Todd shit, too. My name is Eric."

"All right, Eric. Can you hold on a moment?"

"Sure."

Jacqueline muted the call. Then she walked into the kitchen, grabbed a knife, and basically slashed the couch to death. Heaving, her hair a tousled mess, she walked back, picked up the phone, and unmuted the call.

"Sorry about that."

"Dang, what happened? You sound out of breath."

"I thought I saw . . . the UPS man . . . and tried to catch him." Her tone became soothing, flirty. "Listen Todd, Eric, I know how you're feeling. I know I sounded mad at first, but that's just because you quitting the job almost sounded like you're quitting me. The Atwaters got what they deserved. Now I'm done with all that. Let's get out of here, you and me. Go somewhere fun and tropical and far away from this cold-ass winter."

There was a long pause. "That sounds good, Jacqueline, but you'll have to go there without me. See, it's like this. I met somebody."

Jacqueline's entire body began to shake. She picked up a pen and snapped it in two, and then another one. She tried to snap a thick marker but that plastic wouldn't give.

"Did you hear me?"

"Do you think this is news to me? I told you about her weeks ago. Didn't know she had you wrapped like that, though. I took you for someone who was much smarter, whose taste was . . . refined. But, hey. I'm happy for you."

Eric laughed. "You're bullshitting, Jacqueline. If I were anywhere close to you, you'd try to beat my ass."

"Probably, but only because you like it. Tell you what. Why don't I come over for a drink, give you your final payment, and end this as friends."

"I don't know. Something tells me you're sounding all friendly but you're really pissed."

"Heck yes, I'm pissed. Losing that eight-inch weapon you're rocking, what girl wouldn't be mad?

But I don't own you, Todd, I mean Eric. It's a free country. You can do what you want. I'm not worried about you talking, because that would implicate you. All's fair in love and war, right?"

"Right."

"So you get off work. I'll come over, bring the wine, and toast to your life in Washington."

"My girlfriend comes over when she finishes her waitressing job. So you can only stay for an hour."

"In that case, I'll be waiting when you get there. We'll just have to drink fast."

An hour after Eric, aka Todd Dern, got off work, his girlfriend rang his doorbell. Nothing happened. She rang it again. Miffed, she pulled out her cell phone. "Hey, you. Let me in. It's freezing out here." She rang the bell once more, sure she'd seen his car outside. In a huff, she went to bang on the window. That's when she saw him sprawled on the floor. His T-shirt was covered in blood.

"This is 9-1-1, what is your emergency?"

"I need someone to get here quick. My boyfriend's lying on the floor with blood all over him. His door is locked. I can't get in. Help me! Please help!"

The paramedics made it there in five minutes. They busted down the door and raced inside. Police held the young woman back. When they wheeled Eric out on a gurney, she lost it.

"Eric!" Scuffling with the police, she managed to pull away. "Eric! I'm here."

The police caught her at the same time one of the medics did. "Ma'am, you've got to calm down!"

"Is he alive? There was so much blood."

"Ma'am, calm down. Some of that was spilled wine. He's alive, but his situation is very critical."

The police officer interrupted. "Ma'am, we're going to need you to come down to the station."

They wrapped a blanket around her and led her away.

CHAPTER 40

"Mrs. Givens, please. You must eat."

"I'm not hungry."

"Don't you want to live for your son? I'm sure he misses his mommy. You've got to eat to get well."

It had been ten days since Jessica lost the baby. Once she'd been released from the hospital, she was placed in a home for round-the-clock psychiatric evaluation. After a doctor walked into her room as she was trying to commit suicide, it's what all the doctors knew had to be done.

The nurses had been told about the miscarriage and were very sympathetic to her situation. The psychiatrist, a mother with two children of her own, treated Jessica gently, determined to go slowly. She walked in now, as an exasperated nurse shook her head and placed down the fork on the plate of uneaten food.

The doctor sat, and for a moment simply watched Jessica stare out the window. After about ten minutes, she spoke. "It's not any better today?"

Jessica shook her head. Five more minutes passed.

"Sometimes it's better to talk about it." Her response, tears. "I know right now it feels the hurt will never lessen, and it will certainly never go away. But I'm told by other mothers who've faced your sorrow that in time, the pain becomes bearable enough for them to live again."

After another fifteen minutes, the doctor prepared to leave. Every visit had been a one-sided conversation. Today looked to be no different. She gathered her papers.

"She took everything."

The doctor leaned forward, barely able to hear her patient's soft voice. "Who, Jessica?"

"Sissy."

"Who's Sissy? Is that your sister?" Jessica nodded. "What did she take away?"

"My family."

"How'd she do that?"

Silence was her answer. Silence laced with tears.

"Your son misses you."

"Where's Dax?"

"He's with his father."

Jessica looked up. "He's with Nathan?"

The doctor frowned. "No, Vincent. His dad. Your husband."

"Oh."

The doctor quickly scanned her notes and the file. The name Nathan didn't appear anywhere. "Who is Nathan, Jessica?" Silence. "Is Vincent your son's step-dad?"

"No."

"He's his biological father."

Jessica slowly nodded.

"Do you want to tell me about Nathan? I think you'll feel better if you do."

Another slow nod, and then an answer. "Yes."

Nathan reached the building where he and Vincent had agreed to meet. He pulled into the parking lot and saw a sports car that he correctly guessed belonged to Vincent, who sat inside. He parked in the next stall.

Once inside, he walked into a small conference room. Vincent was there, talking to Dax. He stood when Nathan entered.

Nathan met him with hand outstretched. "Thanks for meeting me, man."

"Hey, it's not easy. But it's the right thing to do." Vincent shrugged. He looked at his son. "Dax, say hi to Nathan."

"Hi, Nat-tan."

"Hey, Dax. Give me some, man." He held out a fist. The little boy bumped it with his fist, and smiled.

"Here you go, Dax. Want to play your video game?"

"Yes."

"Okay. Daddy and Nate are going to talk a little bit, okay?"

"Okay."

The two men sat at a table several feet from where Dax played. Nathan looked at how Dax's face scrunched up as he concentrated. Both he and his nephew, Aaron, did the same thing. "Nobody could have told me I'd ever be in this type of situation."

"It's one hell of a mess," Vincent agreed.

"I'm just glad not to make this public, or have to

drag it through the courts. I can't imagine how you're feeling through all this."

Vincent looked at him. "I can't imagine how you must feel, either." They both watched Dax play for a while. "How did you find out?"

"Got an anonymous e-mail with his picture attached."

Vincent's chuckle held no humor. "No doubt as to who sent it."

Nathan looked at him "Who?"

"Jessica's diabolical sister, Jacqueline. She's the one behind all this shit."

At the mention of Jacqueline's name, Nathan's blood ran cold. "Is that what Jessica told you?"

Vincent nodded. "She didn't have to, though, when I really thought about it. Jacqueline was the only way all the puzzle pieces fit."

"How can a woman cause so much trouble all the way from Australia?"

"The Internet, man. You can reach anybody from anywhere."

"But why, man? I thought she and her sister were cool."

"Jacqueline isn't cool with anybody but herself. She's a narcissist, a sociopath, a psycho. You of all people should know something about that. Look what she talked Jessica into doing to you!"

"Yeah, you've got a point there." Nathan fiddled with his cell phone on the table. "Though there's not enough conversation in the world to get me to kill somebody."

"I understand your position, but don't judge Jessica too quickly. Given the right situation, we could all take a life."

"How is she?"

Vincent shook his head. "Not good. I partly blame myself for what she's going through."

"You're not the only one who saw her that day."

"I know."

"Do you think the two of you will be able to work this out? It's none of my business, but I feel all up in the mix."

"You are in it. You're right in the middle of it because of that little one there." He looked at Nathan. "I love him like a son, man."

"He is your son."

Vincent nodded. "He's yours, too."

Nathan sighed. "How are we going to work this out, make it right for everybody?"

"That's the million-dollar question, Brother. And I ain't got a dime."

CHAPTER 41

A group of police officers, Ralph and two other detective huddled in the Atwater great room along with Randall, Sherri, and Mom Elaine, who'd finally been told much of what she'd already suspected. Their home had become a command post of sorts, a central meeting place for Operation Get Jacqueline. Several jurisdictions and law enforcement departments in three states had come together to form a team. Nathan's friend Ralph was one of the men listening intently to the D.C. detective who'd been assigned the Eric Martin case.

"How's he doing, Officer?"

"Better, but still critical. The large amount of arsenic and ethylene glycol in his system caused his major organs to begin shutting down. The doctors are cautiously optimistic that he'll survive."

"So let me make sure I've got this straight." The detective from Alexandria leaned forward, using a finger to make each point. "This Eric guy, speaking on condition of immunity, says that Jacqueline Tate, who we know went to Australia, somehow snuck back into the country and wreaked all this havoc from an apartment in Baltimore: naked pictures in Alexandria, paternity issues in Atlanta, breaking into your computer remotely," he said with an incredulous look toward Sherri, "then moseyed over to an apartment in Washington, D.C., to ply him with poisoned wine."

Randall, Ralph, Sherri, Nathan, and Mom Elaine answered in chorus. "Yes."

"Wait just a minute." A tobacco-chewing detective from North Carolina joined the talk. "Do y'all hear yourselves talking? In order to do all of what you're saying, she'd have to be two, three, hell, five got-damn people."

"Trust me," Ralph deadpanned, "she can pull off being several different people in her sleep."

The D.C. detective who'd joined Ralph on the case nodded his agreement. "We know of at least one alias she was using—Kate Freeman. There very likely could be more. We also know that someone using Jacqueline Tate's identification flew to Australia. We're working with the authorities there to try and track whoever that is down."

Randall's frown deepened. "So Jacqueline never left the country at all?"

"There's nothing saying she reentered the country, so we have to check out every angle. And there's another piece to this, Dr. Atwater, one that we believe you'll find quite interesting, that we learned just before coming here." Randall said nothing, only looked. "The name Todd Dern ring a bell?"

"Yes, he's the security manager guarding our offices; came on board, oh, a few months ago."

The D.C. detective fixed him with a look. "Todd Dern is Eric Martin."

All the Atwaters reacted.

"No!"

"You have got to be kidding!"

"I don't believe it."

"Get the hell out of here."

The news picked Randall up out of his chair. "That means my office has been compromised. Excuse me. I've got to handle something right away."

Ralph watched Randall leave the room, then looked at the D.C. detective who'd just spoken. "Just when you think it can't get worse, it up and does. Any word back from the Aussie authorities?"

"Not yet. But as soon as they find her, they'll take her DNA and fingerprints and send them over. Those are two things that don't lie. And one is impossible to change."

"DNA," Nathan said knowingly.

"No, sure can't change that," Mom Elaine agreed.

The Alexandria detective's tone softened as he turned to Sherri. "How is your daughter doing, Mrs. Atwater?"

Sherri shook her head. "It's still very much day to day. We've pulled her out of school. She's seeing therapists. We finally put her on a low dosage of an antidepressant just to get her stabilized enough to eat and sleep. It's also difficult for her brother, Aaron. They're very close and her pain has definitely affected him. Some of his classmates have not been kind. He's been holed up in his room for days, stuck to his computer and various gadgets. He fancies himself the next Bill Gates," she explained. "I'm glad he has a diversion." Sherri rubbed her arms against an imaginary chill. "It's unfathomable how someone could do this to a child."

"I know the police are still working on finding out who did this."

"We know who did it," Sherri said through gritted teeth. "Corvales Mitchell."

The Alexandria detective nodded. "There's reason to believe that he was involved, but no solid proof. One of his neighbors spoke of seeing a strange couple in the complex on Christmas morning, but neither Corvales, his family, nor any other neighbors would talk to us. Unfortunately, this isn't uncommon. Where he lives, law enforcement isn't popular and cooperating with authority is very rare. We won't give up. But right now, it's doubtful we'll come up with enough evidence to file charges."

"That girl's capable of anything," Mom Elaine said to Sherri. "This family knows that all too well."

Ralph's expression softened as he took in the elder Carver. "We've got law enforcement across the country on high alert. BOLOs and APBs are everywhere. Her picture has been sent through the national database. If she gets seen or stopped between here and Tijuana, it's a wrap."

The Baltimore detective's cell phone vibrated. The room became still. "Detective Tierney." He frowned. "Damn! Are you sure?" He listened, nodded. "Well, stay on it. Let me know as soon as you hear anything, anything at all."

He ended the call. "Eric Martin is still talking. Says he rented an apartment for Ms. Tate in Baltimore. My men just came from checking it out. Furniture's there but it looks like whoever occupied it is gone. There are no clothes or personal items. They said one room looked like it had been set up as an office with quite a few surge protectors and cables, suggesting a bunch of electronics were used in there."

Sherri looked at Randall. "It's just like last time, baby. Somehow she got on my computer."

"Dammit!" Ralph smacked his fist against his palm in frustration. "How does she manage to stay one step ahead of us?"

"Y'all keep digging," Mom Elaine offered. "It's a long road that don't have a turn in it. You mark my words. Her luck is not only going to change, it's going to flat run out."

The group broke up then, with each division or state detective checking in with the local team. An hour later, there'd not been much in the way of news. Jacqueline hadn't been spotted in Baltimore, Alexandria, Atlanta, or D.C., and there still was no sign of her in Australia.

The North Carolina detective sought out the one from D.C. "Can I speak with you for a minute?"

"Sure."

"I'm going to need you to send what you've got on that Martin poisoning over to my boys in Raleigh. The more I got to thinking about that thing, the more it sounded familiar. We had a corrections officer die the day that Jacqueline got out of prison."

"No kidding?"

"The very day, one of the persons who'd guarded her ended up dead. During the investigation I found out that there'd been an alleged sexual assault followed by a physical one that ended with Tate getting time in solitary confinement and extra time on her sentence. The case had gone cold, but in light of all that's happened here, and since the first murder case also involved a poisoning, it's being reopened."

"We'll be happy to share all of our files and find-ings, to help in any way we can."

"I appreciate that."

Down the hall and around the corner, Nathan and Sherri shared some sibling time. "Can you believe all of this madness?"

He shook his head. "Sometimes I look in the mir-ror and wonder who's staring back at me and where is my life."

"Do you feel like Daddy yet?"

The question elicited the first true smile from Nathan all day. "Vincent is his father. I feel more like an uncle, or friend. He's my biological, but I don't know him, Sherri. And he doesn't know me."

"Are Vincent and Jessica going to stay together? Can their marriage withstand all of the lies he said Jes-sica told?"

"Right now both of them are focused on Jessica getting better and taking care of Dax. One of Vincent's aunts is helping him. During the weekday while he's working, Dax goes to day care."

"How do you feel about Jessica?"

Nathan thought for a long moment. "That's a good question that I'm not sure how to answer. I've been through every emotion with that girl, and for some rea-son . . . love is still the strongest one."

Randall joined them in the kitchen. His face was a mask of worry. Sherri walked over to him. "Were you able to check everything, make sure all of your re-search is secure?"

"I just spoke with the same guy who swept the of-fice the last time to make sure there are no hidden video or audio recording devices. Baby, do you think you can hold it down here? I really need to go to the office and handle matters, just for a few hours."

"Of course, go. We'll be fine."

"I'll keep an eye on things, Brother," Nathan added. "Handle your business."

Another hour passed, and except for minor snatches of information, the situation remained the same. Sherri and Nathan rejoined law enforcement in the great room. Mom Elaine had gone upstairs for a nap. The therapist assigned to take care of Albany had returned from gathering clothes and other items for an extended stay. The chef was making dinner. Law enforcement was preparing to leave.

"You've got my number, Mrs. Atwater. Please don't hesitate to call with any questions or concerns. If you see or hear anything out of the ordinary, call this number." The Alexandria police officer handed her a card. "A car will be guarding the house and a couple more will circle the perimeter for the next several days. Be attentive. Be alert." He looked from Sherri to Nathan. "I don't have to tell you two about the potential danger of this situation. We're doing everything within our power to find her. It's just a matter of—"

The sound of feet clamoring down a staircase caused the officer to stop short. Instinctively he and the others placed their hands on their weapons. Aaron, carrying his mother's computer, burst around the corner. He was trying to talk so fast he couldn't catch his breath, and no one could understand a word.

"Aaron." Sherri walked over to where he hopped from one foot to the other. "Honey, slow down and tell us what's the matter."

"I think I found her."

"Jacqueline?"

He nodded his head rapidly. "I found her program, Mom. It was buried on your hard drive, hidden behind these other codes. That's why it took me so long to crack it."

The D.C. detective walked over. "What are you saying, Son?"

"She bugged my mom's computer, got in and changed some things around. At first I couldn't find it. But I copied Mom's hard drive and attached it to my computer so I could run a different program." He was still talking fast, but his breathing had evened, so he could be better understood. "She was able to access this computer from a remote location. I finally found a way to reverse the signal. See." The team of detectives gathered around the twelve-year-old, who in his Mario Bros. T-shirt and thick black rims looked even younger than that. "This is her computer." He clicked on a few keys. The screen split, revealing the one where he typed alongside another. "She's encrypted a lot of the material so I can't read the files. And she skewed the IP address. I think it's behind a proxy. But if you get with whoever issued this IP, they might be able to help narrow the places it could be. And then you could find her!"

"Burt!" the D.C. detective yelled out to one of his officers. "Get over here." He looked at Aaron. "Now tell the officer everything you just told me."

By now, Aaron had totally calmed down. He went through the process slowly with the officer, one of the computer pros in the office, throwing around technical language that only they understood. After five minutes, the officer walked up to his boss. "He's on to something, that's for sure. I'm going to call the office with this info and have them get on it right away."

Sherri walked over to her son. "Thanks, Aaron. I'm proud of you, baby."

Aaron nodded. "I want to get the woman because she messed up my sister and keeps bothering our family! This time when they put her in jail, they'd better not ever let her out."

CHAPTER 42

"Shit!" Jacqueline sat in the parking lot of a large shopping mall, accessing the Internet through someone else's wireless account that she'd broken into. Things were much too hot for her to chance using even the burners right now. Even being on the tablet was risky. All she wanted to do was make her flight reservation so that when she reached the airport she could bypass the counter, print her ticket at a kiosk, and be on her way.

The past seventy-two hours had been a roller coaster. She hadn't even had time to stop and think of what all had gone wrong. She'd plied Eric with enough poison to kill six horses. Five minutes. If his girlfriend had showed up just five minutes later, he would be dead. But he wasn't. This she knew for sure because she'd snuck into the hospital to finish the job, only to find a police officer guarding his door. That's when she knew the jig was up. Kris had been right all along. He was not to be trusted, a lesson Jacqueline well knew.

Every time she'd trusted someone, it had come back to bite her.

Credit card . . . which one should I use? My choices are limited. With Alice Smith's ID being international, it might draw extra attention and send me through customs. Plus, they may have flagged that passport. Kate's has been used the most, especially in Raleigh. Should I chance it? She'd have to. Jasmine was out. One turn of the security system's X-ray arm and they'd be on to the fat suit. She purchased the ticket under the name Kate Freeman, and after looking around for cameras or nosy shoppers, began the transformation into the curly-haired woman who'd entered the Raleigh-Durham International Airport a lifetime ago.

Across town, at a Baltimore police station near downtown, excitement crackled through the air like electricity. "A car matching the description of the one rented under the name Kate Freeman was spotted on the 695."

"Are they sure it's Jacqueline Tate?"

"No, but they don't want to take any chances, so they're calling for backup before they make the stop."

"Don't underestimate this woman. Whether or not she's armed, she is extremely dangerous. I have no doubt she's killed before and if backed into a corner, she will kill again."

Jacqueline weaved in and out of traffic on her way to the Baltimore-Washington International Airport. It was hard for her to stay under the speed limit, but she forced herself. To do all she'd done and get popped for a speeding ticket would definitely not be a good look.

"Almost there, almost to the exit."

She gripped the wheel, tried to slow down her heartbeat. The radio blared a hard-hitting "Welcome to the Jungle." To rid herself of adrenaline, she sang along at the top of her lungs. The loud music served to drown out the sound of the sirens until they were right up on her.

"What the hell?"

She put on her blinker and changed lanes. So did the two squad cars. She sped around a Dodge truck and changed lanes again. The police followed suit. She turned off the radio and cracked the window.

"Pull over. Driver of the silver Hyundai, pull over now."

She thought she heard voices. Unusual in that these were coming from the patrol car behind her, and not in her head. Once again, the command to stop was issued. Jacqueline's heart beat a mile a minute. She had to think fast. Pulling over was not an option. There was no doubt that she'd go straight to jail.

"Had I known I'd be trying to outrun a cruiser, I would have rented that flashy red Corvette." She jumped into the carpool lane. "Come on, Kris! Let's do this!"

She pressed her foot to the floor and challenged the Sonata to live up to its 140-mile-per-hour odometer claim. The police cars stayed in hot pursuit. Motorists pulled over as they noticed the drama unfolding in their rearview mirrors. It gave Jacqueline an opening. She shot over four lanes and took the exit at seventy miles per hour. Neither police car accepted the challenge.

Jacqueline screamed with excitement. "That's right, pussies! Back up off me. Because I'm one bad bee-atchi!"

She held the last syllable like a note to a song, and threw a fist in the air. "Yes!" she exclaimed, closing her eyes for one split second. They opened just in time to see an 18-wheeler pull out into her lane.

And then her world went black.

CHAPTER 43

Toronto, Ontario, Canada
One month later

Jessica couldn't stop staring at her, the woman for whom she'd been named. It was like staring into the future and how she might look in twenty-five years. Jessica Clarke, her mother's older sister by eight years, had lived a hard life that showed on her face yet hadn't erased all of the beauty that was once there. The shape of the eyes, tilt of the mouth, and cheekbones were identical. Though gray now streaked through it, she was sure Aunt Jessie had once possessed thick, curly black hair, the same as hers.

While staring at her aunt, Jessica was being peered at just as intently.

"I can't get over how much you look like Sandy and me. If I'd seen you on the street, I'd have known you were family."

Jessica smiled. "I would have recognized you,

too." An awkward silence descended before she continued. "My mother's name was Sandra."

"Aye. Cassandra Eileen, to be exact."

Jessica repeated the name, marveling at how it was
at once foreign and familiar on the tip of her tongue.
"Did something happen between you and my mom that
made you lose contact with each other?"

"Yes," Aunt Jessie responded. "Something called
life. While Sandy and I both partied at the bottom of
bottles of gin, I added heroin to the mix. There's five
years of my life that I don't remember and will never
get back. They began when I read the news article
about her dying and ended when I met William, my
angel of a husband who helped get me back right. I've
been clean and sober for the past ten years, and during
this time have been so busy repairing my splintered
family that I had not the time or inclination to look beyond it." She placed a hand on Jessica's arm. "I'm
sorry. I had no idea of your life, had no thought as to
what you must have gone through. Forgive me?"

Jessica nodded. "I forgive you."

In the month since she'd left the mental institution,
Jessica had had to forgive a lot of people, starting with
herself.

"So tell me a little about your life," Aunt Jessie
urged her. "Are you married, children, any siblings besides Jacqueline?"

"I'm married but it's . . . complicated. I have a son,
Dax. He's almost two. No other brothers or sisters. It
had always been just Sis . . . Jacqueline and me."

"When is the last time you saw Jackie?"

Jessica swallowed. "A few months ago. We're no
longer in contact."

"That's a shame. Family's all we've got. I know that's pretty hypocritical sounding coming from me, but it's true. When life is at its toughest, that's who will be there for you."

"Jacqueline is no longer a part of my family." The words came out harsher than intended. Jessica changed her tone. "There's a lot about the two of us that you don't know. Bad things, unfortunate events that have happened between us. The bridges have not only been burned, but they've been detonated with dynamite and blown to smithereens. I will never have anything to do with her ever again."

"I can't say too much. Sandy and I were close growing up, but once we got grown and out of the house, we didn't speak for years." She reached over and placed a hand on Jessica's arm. "But don't be too hard on Jackie. Before the abuse at the hands of your father, she was a happy-go-lucky, fun-loving child, and a delight to be around. The last time I saw her, I knew what had happened. I knew why the light had gone out of her eyes. And when I heard about the fire, I knew what had happened then, too."

"That she'd killed them?"

Jessica's aunt eyed her closely, took a long drag off a cigarette. "That she did what she had to do . . . to save her life."

"That's why she's out of my life, Aunt Jessie. Because I'm doing what I have to do to save mine."

There was a short series of taps on Jacqueline's bedroom door before Millie swung it open and marched into the room. "Good morning!"

Jacqueline growled. "What's good about it?"

For Jacqueline, that she was in a guarded assisted-living facility and not prison was of small consolation. Her now-paralyzed body had her on a more severe and secure lockdown than the justice system ever could.

"That you can ask that question, for one thing." The nurse went to the blinds, opened them wide along with a window. Cool air swirled into the room.

"Shut that got-damn window!"

"You shut it." Jacqueline cursed again. Millie laughed. "That cold air will get your blood circulating, which in turn will help me get you circulating."

She walked over to where Jacqueline lay and threw off the covers.

"Dammit, old woman, leave me alone!"

"And take the chance of getting fired? You can poke my patience, nettle my nerves, and eff up my attitude. But you're not going to mess with my money."

If someone had been closely observing Jacqueline's mouth, they would have caught the merest glimpse of an upturn.

Millie lifted Jacqueline's leg and began to exercise it. "A couple years ago I tended to a patient with throat cancer. A cordectomy took out his vocal cords and a partial laryngectomy rid him of half his voice box. He breathed through a hole in his throat, like that commercial on TV of the woman who smoked."

"Is hearing his problems supposed to make me feel better?"

"Not necessarily. But it's sure reminding me to count my blessings. Remembering him is also reminding me of what gratitude looks like. You've been charged with aggravated assault, attempted murder, attempting to evade arrest, resisting arrest, identity theft, evidence tampering, a slew of cybercrimes, and those murders they're reinvestigating, but you'll likely never do prison time."

"What do you call this? A vacation?"

"Bottom line, as hard as the hand is that you've been dealt, there's still a lot for which you can be thankful. If you think being a paraplegic is bad, you should give being a quadriplegic a try. You can still talk, eat solid foods, move your arms and use your hands. You have bladder control." Jacqueline's brow raised. "That's right. Even though they can't feel it, I've had to change their diapers. There is absolutely no dignity in a grown person lying in their own shit."

She finished exercising the other leg and then sat on the side of the bed. "It's time for your shower. After that, why don't we get you outside? We can even use that brand-new van that's only used for your doctor appointments and go to the park, take in some of the beauty of God's creation. The minute you stop feeling sorry for yourself and embrace the life you still have, the sooner you'll stop being a major pain in my ass."

After the shower they didn't go for a ride. Nor did the nurse take her patient outside. Jacqueline insisted on being returned to the room, where she talked to Kris, her imaginary friend.

"You've got to get me out of here."

"And go where?" Kris's smile was sympathetic. "I'm afraid our running days are over, Jack. And if you keep taking those meds, I'll soon be gone too."

"No! Don't go, Kris. I couldn't bear it."

Kris crawled into bed beside her. "I'll stay as long as I can."

CHAPTER 44

Las Vegas, Nevada

Randall, Sherri, Nathan, and Mom Elaine enjoyed a late-night dinner at a well-known restaurant in their five-star hotel.

"I think Renee looked beautiful in her wedding gown. Silver was a nice alternative to white, and complemented her skin."

"I agree," Nate said, reaching for the water pitcher. "Her husband looked quite dapper, too."

"Ooh, I think he's handsome."

"Watch out now, Mom," Randall teased. "Sounds like if she hadn't snagged him, you'd be next in line."

Mom Elaine gave a look but didn't say a word.

"Renee liked to have driven me crazy with her phone calls. But I'm glad she refused to take no for an answer. I think it's doing all of us good to be off the East Coast for a minute. While visiting with Albany and her therapist earlier, I even saw a smile."

"That's because I'd visited her five minutes before

you did and told her she could go shopping with my Black Card."

"Randall! You didn't!" Sherri couldn't believe it.

"I did."

"You do know that shopping is a form of therapy, right? By the time she returns from her shopping spree, you might have to get a second job."

"To see my baby girl like her old self again, it will have been worth it."

Sherri turned to Nathan. "You are definitely smiling more these days."

"Something that a month ago I didn't think possible. When Ralph told me that Jacqueline was Alice, I wanted to cut off my own—"

"Careful, Son," Mom Elaine warned.

"I wanted to cut off my own head."

"And you still went ahead and said it?"

"No, Mom, the one above my shoulders."

"After not being able to recognize a woman who caused holy hell in this family, sounds like the one that should have been cut off!"

"I have Dax to thank for helping to bring me around. I never knew the joy a child could bring to one's life."

"Is he still calling that other boy Daddy?" Mom Elaine asked.

"Vincent will always be his father. He calls him Daddy and he calls me Daddy Nate."

"Is Jessica still in Canada?"

Nathan nodded. "She's supposed to come back next week."

"What's going to be the arrangement once she gets back?"

"I'm not sure. I guess the three of us are going to have to get together and work out a schedule."

"Has Dev changed her mind about ending the relationship?"

"No, she believes at this point it's best to be friends. I agree. Having a child thrust into my life is causing me to have to make several adjustments, including taking the thought of relocating off the table. She wasn't ready to permanently leave the Bahamas and she didn't start out dating a single dad. Life happens. Things change. I wish her well."

"What about Vincent and Jessica?" Randall asked. "Are they still getting divorced?"

Nathan nodded.

"How do you feel about that?"

"Randall, Sherri," he looked around the table, "Mom. I know y'all want me to hate her, but I don't. When everything went down—finding out Dax was mine, her losing the baby, Vincent filing for divorce—she and I reconnected. Since she's been in Canada, we've talked almost every night."

"Oh, God."

"Now, Sherri," Mom Elaine chided. "Go ahead, Nate. What have y'all been talking about?"

"Everything. For the first time in her life, I believe she's told someone the truth about every part of her life. The girl's been through a lot."

"A lot of people have been through things," Sherri huffed. "And haven't tried to kill people because of it."

"I know that, Sherri. I also know that even with all the madness that happened between her and me, my world was brightest when she was in it. I don't know what the future holds but I know a few things. She's asked for my forgiveness. I've forgiven her. She's the mother of my child. She says she loves me and I believe it. She asked me to be there for her." He looked around with conviction in his eyes. "And I will."

A second passed. Two. Five.

"One thing's for sure." Sherri reached for her wineglass. "We no longer have to worry about Jacqueline Tate. While I'm not one to wish harm on anybody, I'd say she got exactly what she deserved."

"Yes," Randall agreed, reaching for his glass. "She's in a prison that she'll never get out of, that of her own broken body. A part of me feels sorry for her. She's only, what, in her early thirties, and is now paralyzed for the rest of her life?"

Sherri shook her head. "You're saying that even though you came this close to having your discovery stolen and sold to someone else who'd make the millions instead of you?"

"Fortunately that didn't happen. I still to this day don't understand why Larry called me. We've been competitive rivals for years. I couldn't believe he acted with that kind of integrity."

"Y'all are going to have to pray for me," Sherri quipped, "because I feel not one ounce of pity for that woman. If she weren't paralyzed and headed to jail, I'd be pushing for the death penalty. And that's real talk."

"Now, Sherri." Mom Elaine fixed her daughter with a look. "There's no need to hold on to anger. I'm not happy that Jacqueline is paralyzed. That's something I wouldn't wish on my worst enemy, even her. I tell you who I also feel sorry for . . . that woman they caught in Australia, the one who'd traveled on Jacqueline's ID." She looked at Randall. "What was her name?"

"Bonita something or other. Yes, I'm still trying to figure out how Jacqueline talked that woman into going to the lengths she did to help her out. I hope whatever she got paid is worth the five years she'll spend behind bars."

Sherri snorted. "If you ask me, anybody who'll change their face to look like Jacqueline Tate deserves whatever punishment Jacqueline Tate would have received. Doing what she did allowed a murderer to roam unnoticed and wreak havoc in our lives. For that, she deserved life. Five years? She got off easy. She'd better be glad I wasn't her judge."

"This family has been granted plenty of grace and mercy," Mom Elaine said softly. "And vengeance belongs to God. Sherri, all of y'all, do what Nathan did with his son's mother. Forgive that woman, let go of the hate. Enjoy your family, live long and prosper. That's the best way to bless your enemies, child. Living a successful, happy, purpose-filled life is absolutely the perfect revenge."

Don't miss the first book in The Shady Sisters Trilogy

The Perfect Affair

Available wherever books and ebooks are sold

CHAPTER 1

"Let's toast to Jacqueline!"

A group of five fashionably dressed and vivacious women, seated in a trendy Toronto eatery, lifted their champagne flutes in the air. The atmosphere was festive. Even the April showers had paused, allowing bright, warm sunshine to surround them.

"To you, Jacqueline Tate," Rosie, the speaker, continued. "A woman who has finally gotten what all of us want."

"A good man?" The plus-size cutie with dimples and curves kept a straight face as she asked this. The others laughed.

"No, Kaitlyn, money. The next best thing."

"Or the best thing," Jacqueline countered, "depending on how you look at it."

"We wish you tons of success on this new venture. Go get 'em, girl!"

"Cheers!"

The ladies clinked their glasses and took healthy sips of pricey bubbly before questions rang out.

"What, exactly, will you be doing?"

"Is this full-time or freelance?"

"How did you get this job?"

Jacqueline laughed as she raised her hands in mock surrender. "All right, already! I'll tell you everything." She took another sip of her drink, eyes shining with excitement. "First of all, it's a freelance writing contract—but," she continued when the other writer in the group moaned, "it's for three months and . . . it's with *Science Today*!"

"What's that?" Kaitlyn asked, looking totally unimpressed.

"It's the magazine for scientists like *Vogue* is for models," Jacqueline replied.

Kaitlyn cocked a brow. "Really? That big, huh?"

"It's a huge deal," Molly, the other writer, commented. "Doing articles for such a prestigious journal will look great on the résumé."

"Wow, that's wonderful!" Rosie said. "Will you work from an office or from home?"

Jacqueline sat straighter, barely containing her excitement. "That's the best part, guys. I'll be spending most of this assignment in America, traveling to events and interviewing the movers and shakers in the science world."

Kaitlyn reached for the champagne bottle. "Somehow 'mover,' 'shaker,' and 'scientist' sound weird in the same sentence."

"That's because your world revolves around Hollywood," Jacqueline countered. "And you consider tabloids real reading and their content true fact."

"It isn't?"

This elicited more laughter from the group, and more questions. Finally, the successful-but-shy one in the group, Nicole, spoke up. "I'm really happy for you, Jacqueline. After what you've gone through, you deserve to have some good stuff come your way."

It was true. Last year had been a doozy. On top of losing a high-paying job due to downsizing, she'd found out that the love of her life was someone else's love too. Walked in on them in her house, in her bed. Guess he'd not counted on the fact that the interview she'd been called out to do might wrap up early. It did, and so did the relationship. They'd been dating for months. Jacqueline had even confided to her friends that he might be "the one." The one to break her heart, maybe, but not the one for lifetime love.

Rosie sensed Jacqueline's sadness, and placed a hand on her arm. "At least he's out of your life."

"I wish."

Kaitlyn cringed. "He's not?"

"Occasionally we'll cover the same event. You guys remember that he's a photographer, right?"

"I remember he's a jerk," Kaitlyn replied.

"And an asshole," Molly added.

Jacqueline laughed, and it was genuine. "Thank you, guys. You sure know how to make a girl feel good."

Kaitlyn peered at her friend of more than five years. She began shaking her head.

Jacqueline noticed. "What?"

"I don't get it. You're smart, funny, and the most beautiful woman I've ever seen in person."

"Oh, girl . . ."

"Seriously? If it weren't for you, I'd think those chicks posing on the magazine covers were make-believe."

"They are," Molly said. "It's called Photoshop."

"My point," Kaitlyn continued, "is I can't understand why you're not married. I'm with my third husband and I look like a whale!"

Jacqueline frowned. "You do not. Stop exaggerating and putting yourself down like that."

"That analogy may have gone a bit overboard. But I don't look like you."

No one would argue that Jacqueline was a natural beauty. Tall, slender, with creamy tan skin, long, thick hair and perfectly balanced features, she was often thought to be a model when out on assignment, and once had even been mistaken for the pop star Rihanna.

"Maybe Kaitlyn's right," Rosie offered. "Maybe in addition to finding great stories, you might find love."

"Oh no. I'm not even going to think like that, and set myself up to be disappointed. I'm going to stay focused and disciplined, never forgetting the reasons for why I'm there. I'll be going to some great places—LA, Vegas, New York—so, sure, I plan to have fun. But guys? Not interested."

"You say that now." Kaitlyn was obviously not convinced.

"True. Anything can happen. So if I do see a hottie and want a good time, I'll view it as just that, a good time, nothing more. For me, when it comes to men and relationships, using words like 'love' and 'forever' only leads to a broken heart."

Rosie gazed at Jacqueline with compassionate eyes. "You've been through a lot and you're still smiling. You deserve to be happy and to find true love. I, for one, will be rooting for that happiness to come your way."

Kaitlyn reached for the champagne bottle and, noting it empty, flagged down the waiter to bring another one. Already outspoken and boisterous, the bubbly loosened her tongue even further and made her talk more loudly. "I'm with you, Jacqueline," she said, trying to further drain her already empty glass. "I say get wined, dined, and screwed out your mind, then tell the muthafuckas to kiss your ass. Don't even give them your phone number if they can't pass the shoe."

Every face showed confusion. "The shoe?" Jacqueline asked.

"That's right. The shoe. Y'all haven't heard of that? It's a test." Noting her very interested audience, including some from surrounding tables, Kaitlyn lowered her voice as if she was about to drop secrets from Camp David. "Okay, here's what you do. Have him take you out, buy you dinner, and then, after a night of partying, when he's trying to get in the panties, take off your stiletto, pour a drink in the shoe, and tell him to drink it. If he can't do that, then he's not a coochie connoisseur."

Ms. Shy, Nicole, was suddenly not shy at all. "A what?" When the waiter brought out the second bottle, hers was the first glass raised.

"Coochie con-no-sir. One who'll lick it, kiss it, nip it, and flick it before he fucks it."

Rosie's cheeks turned as red as her hair. "Oh my," she whispered with a hand to her mouth.

Molly pulled out her phone to take notes.

"Thanks anyway," Jacqueline responded. "But the last man I'd give my phone number to is one who'd drink out of my shoe. That's just foul."

"Whatever." Kaitlyn's countenance was one of pure confidence. "I'm just sayin' . . ."

Jacqueline sat back and crossed her arms. "And you know this because?"

"Because when I met the man who drank out of my shoe? I married him!"

This comment sent the table into another vocal frenzy.

"You're lying."

"No, he didn't!"

"Sounds like a wild and crazy date!"

"Geez! I'll never look at good old Harry the same way again."

Jacqueline sat back and took it all in. These were her girls; some she'd known for years and others a few months. Their sisterhood and support were genuine. Only one of her besties was missing. Kris. Her ride-or-die BFF who'd been there forever. She couldn't wait to share this great piece of news with the main one who'd been beside her during both good times and bad.

"Okay, maybe asking him to sip from your heels is a bit extreme."

You think? Jacqueline's raised brow seemed to imply.

"But there are still good men out there. I finally found one, though it took me three tries."

"Evidently my radar on good men is in need of repair."

"My mother always told me that when you meet him, you'll know." Kaitlyn sat back, thoughtful. "I have to admit, it wasn't until Harry came along that I knew what she meant."

Intrigued, Jacqueline eyed her. "How was he different?"

"It was natural, easy," Kaitlyn said with a shrug. "He felt like an old shoe."

"Ha! What is it with you and shoes?" Rosie asked.

Kaitlyn laughed. "I don't know. Probably time for a new pair." Her voice became serious as she looked at Jacqueline. "I didn't have to try with Harry. I was just myself. He felt right, and good, from the beginning. That's how I knew it. Maybe that's how you'll know it too."

"Sounds easy, but again, with the bad luck I've been having, I'm just not sure."

"I understand your being cautious. Just don't shut totally down. Leave a little space in your heart open to love. A little light, so the right man can find it."

They toasted to that and once the entrées arrived, the conversation moved around to other things. Later, however, Kaitlyn's words still echoed. Jacqueline wanted to find love, really hoped that it would happen. But during this assignment and over the next three months, at least? She wouldn't go looking for it.

Turn the page for a sizzling preview of

STILETTO JUSTICE

By Camryn King

Available wherever books and e-books are sold.

PROLOGUE

"Is he dead?"

"I don't know, but seeing that lying trap of a mouth shut is a nice change of pace."

Kim Logan, Harley Buchanan, and Jayda Sanchez peered down at the lifeless body of the United States senator from Kansas, Hammond Grey.

"I agree he looks better silent," Kim mused, while mentally willing his chest to move. "But I don't think prison garb will improve my appearance."

"Move, guys." Jayda, who'd hung in the background, pushed Harley aside to get closer. She stuck a finger under his nose. "He's alive, but I don't know how long he'll be unconscious. Whatever we're going to do needs to happen fast."

"Fine with me." Harley stripped off her jacket and unzipped her jeans. "The sooner we get this done, the sooner we can get the hell out of here."

"I'm with you," Kim replied. Her hands shook as

she unsnapped the black leather jacket borrowed from her husband and removed her phone from its inside pocket. "Jayda, start taking his clothes off."

"Why me?" Jayda whispered. "I don't want to touch him."

"That's why you're wearing gloves," Harley hissed back. "Look, if I can bare my ass for the world to see, the least you can do is pull his pants down. Where's that wig?"

Kim showed more sympathy as she pointed toward the bag holding a brunette-colored hair transformer. "Jayda, I understand completely. I don't even want to look at his penis, let alone capture it on video."

Harley had stripped down to her undies. She stood impatiently, hand on hip. "I tell you what I'm not going to do. I'm not going to get buck-ass naked for you two to punk out. It's why we all took a shot of Jack!"

"I'm too nervous to feel it," Jayda said as she wrung her hands. "I probably should have added Jim and Bud."

"Hold this." Kim handed Jayda the phone and walked over to the bed. After the slightest of pauses, she reached for the belt and undid it. Next, she unbuttoned and unzipped the dress slacks. "Jayda, raise him up a little so I can pull these down."

Harley walked over to where Kim stood next to the bed. "Don't take them all the way off. He looks like the type who'd screw without bothering to get totally undressed."

Kim pulled the pants down to Hammond's knees. The room went silent. The women stared. Kim looked at Harley. Harley looked at Jayda. The three looked at each other.

"Am I seeing what I think I'm seeing?" Jayda asked.

Harley rubbed the chill from her arms. "We're all seeing it."

"*Star Wars*? Really, Hammond?" Kim quickly snapped a couple pics, then gently lowered the colorful boxers and murmured, "Looks like his political viewpoint isn't the only thing conservative."

She snapped a few more. Harley donned the wig, looked in the mirror, and snickered. "Guys, how do I look?"

"Don't," Kim began, covering her mouth. "Don't start to laugh . . ." The low rumble of muted guffaws replaced speech.

The liquor finally kicked in.

"Come on, guys!" Jayda harshly whispered, though her eyes gleamed. "We've got to hurry."

"You look fine, Harley. As gorgeous a brunette as you are a blonde."

Harley removed her thong and climbed on the bed. "Remember . . ."

"I won't get your face, Harley. What the wig doesn't cover, I'll clip out or blur. You won't be recognizable in any way."

"And you're sure this super glue will work, and hide my fingerprints?"

Jayda nodded. "That's what it said on the internet."

"I'm nervous." Harley straddled the unconscious body and placed fisted hands on each side.

"Wait!" Kim stilled Harley with a hand to the shoulder. "Don't let your mouth actually touch his. We don't want to leave a speck of DNA. I'll angle the shot so that it looks like you're kissing."

"What about . . . that." Jayda pointed toward the flaccid member.

"Oh, yeah. I forgot. Look inside that bag." Harley tilted her head in that direction. "With the condom on, it looks like the real thing."

Jayda retrieved a condom-clad cucumber and marched back to the bed as though it were a baton. "He won't like that we've filmed him, but he'll hopefully appreciate that we replaced his Vienna sausage with a jumbo hot link."

The women got down to business—Jayda directing, Harley performing, Kim videotaping. Each job was executed quickly, efficiently, just as they'd planned.

Finally, after double-checking to make sure her work had been captured, Kim shut off the camera. "Okay, guys, I think we've got enough."

Harley moved toward the edge of the bed. "Pictures and video?"

"Yep. Want to see it?"

"No," she replied, scrambling into her jeans. "I want to get the hell out of here."

"That makes two of us," Jayda said, walking toward the coat she'd tossed on a chair.

"Three of us." Kim took another look at the footage. "Wait, guys. I have an idea. Jayda, quick, come here."

"What?"

"No time to explain. Trust me on this . . . please?"

Five minutes later they were ready to go. "What should we do about him?" Jayda asked, waving a hand at his state of undress.

"Nothing," Kim replied. She returned the phone to its hiding place in her pocket. "Let him figure out what may or may not have happened."

They'd been careful, but taking no chances, they wiped down every available surface with cleaning wipes, which they then placed back in the bag that once again held the condom-clad cucumber. Harley almost had a heart attack when she glimpsed the wineglass that if forgotten and left behind would have been a forensic team's dream. After rinsing away prime evidence, she pressed Grey's fingers around the bowl, refilled it with a splash of wine, and placed it back on the nightstand. After a last look around to make sure that nothing was left that could be traced back to them, the women crept out of the bedroom and down the stairs. Harley turned off the outside light and unbolted the side door.

Kim turned to her. "You sure you don't want to come with us?"

Harley shook her head. "I have to leave the way I came. Don't worry. The car service is on the way. See you at the hotel."

After peeking out to make sure the coast was clear, Jayda and Kim tiptoed out the back door as quietly and inconspicuously as they'd arrived. A short time later Harley left, too.

Once down the block, around the corner, and into the rental car, Jayda and Kim finally exhaled. The next day, as the women left the nation's capital, hope began to bloom like cherry blossoms in spring. Until now their calls for help and cries for justice had been drowned out or ignored. Maybe the package specially delivered to his office next week would finally get the senator's attention, and get him to do the right thing.

Connect with

Visit us online at
KensingtonBooks.com
to read more from your favorite authors, see books
by series, view reading group guides, and more.

for sneak peeks, chances to win books and prize packs,
and to share your thoughts with other readers.

facebook.com/kensingtonpublishing
twitter.com/kensingtonbooks

Tell us what you think!

To share your thoughts, submit a review,
or sign up for our eNewsletters, please visit:
KensingtonBooks.com/TellUs.